Close Call

A novel by

KI STEPHENS

For myself,
another chronically sleepy girl.

Playlist

NEVER BEEN IN LOVE | GATLIN	♥	3:06
MEANS SOMETHING | LIZZY MCALPINE	♥	2:25
SEEDS | YOKE LORE	♥	4:11
HILL THAT I'LL DIE ON | JONAH KAGEN	♥	2:25
PEACE | TAYLOR SWIFT	♥	3:54
SUNLIGHT | HOZIER	♥	4:17
YOUR BONES | CHELSEA CUTLER	♥	2:39
SIMPLY THE BEST | BILLIANNE	♥	2:54
ALL MY GHOSTS | LIZZY MCALPINE	♥	3:17
HEY LOVELY | CHANCE PEÑA	♥	3:43
I'M WITH YOU | VANCE JOY	♥	4:00
THIS IS HOW YOU FALL IN LOVE | JEREMY ZUCKER, CHELSEA C	♥	2:55
BELONG TOGETHER | MARK AMBER	♥	2:28
DANDELION | OLIVER HAZARD	♥	3:11
RECKLESS DRIVING | LIZZY MCALPINE, BEN KESSLER	♥	3:09
DON'T LET ME | MORNINGSIDERS	♥	3:04
DEEP END | HOLLY HUMBERSTONE	♥	2:52
DEAR AUGUST | PJ HARDING, NOAH CYRUS	♥	3:21
WEATHERMAN | WILD RIVERS	♥	3:06
HOME | GOOD NEIGHBOURS	♥	2:37
FOREVER | NOAH KAHAN	♥	4:28

Chapter One

EMMY

"Madison Emilia Fuller, please tell me you did not drop the squad without speaking to me about it first."

I let out a sigh, gaze drifting to the ceiling. "Okay, then. I didn't drop the squad."

"Em, seriously? What happened?"

I sit up, hugging a cushion to my chest. "I just got so tired, Mom."

"Tired?"

"Exhausted, honestly. Do you know how much work it is juggling cheer, my major, and all those shifts at Lawson?"

There's a pause on the other end of the phone, and I envision my mom's all-knowing smile. "Oh, honey, you know that I—"

"Right," I cut in, a mixture of admiration and exasperation in my voice. This woman never fails to remind me of her feats. Not only was she pregnant during nursing school, but she also proceeded to raise me as a single parent, complete her degree, and work part-time while doing it all. "Who am I kidding? Of course you know. Because you're fucking superwoman or something."

"Language, Em."

"Sorry." I shift uncomfortably, shoving the cushion beneath my thighs. "Anyway, I was just calling to let you know that I won't be attending camp this year. But I'm still staying around campus. I need to find a place of my own since the girls are moving back in."

I've been subletting this apartment for the last couple of

months, but my time here is officially running out. The two people who rent this place during the academic term, Shannon and Jade, will be coming back in just a few short weeks. It pains me to admit that summer's almost over.

Unfortunately, I had to stick around campus in order to keep my work-study position. My supervisor, kind as he is, wasn't willing to hold it for me if I gave up the summer hours, and I simply couldn't allow that to happen. I like having the extra spending money, and it also keeps me from having to ask my mom for more help.

"Any leads?" she asks.

"Kind of? It feels too weird to stay with anyone on the team now, and I'm not sure that I'd even want to. I was thinking about asking Matty if he still needed a roommate."

"Aw, Matty's such a good kid."

"The best," I say because it's so unbelievably true. Matty and I have been friends since grade school, and he's always been the best boy—now man, I guess—that I've ever known. Even now that he's some hotshot baseball captain, he still treats me just the same.

I'm his little Emmy from the next street over. The girl with the chronic scraped knees and the embarrassing snort of a laugh.

"I always thought he had a little thing for you when you were younger."

I roll my eyes, a smile tugging at my lips. "Matty's into men, Mother."

"Not both?"

"Not me. That's for sure."

"Right, okay." She clicks her tongue. "I suppose that should be fine, then."

"Wasn't asking for permission. But thank you for the stamp of approval, anyway. I just have to see if he'll agree to it. He was pretty desperate to find someone last we talked."

"If not, would the girls let you stay a bit longer?"

"I could ask, but there's really only two rooms here," I say, ankles crossed, legs stretched out in front of me on the bed. "And I'm sure Jade will have her boyfriend over a lot, so it's a bit of a full house."

Jade's been doing long-distance throughout the summer, and from what I hear, things between them are still going strong. The two were practically inseparable before their first break, and I bet they'll want to make up for lost time now they're back together.

It's sweet, but I'd prefer not to play witness to it if I don't have to.

I'm terminally single and hopelessly romantic, which means I'm not exactly in the best mindset to be around them. I'd rather find my own story than be a background character in someone else's.

And besides, Shannon's still a proud member of the cheer squad. Meanwhile, I'm, well, trying my best to get away from it all.

"Alright. Just keep me in the loop, will you?" she asks. "I don't want to find out you've dropped out of Dayton next."

"I'm not gonna drop out of *school*, Mom." A lump catches in my throat. "It was just cheer. I wasn't—I mean, I never intended on taking that anywhere after college."

"Oh, but darling, you were so great at it."

"I was mostly the back spot on the lower team," I deadpan.

"Don't downplay your successes, Em. I taught you better than that."

"Sure." My shoulders deflate, stomach knotting as I pack up my school bag. "Well, I've gotta get over to Lawson. We'll talk soon."

"Bye, hon."

"Bye."

. . .

ONCE I FINISH my shift at the cafe, I call Matty and ask him to meet me on campus. I'm sitting at one of the low tables, tapping my fingers against the plastic, categorically unsettled. He arrives in a flash, concern etched into his sculpted features.

I must have sounded a bit more frantic on the phone than I intended.

"Em, what's going on?" he asks, pulling out a chair to join me.

"Sorry, didn't mean to worry you." I snort a laugh at his crumpled brow. "It's nothing serious. I was just wondering if you were still in search of a roommate."

He sinks into his chair, visibly relaxing. "Ah, yeah. It's so late in the game now. None of the guys are available anymore. Gabe and Dom already have a full house. Hayes is living with the Donovan brothers since Bash is headed out."

My ears involuntarily perk up at the mention of Hayes. I picture him now, almost fully formed inside my head. His honey-brown hair, those full lips, and his piercing hazel eyes. There's something undeniably captivating about him, like he possesses that classic Hollywood charm.

A young Heath Ledger with lighter hair and the same devil-may-care smile.

It's almost embarrassing—this schoolgirl crush I have on him—especially because we've only spoken less than a handful of times. If I'm being honest with myself, I'm not even sure he'd be able to pick me out of a lineup.

"Right," I say, shaking him out of my thoughts. "Would you consider living with me, then?"

He cocks his head. "I thought you were living with Cass and them?"

"I quit the team."

"You . . ."

"Yes, and please spare me the lecture. I already heard it all from Mom."

"But why?"

"I'm tired, Matty."

"Tired of the girls? The commitment?"

"Just . . . *tired.* I wake up in the morning completely exhausted, like I've barely even slept a wink. It doesn't matter if I get eight hours or twelve. And believe me, I've been erring on the side of twelve for the better half of the summer. I can barely keep my eyes open during the day. I'm taking multiple shots of espresso just to make it through my shifts here. And there's no possible way I'm gonna be able to study at this rate."

"Jesus, Em. Have you been to the doctor or anything?"

"Last time I saw my GP, my labs were fine. He just told me to stick to a *good diet* and exercise routine." I scoff, staring down at the table in embarrassment. "To get some more fresh air."

"Right, because you're not working your ass off at practice."

"So, maybe that's all it is. You know? I'm tired from doing too much all the time. I need a break."

He gives me a skeptical look. "I guess it could be. Are you . . . okay about it all?"

"Yeah." I lift one shoulder in a casual shrug. "Cass and the girls weren't too happy, but I'm easily replaceable."

"Em—"

"I'm serious. I'm not just saying that because I'm fishing for compliments. I'm not like you, Matty. Hotshot, team captain, always the star of the fucking show. But me? They'll be just fine when I'm gone."

"I think Hayes could easily hold down the fort without me."

"Maybe." I force myself not to slip into another impromptu daydream. *Focus, Emmy, focus.* "Anyway, what do you think of the idea?"

"Of us living together?" I give him an emphatic nod, and he lets out a silent, wistful laugh. "Yeah, I like it. But, uh, would you want to maybe switch with me for the main bedroom? That way, you could have your own en suite. Get a little more privacy."

"Aw, no." I frown. "You don't have to do that."

"I insist."

I shake my head, lips turning up in a smile. That's such a Matty Brooks thing to do—to constantly put everyone else before himself. "You really are the best man in my life."

His nose scrunches. "Aren't I the *only* man in your life?"

"Shut up, Matt."

A hearty laugh breaks from his chest. "Point taken."

Fall term starts next week, and I'm about halfway moved into Matty's place by now. The girls won't be taking back their apartment until Sunday, so I've been slowly packing things up over time.

"And where would you like me to put this box, dear Madison?"

I turn, and Matty is holding up a treasure trove of . . . well, adult toys that I discreetly packed away in a cardboard box. He raises an amused brow, gaze unabashedly rifling through the contents.

I rush toward him, ripping the box from his hands, cheeks flushing. "Can you actually not?"

"They were *right* there." He gestures to the middle of his—now *our*—living room. "Just ripe for my viewing pleasure."

"Okay, well, you don't have to draw attention to them."

"*Them*, huh? Do they have names?"

I scoff, tugging the box closer to my chest. "No, they do not have *names*. What kind of person do you take me for?"

"A girl who packs up a box of dildos with glittery tissue paper and thinks that her new roommate won't snoop."

"Yeah, well . . ." I trail off, scampering down the hallway to my new bedroom. I carefully tuck them away in my dresser and then rub my temples as I meander back to Matty. "Do you think we can take a pause on unpacking for a bit?"

He flops down on the couch without a word of protest. "Thought you'd never ask."

I take a seat beside him, pulling out my phone to scroll for a few minutes. After clicking into Instagram, a yawn forces its way out of me, and my eyes drift closed of their own accord.

"Tired?" Matty asks.

"What's new?"

"Do you think you're too tired to go to a party with me tonight?"

I slowly open my eyes and glance over at him. "What kind of party?"

"Baseball team."

I yawn again. "Ah."

"So, is that a no?"

"No, I'll go." I run my fingers through my hair, blow out a breath, and slap some warmth back into my cheeks. I'm exhausted, but if I take a short nap beforehand, I should be able to make it through a night out. "It sounds fun. Just worried some of the squad might be there."

"Are you avoiding them?"

I straighten my spine. "I left and moved out, didn't I?"

"Yeah, but you could still be friends."

"Maybe."

His gaze softens, and he gives me a friendly pat on the arm. "I can stick with you if that makes things easier."

"Thank you for the offer, but I think I can handle a party. Besides, I might meet someone."

That would be the ideal scenario, wouldn't it? To start off my senior year with a boyfriend. Or, at the very least, some sort of mutually beneficial situationship. I've been meaning to put myself out there despite my awful track record.

The last time I went out was during the spring football banquet. My date, as is customary, spent the whole night flirting with other women. In fact, I'm ninety-nine percent sure that he went home with someone else at the end of the night.

Either way, I had to call myself a fucking Uber in order to get home.

"Going after my teammates, huh?"

I flash him a grin. "Exactly."

"Is that what all *this* was about?" He gestures to my half-empty boxes, giving me a warm chuckle. "A clever ruse to get closer to the boys?"

I manage to lift an arm over his wide shoulders, tucking myself against him. "Oh, Brooks, you know me so well."

Chapter Two

HAYES

"COME TO THE PARTY TONIGHT?"

"Can't. I have a thing going on."

"A *thing*?" I ask, aghast. "Come on, Bash, you're heading out in *two fucking days*. I'm barely gonna see you this year."

My little brother, Sebastian Grecco, is somewhat of a prodigy when it comes to baseball. It's my sport of choice, too, but I'm nowhere near his level and never will be. Although we both come from a long line of baseball ancestry, some are still born with innate talent.

Others, like me, have to work their asses off to be half as good.

So, naturally, my brother was drafted by the Blue Ridge Blazers right after high school. They snapped him up in June and spent the last few months working out contracts. He'll be reporting to their minor league complex in a matter of days.

"I'll visit," he says flippantly.

"Fine. Desert me in my time of need."

"Oh, is it that time of the month for you already?"

I flop onto my back on the couch, scrubbing a dramatic hand over my temples. "Bashy boy, why don't you love me like I love you?"

He grimaces at the nickname. "It's not that hard, honestly."

"God, remember when you used to call me all the time? Whining about how much you missed me when I left for college? Asking me for dating advice?"

"You mean that *one* time when you told me to rub a fucking whisk on my hickeys?"

"Exactly." My brow lifts in mock reprimand. "What happened to that beautiful baby boy of mine?"

"He grew up. Had sex. Became a man or whatever."

"Wow, suppose there's no interest quite like self-interest."

He snorts, a very evident pity laugh. "Right, well, I've got to get going, man. I'll catch you before I leave on Sunday, yeah?"

"Because of that *thing* you have going on tonight?"

"Listen, Hayes." His expression turns the tiniest bit contrite. "You're gonna find some chick to hook up with less than an hour into the night. I doubt you'll miss me when you're getting busy."

"I'm a highly efficient multitasker."

"Don't worry, you can tell me all about it Sunday morning."

"Ah, ah, ah." I wag a playful finger in his direction. "I don't kiss and tell, Bashy."

"Sure, you don't."

It's PARTY TIME, and I'm officially on a mission. Sebastian was right, after all. I'm looking for someone to hook up with tonight, if only so I can start my senior year off with a bang. Quite literally.

It's not that I'm hard up for company, but it's just something I enjoy. A healthy extracurricular outside of my academic and sports-related pursuits. If sex counts as a hobby, then I'm a full-on Renaissance man.

As luck would have it, there are plenty of beautiful women here tonight. Not that I'm generally too picky about that, anyway. I like women of all sorts. If I could describe my type in a single sentence, I'd probably go with "girls that are nice to me." Flash me a pretty smile, and I'm yours.

Does that make me a bit on the easy side? Sure, but I never claimed to be hard.

"Hayes." My roommate and best friend, James Donovan, claps me on the shoulder, nodding up the stairwell. "There's a girl up there asking for you."

"What's her name?"

"Didn't catch it. I told Liam to entertain her in the meantime."

Liam, our other roommate, is James' little brother. He's a highly excitable sophomore who recently leveled up to varsity soccer. If I were a better man, I'd let him field the offer himself. But I'm not, so I won't.

"Thanks for the tip." I throw a quick cheers to James and make a dash for the kitchen. I need a Solo cup refill before I head up there, lest this girl actually wants to spend some quality time together.

I tap the second keg and fill my cup to the brim, taking a swig before wiping the back of my mouth. When I wander back to the living room, the place is already ten times fuller than it was a few moments ago. I do a quick one-two scan of the room before glancing back to the staircase.

And through the muddle of people, I spot my buddy Matty standing there at the foot. He's a head taller than the rest of the room, friendly as fuck, and a beast of a co-captain. The kind of teammate everyone wants and the one that I'm lucky enough to have.

"Matthew fuckin' Brooks," I shout across the room, pushing through the crowd toward him. "There's my best friend in the whole wide world."

He rears back as I approach, giving me an amused look. "I thought that was James?"

"Yeah, alright." I wave him off with a chuckle. "*Second* best friend in the whole wide world."

"I see that somebody's already had a few good drinks."

"Who, me?" I place an incredulous hand over my chest. "Nah, just happy you came to my party."

"Happy to be here, bud." He glances over to the girl standing beside him—medium-height, mid-sized, icy-blonde hair, and a cute round face. Her lips are painted a deep plum that contrasts with her pale complexion.

She's fucking gorgeous.

"You know my friend Em," he says, slinging a casual arm over her shoulder. He gives her a quick squeeze and then brings his hand back down to his side. It's not a possessive move, really. No more than a friendly gesture.

"Not sure." I squint, gaze raking over her features one more time. And that's when it hits me. I'm almost certain she's a member of our cheer squad. "Oh, right. You're on the che—"

Matty's eyes go wide, and he draws an index finger across his throat, cutting me off. "She's my friend from back home," he says instead.

I tilt my head but decide not to question it further. Tipping my cup toward her, I say, "Well, cheers, then. Welcome to the party."

Before she can get a word in, someone barrels into me from behind, shoving me up against her. My cup flies out of my hand, beer splashing down the front of her top and instantly soaking through the thin layers.

"Shit," I say, "I'm so sorry."

I step back, gaze flitting across her body. Her mouth forms a perfect O of shock, and her top is devastatingly transparent, the lace of her pink bra fully on display. She hunches over, holding out the hemline of her shirt, and the beer that was once in my cup is now dripping onto the hardwood floors.

"Fuck," I say, "you're really wet."

"Soaked," she squeaks out. "Thanks for noticing."

I give Matty a wide-eyed glance, grimacing at my mistake. He just shakes his head at me, rubbing his temples, amused but maybe not in a good way. "Can I grab you something dry to wear?" I ask and then gesture up the stairs. "My room's just up there."

"Er . . ." She peers down at her shirt, to Matty, and then back to me. "Yeah, I guess that's a good idea. Lead the way?"

"Want me to tag along?" Matty asks, but she just waves him off.

"Like I said, I can handle a party."

"Alright." Matty claps me on the shoulder before stepping back. "Hayes, be on your best behavior. Alright?"

"I'm a Grecco," I say, "I was born a fucking gentleman."

Matty snorts as I take his friend's hand, curling my fingers around her palm. Without another word, I guide her up the stairs a half step behind me and then direct us down the hall toward my bedroom. There are few people crowded up here, but it's a lot quieter than the space downstairs.

On the way, we pass by Liam's room, and I can hear the faint sound of a feminine giggle through the crack in his door. He must have taken his entertainment duties quite seriously. And I must have taken too long to make it up here, so he proceeded to swoop in on my mystery girl.

I have to hand it to the kid. He saw an opportunity, and he took it. Good for Liam. Besides, I lost interest before I made it past the foot.

"After you," I say, waving her inside my room. "Let me find you a shirt really quick."

I turn my back on her, rifling through the top drawer, where I house all my favorites. "I like your room," she says quietly from behind me. "It's . . . clean."

"Clean." I snort a laugh. "Well, at least I have that going for me."

I pull out a dark cotton T-shirt, my last name stretched across the back in bold letters. It's the comfiest shirt I own, with the slightest amount of fade, perfectly worn in. "Here. Will this do?"

She grabs the fabric from my outstretched hand, delicate

fingers brushing mine. "Thanks," she says, brows scrunched, head tilted. "I guess I'll just . . . put it on, then."

"Ah, fuck. Right. Okay, let me just turn around so you can change."

Despite the fact that I can see *everything* she has going on beneath her shirt, I suppose it makes sense to give her some semblance of privacy. I'm a virtual stranger, after all. So, I flip on my heel and patiently wait for her to change.

"Uh . . . Hayes?" she says after an awkward minute of me staring at the wall.

"What's up?"

"Could I use your bathroom to wash up first? Just a quick body shower? I'm really sticky from the beer."

I flip back around to face her, and she's practically naked from the waist up. Her beer-soaked shirt is clutched in one hand, my clean T-shirt in the other. And man, was I dead wrong before. I thought I could see everything, but now I know exactly what I was missing.

The flimsy lace of her bra is nearly transparent, pushing up the fullness of her large breasts. Her nipples—hard, pink, perfect— visibly poke through the thin barrier. *Good fucking Lord.* This woman, hands down, has the greatest rack I've ever seen in my life.

"Fuck," I murmur absentmindedly, and then I slap myself on the forehead. "I should not be looking at your tits right now. *Shit.*"

I turn on my heel again, blowing out a heated breath, mentally kicking myself.

But she just laughs at me, loud and full-bodied. It takes her more than a minute to finally calm down, and then she says, "We might as well stop pretending that's helpful. We both know you've seen, like, all of my boobs now."

"Right." I shake my head, then slowly turn back around. I make a conscious effort to stare directly into her eyes this time. They're a dark navy blue with a ring of light brown around the outside.

Really fucking pretty. Kind of sparkly under the glaring overhead light.

I should consider changing that bulb, shouldn't I? Swap it out for something more glowy and yellow.

"Well, if it's any consolation," I say, "they're really great boobs."

She laughs again, and it's the sweetest sound. "Oddly enough, it is. Thank you."

"I solemnly swear that I won't look again, despite their greatness," I say, lifting a hand in mock salute. "Scout's honor."

"You really just say whatever comes to your mind, don't you? No holding back."

"Sure, why not?"

She steps closer, worrying over her bottom lip. "I don't know. Seems . . . difficult."

"It's the opposite, actually. You just say what you want. Do what you want." I lift a brow, scrub a hand over the back of my neck. "Take what you want."

"Oh." She stares at me for a monumental amount of time. There's an undeniable heat in her gaze, a confidence in the way she straightens her spine, and it feels a lot like a challenge.

"You know how you're looking at me, don't you?"

"How's that?" she asks, a threadbare whisper in the sliver of space between us.

"Like you want me to put my money where my mouth is. Like you want me to take what I want. Right. This. Very. Second."

Her lips part with a tiny gasp, breathy and surprised. It makes me wonder what other sorts of sounds she might make. But then, just as quickly, the illusion shatters. "Look, as much as you've . . . *intrigued* me, I'm really more of a third-date type of girl."

"Good to know." I give her a placating smile, gesturing to the door on the far side of the wall. "Shower's just through there. Let me know if you need anything. Or if you change your mind."

She nods—once, twice, a few more unnecessary times, as if

convincing herself to finally step away. And once she does, she carefully makes her way to the bathroom, slowly opens the door, and tucks herself inside.

"You can use the towels on the rack," I say in a loud voice, and she shouts back a stilted "Thanks."

I flop down onto my bed and pull out my phone to browse through social media. There's a distinct sound of the shower turning on, followed by her shuffling around and stepping into the stream of water.

It's hard to focus when a gorgeous woman is naked and showering in my bathroom, but I push myself to stay mentally strong. As a distraction, I click on Matty's profile and scroll through his tagged photos, searching for a picture of this girl. About three rows down, I find one of them together in a throwback photo from their childhood.

It's cute. Matty's little braces and Em's big, goofy smile.

Curiosity gets the better of me, so I click on her username to do some more direct snooping. But right when I find a cheer picture—her in uniform, plum-purple lipstick, smiling dead-on at the camera—she calls my name through the wall.

Like she was watching me all this time. Like I've been caught with my hand in the metaphorical cookie jar. I nearly drop my phone at the sound.

Once I regain my composure, I manage to shout back, "What's up?" in a totally normal, unalarmed tone.

I wait a few long seconds for her reply, then, "Hayes, I changed my mind."

"*Fuck*, okay," I say under my breath, and louder, "Coming!"

I fumble with my phone, setting it down on the nightstand as I peel off my jacket. It's a scramble to join her, and just before I reach the door, my phone buzzes three incessant times. I'm fully intending to ignore it, to hop into the shower with this girl and pretend I never heard it.

But then there's a call, and it's Sebastian's ringtone.

Sighing, I trudge back to the nightstand, end the call, and check my texts first. If it's not an emergency, there's no reason for me to speak to him right now. It'll just ruin the mood.

Sure enough, I have three unread messages, all from my brother.

BASH

911

siren emoji

Call me

Without hesitation, I hit Call, and he answers on the first ring, talking so fast that he's spewing word vomit. "Bash, hold on. I can't fuckin' understand you," I cut in, concern furrowing my brow. "Speak slower."

"I need your help, man. Cops are on their way . . ." he manages to say through gasps of air, clearly on the verge of a panic attack. "Fuck, *fuck*. If I get arrested and the Blazers—"

"Where are you?"

He spits out the address of some nearby park, and I pull up the location on my phone. It's only a fifteen-minute drive from here. "Hold tight," I reassure him. "And calm the fuck down. I'm gonna help you."

Chapter Three

EMMY

I WIGGLE my fingers under the stream of warm water, working to soothe the jitters, failing to calm my racing heart. It's a surreal moment, really, inviting Hayes into the shower with me. I've had this silly crush on him for what feels like forever, but with nothing to show for it.

And now here I am, drenched and waiting, the pit in my stomach hollowing out.

I steel myself, trying to channel some of that cheerleader confidence I've honed over the years. There's something to be said about constantly putting your body on display for thousands of people. Over time, I've learned to appreciate the good parts of me and to be neutral about the rest.

So, I'm not tiny, toned, and perfectly waxed. I have stretch marks on my thighs, a rounded tummy, and imperfections in places that I'd rather not think about right now.

But my body, mid-sized and powerful, has always been a source of strength, not shame. My thicker thighs have always been my solid base in cheer, grounding me, giving me support. They're part of what makes me, me.

And now that I'm standing here naked, my boobs aren't supported by underwire or hidden by a thin scrap of lace. But I still think they're pretty fucking fantastic. Hayes seemed to think so, too.

I have nothing to be ashamed about. In fact, I'm excited to see the way his face lights up—to watch his gaze hungrily roam over my body—when he finally joins me here.

Turning slowly under the water, I let it cascade over my shoulders, mulling over the idea. It's exhilarating and nerve-racking all at once. But as the minutes stretch longer and longer, a knot of confusion tangles inside my head.

What the hell is taking him so long?

Then there's a scuffle, a muffled shout. "Sorry, I have to go," he calls, followed by the sound of a door slamming shut. Silence blankets the room, and a wave of confusion slams into me. Hard and unrelenting.

I turn off the shower, heart sinking, and wrap a towel tightly around myself. Crestfallen, I peek through the slightly ajar door, only to confirm that Hayes has indeed left me here, alone in his bedroom.

My brain flits through a whirlwind of emotions—confusion, disappointment, anger. I thought . . . Well, I guess I thought wrong. I stand in the doorway for a moment, dripping and bewildered, trying to process the abrupt turn of events.

Then with a deep, steadying breath, I step back inside the bathroom, dry myself off, and slip into Hayes' clean T-shirt. My mind's racing with questions, and my heart's heavy with an unexpected sense of rejection.

What could possibly have made him rush off like that? And why, despite my initial hesitation, does it feel like such a blow to my self-esteem?

When I rejoin the party, I find Matty in the back room, engrossed in a game of beer pong. He takes a shot, his arm moving in a smooth, practiced arc. But the ball pops off the rim of a cup on the back row, bouncing away with a soft tap.

"Well, shit," he mutters, a hint of amusement in his tone. Then, his eyes catch mine, and his whole face lights up. "Emmy! Perfect timing. Be my second."

"Hey," I say, trying to muster a smile as I step to his side. But that perceptive gaze sees right through me.

"Something wrong?" he asks. "Where'd Hayes get off to?"

I snort, unable to hide my bitterness. "Good question."

He holds up a finger to his friends across the table, signaling a brief pause. We step aside into a quieter corner, his expression turning serious. "Did something happen between you two?" He eyes me up and down, a smirk twisting his lips. "Nice shirt, by the way."

"Thanks," I deadpan. "And no, not really. I was in the shower, and he just randomly got up and left."

He lifts a questioning brow, his forehead creasing slightly. "Shower, huh?"

"I was covered in beer, remember? Nothing happened."

"Didn't think so."

"Why not?" I can't help but challenge the assumption, a spark of frustration igniting inside me.

"Well, because you're . . . you're my little Emmy Fuller," he teases, ruffling my hair with affection. Normally, I'd be irritated, but I know he's just trying to be endearing. "And Hayes is . . . well, *himself*."

"I'm well aware of his reputation, Matty."

He gives me a sideways look. "Well, I suppose that's good to know."

"Is that it, then? You think he's open for business to everyone except for me?" I can't hide the hurt in my voice, the feeling of being excluded, even from something as trivial as a potential hookup roster.

He snorts, amusement flickering in his eyes. "*Open for business*. That's a good one."

I fold my arms over my chest, a defensive barrier. "I'm serious, Matt."

"No, that's not what I was saying at all. You're a fucking catch.

It's just . . . hard to picture you two together, that's all." His voice is gentle, trying not to wound, but for whatever reason, the words still sting.

"Well, you should know that he wanted to." I wave a hand dismissively, a mixture of defiance and a desperate attempt to prove my worth. I don't know why I'm even bothering to posture because I already know how Matty sees me. "So, go ahead and picture that."

His expression shifts to a disgusted scowl. "Okay, so he wanted to hook up with you. You hopped in the shower, and he just dipped?"

"I . . . may or may not have invited him to join me first. And then he kind of, like, ran out of the room in some sort of a hurry."

"Oof."

"Exactly."

"Well, I'm sure it's not anything to do with you," he says. "Maybe there's some other reasonable explanation."

"Maybe." A wave of resignation washes over me. "Or maybe you were right before. The two of us together? It just doesn't make sense."

His forehead creases with concern. "Sorry, Em."

"It's fine," I say dismissively. "But, you know, I think I could really use a win right now."

He gestures back to the beer pong table, the red cups arranged in perfect triangles, both sides evenly matched. "What do you say? You wanna play?"

"Yeah, let's play."

Shannon and Jade reclaimed their apartment yesterday, marking the end of my summer residence. Now, once and for all, I'm fully settled into Matty's place.

It was a bittersweet departure, leaving behind the cozy nook I'd called home for the last few months. But moving into the larger room at Matty's feels like a fresh start, a new chapter as I step into my senior year.

The decision seems right, a much-needed change. Still, I can't help but feel a twinge of nostalgia for the routines and rituals I've left behind. Each corner of Matty's apartment, while welcoming, feels unfamiliar, lacking the memories and personal touches that made my summer place feel like home.

My new shelf hosts a carefully curated collection of books, each one serving as a gentle reminder of a past that's slowly slipping away. Beside them, on my desk, there's a tiny glass jar filled with paper stars. I made my first batch of ten while finishing up some pre-term assignments last night.

This newfound hobby of mine, meticulously folding strips of paper, has become a soothing ritual. It's a way to center myself, to maintain focus during long study sessions, and to ward off the sleep that threatens to claim me. The end product is tiny and cute, and I can keep them—collect them in these little jars—like trophies for a job well done.

Now that I've dropped the squad, winning another *real* trophy is out of the question.

After the party—an extended Friday night that stretched into the early hours of Saturday—I've spent the last few days recuperating and unpacking. I've been so tired, but I've been doing my best to be as organized as possible.

Classes start tomorrow, and there's this nagging feeling of being underprepared, despite having all my books and supplies lined up. There's an emptiness, a void left where cheer and game prep used to be, making the onset of fall term feel hollow.

Matty, in stark contrast, epitomizes readiness.

His approach to the new term borders on military precision. His meals for the week are prepped and stacked in Tupperware containers, a testament to his organizational skills. I sat there, watching him clean his backpack with an actual vacuum and wipe his laptop screen with a microfleece cloth.

There's a part of me that envies this level of preparedness, this ease with which he steps into the new academic year. But I'm not there yet, still navigating my own transition, adrift as I adjust to this new chapter.

Now, on the eve of our senior year, we're lounging on the couch together, absorbed in the final NFL preseason game. It's still early, but I wonder if I should retreat to bed now to stock up on beauty sleep. The TV blares in front of us, casting flickering shadows across Matty's concentrated face, and I'm searching for the best way to say good night.

"Fuck," he exclaims, jolting me from my thoughts.

At first, I assume it's related to a misstep in the game, but the screen shows nothing of the sort. Instead, Matty's focus is entirely on his phone, his eyes wide with disbelief.

"What is it?"

He gulps low in his throat. "Hayes got arrested."

"Oh, my God. When?"

"Friday night."

My jaw drops. "For what?"

"Destruction of property. I guess he smashed up a car with a fucking baseball bat." His tone is incredulous, as if he can't quite believe the words even as he speaks them aloud.

"No way."

Images of Hayes, perpetually calm and collected, flash through my mind. Him wielding a baseball bat in a fit of rage seems so at odds with the person I thought I knew. But then again, most of what I know about him is probably just a construct of my own imagination.

"Rookie move, Grecco," Matty mutters, more to himself than to me. His gaze shifts from the phone to the TV, then back again, as if trying to reconcile two conflicting realities.

"Like, this happened right after he left the party?" The pieces fall into place, forming an unsettling timeline. Hayes took me upstairs, I asked him to get in the shower with me, he ran out of the house and then immediately decided to commit a misdemeanor. "Am I the type of woman who inspires petty crime?"

"Must be, considering he spent the night in jail."

"God, I wonder what actually happened that night."

"Me too." He works a thumb over his clenched jaw. "Kid's already been suspended from the team and put on academic probation. Depending on the sentence, he could be kicked off. Or worse, expelled."

"Wow. That's awful."

"I really don't know what the fuck happened," he says with a shake of his head. "None of it sounds like the Hayes I know."

I cross my ankles in front of me, tuck my hands beneath my thighs. "That's so weird, right? Like, he was upstairs with me one second. Then the next, he leaves to go smash up a car?"

"It's very fucking weird," he says.

"How'd you find out?"

"Group chat." He tilts his phone in my direction. New messages are pinging in by the second, the screen lighting up with the rapid-fire conversation. "The whole team's buzzing about it."

"And right before the first day of classes, too. What a way to start off the year."

A twinge of sympathy pangs in my chest. Despite the gravity of his actions, despite the fact that he abandoned me on Friday night, I'm not sure he deserves to lose his spot on the team. He's worked hard over the last three years, and to lose it all over one bad choice is extreme.

The timing couldn't be worse, either, a shadow cast over the start of our final year.

"It sounds like he just had an initial arraignment this morning," he says. "I don't know the rest of the details, but I'm assuming he might get off with a plea bargain or something. Depending on how bad it was, obviously."

"So he might get the charges cleared, after all?"

"I don't know, but I sure as shit hope he does," he says, rolling his shoulders back. "I need him to play this year."

I nudge him with my elbow. "And because you care about your friend, right?"

He flashes me a half-grin. "That, too."

"Well, fuck."

"Yeah, you can say that again."

"*Fuck.*"

Chapter Four

HAYES

I AM so beyond fucked right now.

I'm supposed to be sitting in my first class of the semester, but instead, the cold, sterile hallway of the administrative building has become my temporary prison. I'm posted outside the dean's office, waiting to find out if I'll even remain a student here.

Expulsion. The word makes my stomach churn. It's like a dark cloud hovering over me, threatening to burst and wash away everything I've worked so hard to achieve. Everything I've spent my life agonizing over—my spot on the team, my degree, my future—it could all be wiped away with one swipe of the dean's pen.

And it would be no one's fault but my own.

My mind replays the events of Friday night, each moment a piercing reminder of the chaos that unfolded. I may not have swung the bat, but I'm the one who decided to take the fall for my little brother.

The initiation rite came from one of his new teammates, just a rookie tradition. They gave him an address, told him it was part of proving himself, smashing up the hood of some old, abandoned car parked there.

But what he didn't know, what none of them told him, was that the car belonged to a guy rumored to be sleeping with a player's girlfriend. The whole thing was a setup—a twisted game of loyalty and betrayal. It was supposed to be a harmless prank, but it turned personal, fast.

After Sebastian did the deed, the car's owner came out—turns out he was home. The scene played out like a badly scripted movie, complete with shouting, threats, and a fucking shotgun pointed in my brother's direction.

His teammate, who was supposed to back him up, bailed the moment he heard police sirens. That fragile loyalty dissolved as quickly as smoke in the wind. And Sebastian was left alone, panicked and desperate.

That's when he called me, and something protective inside of me unleashed. I couldn't let him face the consequences by himself. Not after watching him crumble under the pressure all summer.

So, I showed up just in time to cover for the whole thing, adrenaline coursing through my veins. The police arrived on the scene, I told Sebastian to keep running, and then I laid myself on the sword for him.

The memory of the flashing lights and stern faces of the officers is still vivid in my mind. It was my first official run-in with the law, but it wouldn't have been my brother's.

He may be trouble—naive and overly trusting—but the kid has more talent in his body than anyone would know what to do with. And he's only eighteen. He deserves a real shot at making his life count for something. At following his dreams, at playing with the Blazers.

If I allowed him to get arrested—if he was the one who ended up in jail that night—he would've violated his contract and lost his spot. His record isn't spotless like mine, and our old family friend wouldn't have been able to rustle up a simple plea bargain. So, I took one for my brother, again.

But this time, covering for him may have cost me more than I bargained for.

The waiting is excruciating, each tick of the clock echoing in my ears like a countdown to my fate. My stomach churns, and I force myself to swallow down the acid that burns in my throat. As if on cue, the office door creaks open, and a secretary with a tight bun and tighter expression gestures me inside.

I step into the office, my knees weak and palms slick with sweat. Dean Franklin sits behind his large oak desk, fingertips pressed together as he surveys me over his reading glasses.

"Have a seat, Mr. Grecco," he says, gesturing to the chair opposite him.

I sink down, perched on the edge like a diver on a high cliff, bracing for the inevitable plunge. My heart pounds against my rib cage.

"I'm sure you know why you're here," the dean begins. His voice is calm but tinged with disappointment. The room feels colder, the air thicker, as if every word he speaks adds another weight. "Your actions on Friday night were reckless. You endangered not only yourself but others. This behavior is unacceptable for a student representing Dayton University."

He pauses, letting the words fully sink in. The silence in the room is nagging, and I find myself counting the seconds, each one clanging around inside my head. I stare down at my hands, clenched together in my lap, knuckles white from the tension.

"However, given your otherwise clean record, the board has agreed to place you on probation for the time being."

I nod, relief flooding my system. It's a small reprieve in the storm, a fleeting moment of respite. "Thank you, sir. I really appreciate you giving me another chance."

He holds up a stern hand. "Don't thank me yet. Your actions still warrant serious consequences." He slides a document across the desk. "You'll be placed on disciplinary probation for the remainder of the academic year. Any further infractions and you'll face immediate expulsion.

"You'll also need to complete two hundred hours of community service on campus," he continues, his words methodical, each one a nail in the coffin of my college athletics career. "And provide us records of your mandatory counseling obligation."

"Of course. I understand," I say quickly. My mind races through the implications, the added workload on top of my already demanding schedule. But I'll do anything to stay at school, to play with my team.

"And lastly, you're hereby suspended from all sports activities. Indefinitely."

This time, I shoot up from my chair.

"What?" My heart plummets to my shoes. This news hits me like a physical blow, knocking the wind right out of me. *Indefinitely.* The ambiguity, the hopelessness of the situation hits me all at once.

My dreams, my aspirations, everything I've worked for, now hang in the balance, teetering on the edge of uncertainty. The anger, the disappointment, even the community service and counseling made sense.

But being pulled from the team indefinitely? It feels like someone just ripped my soul out of my body.

"Sit down, Grecco." The order is stern, brooking no argument, and I obey. "I understand this is hard for you, so don't think this decision was taken lightly.

"Your actions on Friday night have consequences that extend beyond mere punishment. It sends a message to the rest of the student body about what we will and won't tolerate, especially from those chosen to represent our university. Until you've demonstrated a commitment to better behavior, you won't be participating in any sports events or activities."

"Sir, if I—"

"No," he interrupts me with a raised hand, a barrier to any further discussion. "This is not a negotiation."

I sit back in my chair, stunned into silence. This isn't how things were supposed to pan out. I was meant to protect Sebastian, keep his future intact while somehow salvaging mine. Instead, I've been sidelined, cast aside like a broken toy.

I swallow down the bitter taste in my mouth and force myself to nod. "Yes, sir."

He leans back in his chair, watching me with an unreadable expression, as if trying to gauge whether I've truly understood the magnitude of my actions. "This is your second chance, Grecco. Make it count."

As I stand to leave, I'm already planning my strategy for redemption: extra hours in the gym, extra effort on my studies, extra humility in my daily life. I'm willing to put in the work because being a part of this team still means something to me.

I may have risked it all for Sebastian, but I'm not willing to go without a fair fight.

BACK AT THE HOUSE, I open the door to the sounds of booming video games and raucous shit-talking. The energy is a stark contrast to the solemnity of my day. But the Donovans are home now, so it's time to switch gears.

"Hey, guys," I announce, letting the weight of my backpack hit the floor with a thud.

"Welcome home, bad boy." James chuckles, tossing a cushion in my direction. "How's life on the edge?"

"Aren't you supposed to be in class or something?"

"Couldn't eat, couldn't sleep, couldn't breathe until we found out what was gonna happen to you," James says.

I snort. "Right, but you could still play COD."

"Well, we're not terminal," he mutters, lifting a brow. "So? What's the verdict?"

"You're looking at DU's latest king of probation."

Liam doesn't even glance away from the screen. "Did they crown you with an e-collar this time?"

James slaps him on the back of the head. "Bro, what?"

"You know, to keep him from batting at unwanted places?" Liam finally looks at me, his half-hearted attempt at humor tinged with concern.

"Well," James says, "that was an interesting thing to say out loud."

I appreciate the effort to keep things light, but my stomach roils as they chuckle, and I do my best to brush past it. "I got off with community service. I'm still doing the court-mandated counseling. And, well, they suspended me from the team. Indefinitely."

The sound of gunfire from the game fades as the room goes silent, all eyes on me now. "Are you fucking serious?" James asks, his playful demeanor dissolving into shock.

I give him a weighted nod.

"Shit," Liam curses under his breath. "Sorry, man."

"It's whatever. I knew what I was doing." I flop onto the sofa beside them, grabbing a controller before I give them a shit-eating grin. "But you know, if picking up trash on campus ever becomes a sport, I'll probably be team captain of that, too."

James laughs, but the humor doesn't quite reach his eyes. "Blue-collar criminal turned captain of community service. Dude, your résumé is getting wild."

"You know we got your back, though, right?" Liam asks. "Whatever you need, man."

I tilt my chin, appreciative of their support. Other than Sebastian, they're the only two people who know the whole story, and it's going to stay that way. The last thing I need is my teammates, coach, or parents finding out I risked my future—and the team's—for my little brother.

So the truth will stay between us, locked down tight.

As soon as the boys venture back to the game, my phone vibrates in my pocket. "Gotta take this," I mumble, standing up and stretching my tense muscles. "You should go to class, guys. I'm calling this day a wash."

I quickly make my way upstairs. Once in the sanctuary of my bedroom, I answer the phone. "Hey, Bashy boy, everything okay?"

I've been worried about the kid over the past couple of days. He was forced to leave me here to fend for myself, and I know the guilt must be eating him alive. Not to mention, he's had to face the teammate who hung him out to dry on Friday night.

If he had just given me a name, I may have already wound up behind bars for a second time.

"Yeah, bro. All checked in. Starting pre-programming tomorrow." His voice is a mix of excitement and lingering guilt, the latter of which I can almost feel through the phone. "I've just been waiting for an update from you."

"Well, the dean's office wasn't exactly a party," I begin, recounting the dirty details in as few words as possible. I make a conscious effort to keep my tone light; Sebastian doesn't need to worry about me right now. He needs to focus, keep his head on straight.

"Hayes, I'm really fucking sor—"

"Stop. Enough with the apologies. I made my choice, and that's on me," I cut him off before he can spiral into another round of self-blame. "Focus on your training. Make this all worth it."

An uncomfortable silence lingers between us before he speaks up again, his voice softer this time. "Thank you, bro. Seriously."

"Sure, man. We'll talk soon."

I end the call, rub my temples, and slowly wander to the bathroom for a much-needed shower. As the hot water washes away the grime of the day, I let my thoughts drift, trying to process the turmoil. The steam fills the room, wrapping me in a warm, foggy cocoon.

I close my eyes for a beat or two, drowning out all the noise. And when I open them again, my gaze lands on something glinting on my bathroom counter. It's something I must have missed before —a delicate necklace bearing initials in gold cursive.

Memories from Friday night flood my mind in vivid detail—that sweet girl slipping into my shower, the panicked call from Sebastian that shattered the moment, and how I hastily threw on my jacket and bolted out without a second thought.

Once I towel off, my fingers trace over the intricate design of the necklace, the letters M.E.F. dangling there in my palm. The cool metal is a strange sensation against my warm skin, a reminder of an encounter that feels like a lifetime ago.

Thinking of it now, I probably owe her some sort of an explanation.

With a sigh, I carefully place the chain back on the counter. I'll return it to her later, tell her I'm sorry for bailing, and that'll be that. But for right now, I'm going to focus on untangling my other messes first.

Chapter Five

THE FIRST WEEK of the semester is done and dusted, leaving me exhausted and in need of a relaxing Friday night. So here I am, drinking a glass of red wine in the cozy comfort of my summer sublet.

Shannon and Jade invited me over for dinner, insisting that I join them. At first, I hesitated, not wanting to encroach on their time or be around a former teammate. But they persisted, and I'm grateful for it.

They're both incredibly sweet and welcoming girls. They came through for me when I needed a place to stay during the summer, and I would've considered staying here longer had there been extra space. Especially since I had been leaning on Shannon for a while now.

Last year, I confided in her about the headaches and fatigue that were plaguing me. She never dismissed or belittled my concerns, always offering support. In fact, she was the one who encouraged me to leave the squad if it became too much.

Not all of my teammates were as accepting of my decision. But tonight is about leaving those troubles behind, about moving forward and enjoying time with the people in my life who are meant to stay.

Earlier, the three of us gathered in the kitchen to make our own personalized pizzas. Shannon stuck with classic cheese, while Jade opted for a weird combination of pineapple and jalapeño. As for me, I piled on a load of black olives.

It's probably just a placebo effect, but I've been craving salty foods. And the more I eat them, the better I convince myself that I feel.

It's nearing nine o'clock by the time we all settle in to chat on the couch. The wine helps me to relax, and I find myself more comfortable, more at home than I expected.

"So, Em, how's life post-squad?" Shannon asks, tucking one long leg under her knee.

"There are things I miss about it, obviously," I tell her, picking at a loose thread on the couch cushion. "But then there's also less headaches, less sleeping for hours on end after a rough practice. I don't know, I think it will be good for me."

Her expression softens. "It sounds like you made the right choice for your health."

"And how was your first week living with Matty?" Jade asks, dark eyes sparkling with curiosity.

"Actually, it's been great. He's . . . very organized and clean. He's probably the only guy I could actually tolerate living with. Plus, he got me out of the house last Friday night for a party."

"Oh, my God," Jade cuts in, eagerly leaning toward me. "Did he tell you about what happened with Hayes that night?"

"Uh . . . well, yeah, he did." They both give me a sideways look, silently urging me to continue. "I was with him right before he got arrested."

"Wait," Shannon says, "you were there when he smashed up that car?"

"No. I was taking a shower in his bedroom, actually."

Shannon's eyes go wide, and Jade slinks even closer to me as she says, "Okay, hold on, I feel like there's a whole lot to the story that we're missing out on."

My cheeks flush with heat, so I take another slow sip of my wine to hide it. "It's not a big deal, really."

"No way, spill," Jade insists. "Did you two finally hook—"

"Jade!" Shannon cuts her off with a faux glare, but the corners of her mouth twitch in suppressed amusement. She carefully turns back to me. "You don't have to share anything you don't want to."

"It's fine." I wave off her concern. "He, um, he spilled his beer all over me. Took me up to his room to change. There was . . . a moment between us, I guess you could say."

I quickly recount the rest of the story, ending with the fact that Hayes spent the night in a cell while I ruminated over being left alone—naked and waiting—in his shower.

"Damn." Jade gives me a wistful sigh. "So, you didn't even get to sleep with him first?"

The heat climbs from my cheeks up to my ears as I swat at her arm. I may have mentioned my unrequited crush, but it doesn't mean that I've just been waiting around, hoping that Hayes would give me a chance.

"I didn't *intend* to hook up with him that night."

"No," Shannon says sweetly. "Of course you didn't."

I tilt my head. "What does that mean?"

"Nothing bad," she rushes to assure me. "I just mean that you like to be wined and dined first. Like, you're a relationship kind of girly. And just because it's Hayes Grecco doesn't mean you're going to forget about your own standards."

"Even though he's ridiculously hot," Jade adds.

I laugh. "You better not let West hear you say that."

"Surely Theo would survive," she says.

Theo Westman-Cooke—known as West by everyone but Jade —would, in fact, not survive. He's the obsessive type. So blatantly in love it's almost hard to watch. A complete simp from the day he decided he was all in on their relationship.

It's sweet, really. He went from a guy who was solely focused on football to a man who made her his top priority. It's what every woman wants. Someone with their own ambitions and goals, but when push comes to shove, they won't hesitate to put you first.

"Anyway, I haven't heard from him since then," I say. "Not that he has my number or anything."

"And you have no idea why he left to, like, randomly commit a crime in the middle of the night?" Jade asks, her brow furrowed.

"Zero idea."

Shannon squeezes my arm. "Do you think you want to talk to him again? Figure out what went wrong?"

"I don't know, honestly," I say. "The whole thing is so weird. I feel like he has so much going on now, too. I probably haven't even crossed his mind since he darted out of the room. And I'm not so sure he recognized me in the first place."

Shannon's voice is gentle, coaxing as she asks, "What do you mean?"

"Like, when Matty introduced us before he spilled the beer. He didn't seem like he knew me at all. And it's fine, we've barely interacted before that night. But it's kind of, like, do I want to pursue someone who finds me that unmemorable?"

"Well, if you're curious, we could find out."

I blink. "What?"

"Like, tonight," Shannon continues. "There's another party going on. We could show up, see if you're really as *unmemorable* to him as you think you are. Or, at the very least, you could confront him and find out what really happened that night."

"Oh, that all sounds like . . . way too much." I fiddle with my fingers in my lap. "Don't you think?"

"You're worried about coming on too thick?" Shannon asks, and I nod my confirmation.

"Em, you were completely naked in his shower, offering yourself up to him," Jade says softly. "He got you to that point, so I think he can offer you some sort of explanation, at least."

I lift my shoulder in a half shrug. "I guess."

Shannon pushes up from the couch, standing before me with both hands planted on her hips. "Okay, I've decided," she says. "We should go."

"Are you guys sure?" I glance back and forth between them. "We had planned for a nice, quiet night in. I don't want you to feel like you *have* to take me to the party."

"You're not the one who suggested it, Em. I am," Shannon says, and her decisiveness is oddly comforting. "Let me live vicariously through you, okay?"

"Yeah, I'm also in," Jade says, standing up to join her. "Let me just call Theo real quick to let him know we're going out. He might want to join us there."

"Okay, fine." I shake my head in defeat. "Let's go. If worse comes to worse, I can just say I'm there for Matty."

I stand, and Shannon wraps an arm around my shoulders. "You never need an excuse to go to a party, Emmy. They should just be grateful that you showed up."

I snort a laugh. These two are exactly the ego boost I needed.

THE PARTY IS ALREADY RAMPED up by the time we arrive. I haven't been to this house before, but it must be where a big group of the younger players live. Music pulses through the open windows, and groups of people mingle on the front lawn, holding red Solo cups.

"Let's go in through the side," Shannon says, steering us toward the gate leading to the backyard.

It's calmer back here, just a handful of people sitting around a firepit. The back door is propped open with a case of beer, and we slip inside the house.

I scan the bustling kitchen and living room, but Hayes is nowhere to be found. Given the mess he's tangled himself up in, it's possible he's not even at the party tonight, and the thought has me torn between relief and disappointment.

"Want a drink?" Jade asks, nodding toward the array of liquor bottles and mixers spread across the counter.

"Sure." I choose a hard lemonade from one of the coolers, hoping the sweetness will help calm my nerves.

We meander through the party, Shannon and Jade chatting with people they know while I trail behind them quietly. I don't see Matty, either, which is odd. He said he was going out again tonight, and this is most definitely his scene.

Thirty minutes in, I'm contemplating calling it quits. Coming here with the naive expectation of bumping into Hayes and effortlessly confronting him was foolish. Wishful thinking, to put it lightly.

"Hey, let's check out the basement," Shannon says, tugging at my sleeve. "Sometimes people hang out down there when it gets too crowded."

I follow her down the carpeted steps, my empty bottle dangling loosely in my fingers. And that's when I see him.

Hayes sits on one of the couches, a beautiful brunette sitting so close she's practically in his lap. His arm is draped over her shoulders, their heads bent together as they talk. The girl says something that makes him laugh, his eyes crinkling at the corners.

My stomach drops, and I freeze on the bottom step. It's not like they're making out in plain sight, but I'm fairly certain they're at least flirting. Clearly, I'm as forgettable as I thought.

Shannon frowns beside me. "Come on," she murmurs, pulling me back toward the stairs.

As we shuffle out, I blink against the sting of tears, though I'm not genuinely upset. After all, he owes me nothing. It's more a sense of embarrassment that I allowed myself to be swept up in the idea. I should've known better.

"Hey, Emmy!" I turn to find Hayes standing from his spot, rushing toward us at the foot of the stairs. He seems a bit out of sorts tonight. Not drunk, but at least tipsier than he was when I saw him last. "I'm so glad you're here."

My brow crinkles. "You are?"

"Uh-huh." He nods enthusiastically. "You left something at my house, and I've been wanting to give it back to you."

"Oh."

"Your necklace," he says. "I don't have it on me now. But we could go back to my place and I could get it for you."

"You want to leave the party . . ." I glance behind him, taking in the shell-shocked expression of the brunette he just left behind. "To get my necklace . . . *right now?*"

"Sure." He beams. "No time like the present."

"Well, I think you might be kind of tipsy." I chance a look at my friends, and they're staring at us in wide-eyed amusement. "And I didn't drive here myself."

He rubs his chin, contemplating. "We can Uber."

"Sorry," I say, "I'm just a little confused. If you had my necklace all week, why didn't you text me to come pick it up?"

"Oh, right. Well, I didn't have your number."

"And you couldn't ask Matty for it?"

"I *did* ask Matty."

"You did?"

"Uh-huh."

I narrow my eyes. "And?"

"Oh, he said 'no.' See for yourself." He rummages in his pocket, pulls out his phone, scrolls to their conversation, and then hands it over to me.

HAYES

hey, can I get Emmy's #? she left something here the other night

MATTY

yeah, I'm not in the habit of giving out girls' numbers without their permission

HAYES

okayyy, then can you ask her if you can give it to me?

MATTY

you should have asked her yourself, dipshit

HAYES

noted

Hayes frowns as I hand back his phone. "Yeah, I wanted to ask you myself, but I haven't seen you around. I was hoping you'd just show up somewhere."

"Well, I guess you got your wish."

"Right." He shoves his hands in his pockets, swaying slightly, an earnest expression on his face. "The necklace. It looks expensive, and I figured you'd want it back. And I, uh, also wanted to talk to you about that night."

I glance uncertainly at my friends. Shannon gives me an encouraging nod while Jade mouths, "Go for it!"

"Okay," I say finally. "We can grab an Uber to your place."

His features light up. "Sweet! Let me just say bye to some people, and I'll meet you out front in five?"

I agree, and he turns on his heel. I follow the girls up the stairs, and once we're out of earshot, Shannon grips my arm. "Em, you sure you want to go?"

"Yeah," I say. "I'll get my necklace, we'll talk, and then I'll come right back."

Jade waggles her brows. "What if he wants to give you more than just the necklace?"

"Not happening," I say. "He's clearly not that interested."

She gives me a skeptical look, poised to disagree, but we're interrupted by Hayes bounding toward us. He slips an arm around my shoulder, turns to my friends, and says, "Hey, don't you worry, you little sweethearts. I'll take care of this one."

And then he pulls me straight out the front door.

Chapter Six

I TAKE Emmy into my room, fumbling a bit with the door on our way in. "Sorry it's a bit of a mess," I say, motioning toward the untidy bed strewn with laundry. "It's been a hell of a week. But, uh, make yourself comfortable."

She just stands near the door, arms crossed over her chest as she eyes me warily. "Thought I was just here for my necklace?"

I give her a cheeky smile. "Ah, you got somewhere else to be?"

"Hayes."

"I'll go grab it right now." I walk into my bathroom, where, sure enough, her necklace still sits on the counter. I carefully pluck it off, curling my fingers around the small pendant.

When I return, Emmy's perched tentatively on the edge of my bed, her gaze fixed on my nightstand. There's a picture of me and Sebastian sitting there, big smiles on our faces after winning some Little League game.

"Found it," I announce, holding up the necklace.

"Thanks." She stands to reach for it, and as she does, I gently catch her wrist. "What is it?"

"I just wanted to say I'm sorry for bailing on you." I rub my thumb softly along the inside of her wrist before pulling away. "You should know it had nothing to do with you or anything that did or *did not* happen between us that night."

She pulls her bottom lip between her teeth, nibbling as she contemplates my apology. "So, what *did* happen, then?"

"It's a long, complicated story," I say. "I made a split-second decision, and now I'm paying the consequences."

"I kind of already heard."

I wrinkle my nose. "Matty told you about the car?"

"Yep." She gives me an apologetic smile. "And your arrest, the probation, all of it."

"Damn." I rub the back of my neck, roll out my shoulders. "A guy can't even tell his own stories these days."

"I mean, you can tell me in your own words." She laughs, cheeks flushing a deep crimson. "I'd love to know exactly what happened while I was naked in your shower."

"*Fuck*, don't remind me."

She gulps, looking away. "Sorry."

I scrub a gentle thumb across her chin, tilting her face back to me. "Not like that. I just . . . that's probably my only real regret from that night. Not getting to *spend time* with you before it all went down."

"That's your one regret? Not destroying that car or anything?"

I give her a lighthearted chuckle. "Like I said before, it's complicated."

"Well, thank you, I guess. For trying to explain. For giving me back my necklace." She holds up the delicate gold chain. "This week was so chaotic. I didn't even realize I lost it. Mom would have been devastated."

"A present from her?"

"Yeah, a hand-me-down of sorts," she says. "My grandma, her mother, gave it to her before she passed. All three of us share the same initials."

"M.E.F.?"

"Exactly."

"And for you, what do they stand for?"

"Madison Emilia Fuller."

"Madison." The corner of my lip lifts in a small smile. "That's really pretty. Why pick Emmy for a nickname instead of something like Maddy?"

"I started calling myself that when I first learned to write," she says. "It was just easier to spell out my first initials, M.E., and then slowly, that turned into just *Emmy*."

"It's cute. Suits you."

"Thanks."

I nod to the chain in her hand, now dangling by her side. "You want me to help you put that on?"

"Oh, um, yeah. Sure."

I take the necklace and step behind her. She lifts her hair off her neck, and I drape the delicate chain around it, fumbling a bit with the clasp. As I fasten it, my fingers brush against the soft skin on her nape.

"There you go," I say, my voice coming out low, breathy.

I want so badly to press my lips right there, to kiss her neck and take her to my bed. But I've already fucked things up with her once. I'm bound to do it again.

She turns to face me, letting her hair fall back over her shoulders. "Thank you."

We're standing closer than is probably appropriate, barely a few inches between us now. Her breath hitches slightly, and I can tell she's feeling it, too—the pull, the undeniable attraction. I can smell her shampoo, something light and floral. Her eyes flick down to my mouth, and I swallow hard.

I know I should step back, put some distance between us, but instead, I find myself leaning in. She doesn't pull away. Our lips almost touch—a light, fleeting graze—when the door to my room swings wide open.

"Hayes, I thought you were trying to forg—oh!" James stops short as he takes in the sight of me and Emmy. A wicked grin spreads across his face. "My bad. Was I interrupting something?"

Emmy's cheeks flame. "No, uh, I was just about to head out.

Thanks again for returning my necklace," she mumbles, brushing past James on her way out of the door.

I'm left standing here without her, confused as hell. The two of us Ubered here together, so I'm not sure how she thinks she's just gonna leave. James looks at me, brow raised, clearly amused by the situation.

Fortunately for me, Liam rounds the corner at that exact moment, stopping her in her tracks. "Oh, hey," he says in that quiet, confident voice of his. "You're Emmy, right?"

She gives him an odd look. "Yeah, I am."

"Right, you're Matty's friend," he says by way of explanation. "The hot cheerleader with the bleach-white hair."

"Again, bro," James says, eyeing his little brother. "Very interesting thing to say out loud."

Liam waves him off. "Anyway, are you here to hook up with Hayes or James?"

She breaks into a coughing fit, that blush of hers slowly making its way up her neck. "Neither."

"Oh, thank God," Liam sighs with relief. "Because I was going to say you can do better than these two losers."

I shoot Liam a warning glare, trying to communicate with my eyes for him to shut the hell up. But of course, subtlety has never been Liam's strong suit.

"Oh, sorry," he says, though he doesn't sound the least bit apologetic. "I just meant that James doesn't really have his head screwed on straight. And Hayes is, like, a complete man-who—"

"Okay!" I interrupt, clapping my hands together. "I think we've all had enough excitement for one day. Emmy, let me walk you out."

I place my hand gently on her lower back, guiding her down the stairs and toward the front door. She goes easily, head ducked to avoid looking at either of the Donovan brothers.

Once we're outside and the door is shut firmly behind us, I turn to her with an embarrassed smile. "Sorry about them. Liam especially has zero filter."

"It's fine," she says quietly, arms wrapped around her midsection.

We stand there awkwardly for a moment before I speak up again. "I'm all sobered up by now. Did you need a ride home or anything?"

She shakes her head, bright blonde waves swinging around her face. "I can call another Uber. But thanks."

"You sure? It's really no problem—"

"Hayes." She fixes me with those navy blue eyes. "I think maybe we should just . . . keep things simple between us. Like I said last weekend, I'm really more into the whole dating thing."

"Dating?"

"You know, that thing people do when they want to get to know each other better."

"Well, what if I want to get to know you better?"

"That's fine." She tucks a loose strand of hair behind her ear. "But I'm gonna go out on a limb here and say you're not interested in a real relationship."

My eyes go wide. "I mean, we're not—"

"Not with me, *right now*. I just mean in general. I want someone who *wants* to get there with me. A guy who's looking for something a little more serious. You know, at least as an end goal."

"I can be serious."

She snorts. "Have you ever been in an actual relationship before?"

"Not exactly."

"There's my point."

"I'll be honest," I say. "I don't know what I'll want in the future, but I know that I'm attracted to you. I know that I wanted to kiss you earlier. I know that you wanted to kiss me, too. Doesn't that count for something?"

"Yeah, sure." She gives me a half-hearted shrug. "It means we're both good-looking people who are chock-full of hormones. I'm sure there are lots of other girls that you'd like to kiss, too."

"Em—"

"Look, it's fine. I just think we'd be better off as friends for now."

I sigh in defeat, not willing to argue the point any further. "Okay, I understand. I am a great friend, after all."

She offers me a small, sad smile. Then, she turns and walks down the driveway, fingertips trailing along the cars as she goes. Her Uber pulls up, and she slides inside while I'm here wishing I could rewind time. Go back to my bedroom when we were so fucking close to kissing.

With a defeated sigh, I head back inside the house. James and Liam are waiting expectantly, identical shit-eating grins on their faces.

"Shut up," I mutter, stomping past them toward my room.

"We didn't say anything!" James calls after me, laughter in his voice.

I slam my door hard, blocking out their snickers. Flopping down on my bed, I scrub my hands over my face and groan.

I suppose Emmy's right. I wanted to kiss her tonight. I wanted to do a whole lot more with her last Friday. Yet as much as I'm drawn to her, I know deep down that we want different things.

She's obviously looking for a real relationship, something meaningful and long-term. And right now, I'm not sure exactly what I'm searching for. I don't even have the bandwidth to find out.

THE REST of the weekend passes by in a haze of video games and junk food with the guys, a welcome distraction from the mess I've got myself into. Now that it's Monday, I'm set to attend my first court-mandated counseling session.

Anger fucking management.

It was part of the plea bargain we made. I promised to complete three months of weekly sessions with Dr. Vargas. I need to learn to control my urges, show that I won't become a repeat offender. That I won't smash up someone else's car just because I'm pissed off in the middle of the night.

If that were even close to the truth, then I might not resent these sessions as much. But here I am, standing outside of my counselor's office, dreading what's to come.

I take a deep breath and wait for her to answer the door. When she does, she greets me with a warm smile and gestures for me to take a seat inside.

"It's nice to meet you, Hayes," she says kindly. "I'm looking forward to getting to know you over the next few months."

"Same here."

The next hour goes by slowly as we discuss my "anger issues" and what led up to my "outburst." Dr. Vargas is a good listener, nodding along, encouraging, as I half-heartedly divulge information about my past.

"So, you said your parents were never around much. It sounds like they allowed you and your brother to fend for yourselves for quite some time," she summarizes, jotting some notes down on her pad. "Do you think that has anything to do with what happened?"

"I don't know," I mumble, crossing my arms over my chest. "Maybe."

"Anger is a secondary emotion, Hayes." She peers at me over her notebook. "What do you think you were feeling right before you destroyed that car?"

"I told you, I don't—"

"Were you sad? Lonely? Hurt?"

I shift uncomfortably in my chair. Keeping up this lie, this complete fabrication of events, is difficult enough. The idea of having to fake my emotions sets me even more on edge.

"I guess," I begin, then stop. "I don't know."

Dr. Vargas gives me a knowing look. "It's okay to not have all the answers right away. We'll figure it out together, all right?"

"Right." I fake a smile, dying inside for this charade to be over.

The rest of the session flies by in a flurry of emotions I don't actually feel, and by the time I'm out the door, I'm more than ready to put this whole ordeal behind me.

Only twelve sessions left. Less than three months until this is all over. It'll be fine in the end. After all, there's nothing I can't handle for just a few short months.

Chapter Seven

EMMY

Matty and I walk slowly through the quad, enjoying the late-summer weather. It's a welcome change from the cramped and stuffy classrooms we've been stuck in all morning. There's nothing quite like a breezy afternoon in North Carolina.

Although today, my knees are particularly achy. It's a common issue for me lately—sore muscles and inflamed joints. Some days are tougher than others. But I'm determined to push through, to enjoy this simple afternoon walk with my friend.

"When we get back home later," I say, "I think I'll take an extra-long bath."

"We should pick up some Epsom salt."

"I've never actually tried it before."

"My dad swears by it. Says it's the best way to unwind after a hard day's work."

I scrunch up one side of my face. "So, I remind you of your sixty-year-old father?"

Matty snorts a laugh, gently nudging me with his elbow. "It'd be an honor for you to be compared to Joe."

"Fair enough."

I lean into the thought, relishing in the fact that I'll be lying in hot water in less than three hours. If only we had one of those whirlpool tubs at home. The kind that are round, luxurious, and could easily fit two people with room to spare.

Sadly, my daydream is interrupted when I spot Hayes across

the quad. He's wearing an emerald-green vest with the campus logo, picking up trash and depositing it into a large bag.

Even doing manual labor, he looks unfairly handsome. Toned and rugged in a classic sort of way. The afternoon sun glints off his golden-brown hair while he works, muscles flexing beneath his thin T-shirt. If I wasn't in public, I might as well be drooling over him.

At this point, I'm well aware that I'm staring, and it's not long before our eyes meet. When he spots me, he offers a crooked smile. Something deviously sweet. My traitorous heart actually flutters in my chest, and I beat myself up for the reaction.

I quickly look away, trying to focus on whatever Matty is saying now. But, of course, I'm not off the hook just yet. Hayes jogs over to meet us, slapping Matty on the back with his gloved hand.

"Would you look at that," he says. "It's Matty Brooks and Emmy Fuller, as I live and breathe. Two of my favorite people."

"Did you just touch me with your trash hand?" Matty deadpans, expression contorted with disdain.

"Nah." He holds up his other hand, swiping it across Matty's upper arm. "This one is my trash hand."

"Disgusting," Matty says, playfully shoving him away.

I haven't seen Hayes in a few days now. Not since our almost-kiss. Not since I told him that I just want to be friends. I honestly don't even know where that came from, considering the fact that I've been crushing on him for months—maybe even years—before that.

But I'm trying to be strong here. To do what's best for me in the long run and not give in to hormone-induced urges. No matter how undeniably attractive I find him.

"Oh, Emmy," he says, dropping the trash bag and clasping his hands together. "I've been thinking about it, and I really should get your number."

"Oh, uh, why?"

"So we can hang out, obviously."

I raise a confused brow. "You want to . . . hang out?"

"Well, yeah, you said we were gonna be friends, didn't you?" He tilts his head. "Don't tell me you were just saying what I wanted to hear. You're gonna break my heart, Fuller."

Beside me, Matty rolls his eyes, coughing some half-assed insult under his breath.

"Fine," I say, a sigh escaping my lips. "If you really want to be friends, then give me your phone."

He spreads his fingers wide, showing off his gloves. "Trash hands, remember? But I give you full consent to reach into my pockets."

I scoff. "Very generous of you."

Matty shoves him again. "My brother in Christ, I know you did not just go there."

"Kidding." Hayes chuckles. "I'll give you my number, and you can text me yours."

I pull out my phone, typing in the digits as he rattles them off. And then he waits there, both brows raised, until his phone vibrates with the promised text.

"Is there something going on here that I should know about?" Matty asks, gaze lingering on his teammate.

"Yes," Hayes answers immediately.

"No," I correct. "There most definitely isn't."

Hayes picks up the trash bag and then gives Matty an exaggerated wink. "Sorry, I meant *not yet*."

"Just give it up, yeah?" Matty laughs softly. "She's way too good for you."

"That's probably true. Anyway, duty calls." Hayes raises a hand to his forehead in a salute, the sunlight glinting off of his fingers as he turns and walks away.

"What a tool," Matty says, shaking his head.

"He's one of your best friends."

"Yeah, he is." The corner of his mouth quirks up. "And you like him, don't you?"

I stop in my tracks, frantically glancing over my shoulder. But Hayes is already yards away by now, sucked back into his community service, and I'm totally in the clear. "I, um, I don't know what you're talking about."

Green eyes light up, and something heavy lodges in my throat. "Em, you're an actual tomato right now."

"Okay, well, that's just 'cause you caught me off guard."

"And because you like him."

"Maybe." I fill my lungs with a big gulp of air. "A little bit. But I'm not that naive. I know he's not interested in me, not *like that*. So we're just going to be friends."

He gives me a tight-lipped smile. "I think the idea of a challenge might be getting to him."

"I'm not playing games here."

"I know you're not, Em." He tosses an arm over my shoulder, tucking me against his side. "Because you're not hard to get. You're hard to earn."

I stare up at him, give a goofy smile. "Isn't that right?"

Joe Brooks is right about a lot of things in life, but I think his penchant for Epsom salt baths is his best discovery yet. I haven't felt this relaxed in ages. My joints feel warm and loose, not at all achy like they have been lately.

I think I could stay inside this tub forever.

I sink deeper into the warm water, letting my eyes fall shut. The lavender-scented bubbles tickle my chin as I breathe in deep. It's warm, all-encompassing,

But then, like an annoying reminder of reality, my phone buzzes from its perch on the ledge of the tub. I consider ignoring it, but curiosity gets the best of me. I peel one eye open and grab for my phone.

It's a text from Hayes. Because of course it is.

HAYES

hey. what are you up to?

EMMY

taking a bath. can't really text

I set my phone back down, relaxing into the water once more. All my thoughts and worries drift away as I settle in—warm, cozy, and complete. But that irritating device instantly buzzes again, and this time, it's an incoming call.

Against my better judgment, I answer. "Hayes, I'm busy," I say as soon I pick up.

He breathes off an easy laugh. "You can put me on speakerphone. Set me on the ledge of the tub."

With a sigh, I follow his foolish command. "So, what's the emergency?"

"No emergency," he says, voice loudly crackling through the phone. "I just want to talk about our plans for this weekend."

"*Our* plans?"

"Yeah, does that suit you? I mean, I've got Mondays full because of counseling, classes are busy midweek, and Thursdays are reserved for community service. So, you know, that just leaves the weekends."

Alarm bells ring inside my head. "For what exactly?"

"For us to hang out," he says simply.

"Is this some kind of weird extended apology tour? Because it's really not necessary," I tell him, leaning my head back. "I've got my necklace, and I've already forgiven you for running out that night."

"It's not an apology," he says softly. "It's me making a concentrated effort."

"An effort to be my friend?"

"Yes, Emmy, keep up."

"Don't you already have enough friends?"

"You're right," he says. "I do have a lot of them. But that's just because I'm a really good one. My friends are always first priority after baseball and my brother. And, well, my brother's off living the dream while I'm suspended from all sports-related activities. So it looks like you're in luck. There's a vacancy in the Grecco social calendar. "

That drags a laugh out of me. "Wow, I feel very special."

"You should," he says. "So, this weekend?"

"What do you propose we do?"

"We could go to the drive-ins."

"The drive-in movie theater off of Sunnybrook? That's so . . . oddly romantic for a couple of pals."

He chuckles, warm and deep. "What about the park? We could, like, do a picnic or something."

I swat at the bubbles in front of me. "Hayes, these are blatantly date ideas."

"Believe me, I'm not trying to date you," he says boldly, as if the idea is simply laughable. "I know better than that."

"Wow, thanks a lot."

"I mean that in a good way."

I scoff. "I can't wrap my head around how that could possibly be in a good way, but do go on."

"I agreed to be friends because that's what you wanted," he says. "And I already know I'd fuck up anything else between us. The thing is, I don't want to do that. I may not know you very well yet, Em, but I really like what I do know. And I'm curious as hell to learn more."

I flush from head to toe, thanking the stars above that he can't actually see me right now. "So, a picnic, then?"

"A picnic," he affirms. "How's Saturday around noon?"

"Pick me up at Matty's?"

He clears his throat through the line. "Matty's?"

"Yeah, I kinda live here now."

"Oh, shit, really? How'd that come about?"

I recount the whole story, starting with my summer sublet and ending with the fact that I quit the squad. There's a long pause after I finish explaining. For a second, I wonder if the call disconnected.

"You still there?" I ask tentatively.

"Yeah," he says, his voice tighter than before. "I'm here." Another beat of silence passes before he speaks again. "So, you quit on your team after three years? Just like that?"

I frown, thrown off by the iciness in his tone. "I mean, it wasn't exactly a spur-of-the-moment decision."

He lets out a small laugh. "Hm."

"*What?*"

"Guess I didn't peg you as a quitter."

Stung, I sit up straighter in the tub. "Excuse me?"

"I'm just saying, I think a lot of people would kill for a spot on the squad. It's hard work, but that's what it takes to be a D1 athlete."

My jaw drops. I just opened up to this guy, confided in him about things that I definitely didn't need to. But he's the one who fucking asked me to explain. Now, he has the audacity to judge my decisions.

"I didn't quit just because it was *hard*." There's a harsh prickling sensation in my nose, but I force it back. "No, actually, you know what? It's really none of your business in the first place."

He sighs, long and hard. "I'm not trying to be a dick, Em. I just don't get why you'd bail."

"You're the last person who gets to judge me for quitting," I say, indignant. "At least I'm not suspended from my team because I went to jail."

A tense beat passes. When Hayes speaks again, his voice is devoid of emotion. "Wow. Low blow."

I close my eyes, instantly regretting the harsh words. But before I can apologize, Hayes continues. "I think we should put a pause on this conversation. Let's wait until Saturday to finish."

I jolt back. "You still want to go ahead with the picnic?"

"Yeah, do you?"

I contemplate my response for a long moment. He reacted poorly to my story, and it struck a chord. I don't like feeling judged, especially when I've been so harsh on myself for the past year and a half.

I'm still working through that, and Hayes doesn't know the full story. He couldn't. All the aches, the pain, the lonely nights I spent ruminating over my decision. Plus, I have a sneaking suspicion that his reaction is more about himself than it is about me.

"Yeah, okay," I confirm quietly. "I'll see you at noon."

"See you then," he says, and the line goes dead.

With a weighted sigh, I scrub my hands over my temples and sink back beneath the bubbles. This time, my head is spinning. So much for relaxing.

Chapter Eight
HAYES

PERHAPS EMMY WAS RIGHT. A picnic in the middle of the park is oddly romantic. But that's not necessarily a bad thing. In fact, I'm partial to it.

It gives me a better opportunity to apologize. You know, for being such a judgmental dickhead the other night. I picked her up at Matty's earlier, and the car ride over was tense, to say the least.

She's still uncomfortable about our conversation. The idea of bringing it up on the ride over—rehashing exactly where I went wrong—didn't seem like the greatest idea, either. There's nothing like being trapped in a car to make a situation even more awkward.

Walking through the park, I have the urge to lighten the mood, maybe bump her hip with mine or shoot her one of those classic grins. The kind that'll make her roll her eyes but end up smiling anyway. Instead, I hold back, keeping it all inside. The last thing I want is to push her further away when all I'm trying to do is get closer.

Once we find a good spot, I spread out a checkered blanket beneath us. Above, there's a large oak tree, its leaves just starting to turn with the arrival of fall.

Emmy sits down, smoothing her white cotton dress over her knees. She's quiet as she helps me unpack the food from the cooler —sandwiches, macaroni salad, fruit, and cookies for dessert. I didn't make it all myself, but I sure did spend a good chunk of time picking it out this morning.

"This looks great," she says, though her tone lacks enthusiasm.

An uncomfortable silence passes between us as we settle in. I clear my throat, steeling myself to finally say my piece. "I'm really sorry about the other night," I say. "For being so judgmental about you quitting the squad. It wasn't my place to talk to you like that."

Her expression softens a bit, but she doesn't say anything.

I run a ragged hand through my hair. "I was way out of line. And you didn't deserve it, especially from someone you've just started getting to know. I hope you can forgive me for being an ass."

The corner of her mouth twitches up with a hint of a smile. "Apology accepted. And . . . I'm sorry, too, for what I said about your suspension."

I wave my hand. "Don't apologize. I deserved it. I was being a big fucking hypocrite. And honestly . . . I was just projecting. You leaving the squad made me think about my own screwed-up situation. But that's not fair to you."

"Two apologies in two weeks, Grecco," she says, laughter in her voice. "Is that a new record for you?"

"Well, if we count the apologies I made to my parents, to the team, to the court, to the Dean, and . . . to the man whose car I totaled." I tick each target off with a finger. "Then yeah, I've definitely set a new record."

She laughs again, something soft and sweet. "What a mess."

"No shit."

She picks at the stem of a strawberry. "Should I instill a third-strike rule for you?"

"Nah, I won't need one," I say, leaning back on my hands.

"You don't think you'll ever make another mistake?"

"Not before I hit a home run." A slow smirk spreads across his face. "And then, hell, the clock restarts."

She tosses her strawberry, and it hits me square in the chest. "You better not be talking about what I think you're talking about."

"A different metaphor, Em." I chuckle. "My version of a home run is me weaseling my way into your good graces. Then, after that, you're sort of stuck with me. Mistakes and all."

"Wow, the confidence you have in yourself is astounding."

"Well, someone has to have some."

"Is that self-deprecation I'm sensing?" She rests her chin on her hand, leaning forward. "I know for a fact your teammates have confidence in you."

I work through a hard swallow. "They did."

"They do," she corrects. "I know Matty does. He believes in you despite your mistakes. And who knows? Your suspension might be lifted sooner than you think."

A single leaf floats down from above us, the first signal that fall is coming. I catch it in my hand, turning it over as I say, "You're quite the personal fortune cookie."

"Yeah," she murmurs, fiddling with a strand of hair. "I'm trying this new thing. It's called being positive."

"I like it."

She gives a gentle nod of appreciation. "Me too."

I take a bite of the strawberry she lobbed at me, savoring it. "So, I know I reacted like a clown when you brought it up before. But if you wanna expand on the cheer stuff, I'm all ears."

"It wasn't any one thing," she says, staring down at her lap. "More like a bunch of little ones that added up over time. The long hours, the over-exercising, the competition. The way we were judged and critiqued over every tiny thing about our bodies. Our appearances. Not from the team but from the other students. I guess it all just . . . wore me down after a while."

I frown. "I can only imagine."

"And I've just been so exhausted these past couple of years. Brain fog, fatigue, sore muscles, headaches. After a normal practice, it felt like I needed to lie in bed for days on end. It made me start questioning myself and who I am. So, I decided enough was enough."

I chew on her words, turning them over in my mind. "I get that. It's a lot of pressure to deal with. And if it was making you unhappy, then you did the right thing."

"Yeah." She rewards me with a small, grateful smile. "It was hard, but a weight lifted off my shoulders when I finally quit. I'm still trying to figure out what I want to do next. But it's nice not feeling so overwhelmed all the time."

"I'm sure you'll find something new that makes you just as happy."

Her cheeks flush. "I know it sounds silly . . . but I've been busy making stars. It helps me concentrate, but I also think it's sort of fun."

"Stars?"

She shifts onto folded knees, smoothing down the skirt of her dress. "Yeah, like those little paper stars? You can make them yourself, or you can buy special strips of paper for it. And then you just fold them up."

I scoot closer. "I want to see. I love stars."

She gives me a sideways glance. "You *love* them?"

"Since I came out of the womb."

"Oh, yeah?" she teases, her head tilting lightly, her laughter hidden in the curve of her lips. "Tell me more."

"For starters, I'm a huge fan of celestial events. Eclipses, meteor showers, those goddamn Northern Lights."

A glow of affection lights up her face, and she swiftly brings both hands to her cheeks, framing a smile that sparkles with amusement. "You are such a great bullshitter, you know?"

"I'm serious."

"Are you an astronomy major or something?"

"No, kinesiology."

"Hm, sounds like you may have missed your calling."

I pop another strawberry into my mouth, chewing thoughtfully. "Speaking of, we should go sometime."

"Go where?"

"To visit the astronomy tower," I say. "Or even just stargazing in general."

"Stargazing." She shakes her head, giving me a wistful sigh. "Again, a very date-like idea from you."

"At this point, I think you're intentionally misinterpreting things."

"You're telling me you'd take any one of your baseball buddies on a picnic, to stargaze, to the drive-in movie theater *alone*? Just the two of you?"

I give her a crooked smile. "Sure would."

She snorts. "Whatever."

"So, how about it? You gonna let me see these stars of yours?"

"I don't have any with me right now," she says. "But, um, I do have a picture."

She pulls out her phone, scrolling through her camera roll before passing it off to me. I glance down, and there's a picture of a jar filled to the brim with colorful paper stars.

"This is cool," I say, genuinely impressed. "You made all of these yourself?"

She nods, sheepish. "It's kind of therapeutic. I just started on these last week. I'll sit there with the paper and fold for hours as I read."

"Making something with your hands. Focusing in while zoning out . . . seems like it would be calming."

"Exactly." I hand back the phone, and she gives me a shy smile. "If you want to try it, I can show you sometime."

"Definitely," I say. "It's a date."

Her cheeks flush that pretty pink again, but she doesn't bother to correct me this time. I know it's not really a date. We've both driven that point into the ground. Still, I enjoy watching her reactions when she's flustered.

While she tucks her phone away, I rifle through the cooler,

passing off a sandwich. She takes a bite, and her earlier words float back to me: *It's nice not feeling so overwhelmed all the time.*

I reflect on my own struggles, the pressure of my punishment weighing down on me. It's exhausting, draining me more than I care to admit. Maybe there's something to be said about this creative outlet of hers.

Honestly, though, just being around Emmy is therapeutic enough.

I'm SPRAWLED out on my bed, mind still reeling from the day with Emmy, when the door to my room nudges open. Liam steps in. He leans casually against the doorframe, surveying the scene with a raised brow.

"Hey, man," he says, a slight crease wrinkling his forehead. "Why are you in bed alone on a Saturday night?"

I casually stretch out my limbs. "Had a long day."

"Oh, you mean your day at the park with your girlfriend?"

"Not my girlfriend."

"Oh, and why's that?" He raises a skeptical brow. "She won't let you treat her like crap like the rest of them?"

My head snaps up, and I sit straighter in the bed. "*Sorry?*"

"No need to apologize."

"I'm not apologizing, you dweeb," I shoot back, defensive. "I'm questioning what the hell you're even talking about."

"You know, the girls you hook up with," he says, as if it's the most obvious thing in the world.

I scoff, annoyed. "Yeah, I don't treat them like shit."

"Oh, my bad," he says. "You just use them for sex and then ignore them."

"First of all, I don't ignore anyone. And second, I've had approximately zero complaints from the women I've been with in the past."

He nods slowly. "Alright, bud."

Well, now I'm officially irked. "Where is this coming from?"

"Nowhere." He idly taps on the doorframe. "I'm just saying, Emmy seems like good people. Hell, I'd let *her* treat me like shit if she wanted."

"Oh, fuck off," I say, brushing off the irritation. "Now I know you're just trying to get a rise out of me."

He grins wide. "Is it working?"

This is Liam's schtick. Pushing our buttons, prodding just to see how far he can go before someone snaps. It's that classic younger-brother syndrome—always in the mix, always stirring the pot. Half the time, you can't tell if he's being serious or just pulling your leg, a line he carefully treads.

It's what makes him so frustrating and yet so endearing at the same time. You never quite know where you stand with him, but that's also the thrill of it. He keeps us on our toes, guessing, and sometimes, that's exactly what's needed to lighten the load.

"Not anymore. Not now that I know you're full of shit." I pause, eyes narrowing. "Besides, you were reaping the benefits the other week, and I didn't hear any complaints then, either."

"In what way?"

"The night of the arrest. There was a girl waiting for me upstairs, and you took my place with her. I heard you two giggling in your room." I recall the muffled laughter as Emmy and I walked by, a small smirk creeping onto my face.

He gives me an exaggerated snort. "I was showing her pictures of James with his head in the toilet."

Skepticism replaces my fading smirk. "Really?"

"Yeah, she only wanted *you*, which brings me to Exhibit A. I was entertaining a girl for you while you had another one stored away in your shower."

"She wasn't *stored away*."

"Semantics."

I sigh, steering the conversation back on track. "Are you done?"

"I can be." He glances at his watch, then back to me. "If you change your mind, we'll be at the Cathouse."

"Get out, Liam," I say, a mix of exasperation and affection in my voice.

He gives me a cheerful, exaggerated wave, all his fingers wiggling. "Bye-bye. Sleep tight."

This time, I don't bother to respond.

Chapter Nine

JADE and I are sitting in the North Campus library, poring over our textbooks. We're both frantically trying to cram in a study session before my afternoon shift. As a marketing major, there's never a dull moment, especially with a busy work schedule and extracurriculars on top of it all.

Jade, immersed in her journalism notes, is just as focused on her own work as I am on mine. Well, that is, until her boyfriend shows up to say hello.

"Hey, baby." West saunters up to us, his presence always a mixture of charm and mischief. "How's it going?"

"Hi," Jade says, beaming up at him. "We're good. You know my friend Emmy."

He acknowledges me with a nod. "You used to cheer with Shan?"

"That's right," I say, and for whatever reason, the reminder doesn't sting quite as much this time.

He leans on the table between us, grinning. "And you have a little thing for Grecco, right?"

My face heats up instantly, and I shoot Jade a wide-eyed look of betrayal. She swats West on the arm, apologizing with her eyes. "Sorry," she murmurs.

"Yeah, that's my bad," West admits, rubbing the back of his neck. "We have this thing about no secrets between us."

I try to brush off my embarrassment with humor. "It's not really a secret if you just keep your lips zipped." They exchange a long look, and I opt to shift course. "Anyway, the two of us are just friends now."

"That's probably good," West says. "No shame in the game . . . but the man sure does get around."

Jade chuckles, poking him in the ribs. "You're one to talk."

West shrugs, unbothered. "Okay, think of me before we met and amplify that tenfold. There's Hayes Grecco for you."

Jade gives me a sympathetic smile. "I'm sure he's not that bad."

I sigh, looking down at my notes. "Doesn't matter anyway. I've already written the whole idea off."

"You two have been spending some more time together, though," she points out.

"We've hung out *once*," I clarify.

Jade glances up at West, giddy as all get-out. "They went on a *picnic*."

"Well, that's romantic as shit," he says.

She sighs, her eyes dreamy now. "I know, right?"

"I can be romantic, too." West wraps an arm around Jade's shoulder, pulling her in for a kiss. "I gotta head to practice, but I just wanted to stop by and say hi for a sec. Love you, baby."

"Love you," she murmurs back, flushing.

I watch them with a twinge of longing in my chest. It's consuming, this desire I have for someone to look at me that way—with adoration, love, faith, and maybe a little bit of pixie dust.

Once he leaves, I say, "God, I wish I could have what you two have."

"Aw, do you want me to set you up with someone?" Jade taps her chin thoughtfully. "There are a lot of guys on Theo's team I'm sure would love to date you."

"Yeah, I tried that already. Remember?" The last date I went on was to their annual spring banquet. The night I was left to the wolves while my date, Morgan, flirted with half the attendees.

She grimaces. "There are a few bad eggs, I'll admit."

"Conor, Remi, Morgan." I tick each name off one by one. "Shall I go on?"

"Okay, but you know who's kind of perfect for you? He's a total relationship guy. Super loyal. He was with someone for a couple of years, but she never wanted to make it official."

I wince a little. "You sure he's not still hung up on her?"

"They broke things off for good right before the summer, and I know for a fact he's looking to get back out there."

"Okay, who is it?"

"Noah Elliot."

I laugh, incredulous. "The star quarterback?"

"That's the one."

"Right," I say slowly. "Why don't you just call him up?"

"Yes! He'd be so lucky to go out with you. I'll ask Theo to put a word in."

Bemused, I choose to ignore her complete dismissal of my sarcasm. "Keep me posted, I guess."

She claps her hands in excitement. "This is gonna be great. We can even double if you want. Noah's such a sweetheart."

Her excitement is contagious, coaxing a smile out of me, even though I'm skeptical. From everything I've observed and heard, Noah really does seem like a solid guy. Plus, with Jade's endorsement, he's got to be one of the good ones.

So what if he seems way out of my league? I shouldn't dismiss the idea of someone just because they seem unattainable inside my head. That's never gotten me anywhere before, and it's not going to start now.

It's time to break out of my comfort zone, to challenge these self-imposed limitations. After all, the only real barrier between me and what I want is my own hesitation.

.   .   .

THERE's nothing quite like the vibrant hum of Lucky's on a Friday night. The place is a favorite hangout for campus athletes, and it's usually buzzing with activity. Tonight is no exception. I haven't been here in a while myself, but this is where we chose to have our double date.

West texted Noah earlier in the week, and he was immediately amenable to the idea. He said he remembered me from the games, even mentioned that he thought I was cute.

So now, the four of us are here together. We found a cozy booth tucked away from the main crowd. And Noah has positioned himself beside me, his demeanor relaxed and easygoing. There's a casual intimacy in the way his arm rests over the back of the booth, just inches from my shoulders.

It's not overtly affectionate, but it's there—a quiet presence I'm acutely aware of.

"So, Emmy," Noah's voice breaks through my thoughts, "what's your major again?" He's all smiles, his eyes crinkling at the corners in a way that's disarming.

"Marketing," I say, absently twirling my straw in my drink. "And you're studying . . . ?"

"Business administration, with a focus on sports management," he answers, leaning back comfortably. "Got to have a backup plan, right?"

"Smart," I say, genuinely impressed.

Throughout our conversation, I can't help but notice how Jade's eyes linger on us. It's like she's silently ensuring that we're both comfortable. That we're happy in each other's company. Her motherly, protective instinct seems to be kicking in, even though we're all adults here.

It's endearing, really.

Jade's been the mediator of this entire setup, and her watchful gaze has been a constant presence throughout the evening. Now, as she stands up, there's a hesitant pause, a final check-in. She gives me an encouraging nod, a silent gesture that says, "It's okay, you got this."

West, ever the doting boyfriend, wraps an arm around her as they stand. There's a playful exchange between them, a quick peck on the lips, and then they're off to play a game of darts. As I watch them leave, another pang of longing for that kind of effortless, cozy love strikes me.

Noah and I are left alone in the booth, and the dynamic subtly shifts. Without Jade and West's bubbly energy, the atmosphere becomes more intimate, more focused.

I'm acutely aware of the man's presence beside me, of the warmth emanating from his body, of his arm still casually draped over the back of the booth. But just as I start to get comfortable, my phone buzzes with a text, and I can't help but sneak a peek.

HAYES

what are you up to tonight?

I hesitate. Part of me wants to engage, to dive into whatever conversation he's angling for. But I'm here with Noah, and it wouldn't be fair to him. So I tuck my phone away, attempting to refocus on the date.

He's been talking about his plans after graduation, his hopes for the draft this spring, but my mind is still partially with that unanswered text. I try to focus, nodding and smiling at the right moments, but it feels like I'm only half there.

Eventually, Noah stands up to get another round of drinks, leaving me alone with my racing thoughts. The bar's lively chatter, the clinking of glasses, and the laughter of the crowd around us intensifies in his absence.

I can't resist any longer; I pull out my phone.

EMMY

I'm out at the bars

HAYES

you're in luck. me too

EMMY

I'm actually on a date

HAYES

with who???

I'm about to respond when Noah returns, placing a drink in front of me. His smile is genuine and comforting, and I force myself to put my phone away to give him my full attention.

But the thought of Hayes being nearby, possibly in the same bar, lingers in the back of my mind. I try to push it away, focusing on Noah's stories about his teammates, his questions about me, but it's difficult.

And then, like a scene from a movie, Hayes walks right into Lucky's. He's all arrogance and effortless charm, sauntering through the front door like he owns the place. It's impossible not to notice him—his presence has a way of demanding attention. And when he finally scans the room, it's like his eyes are instantly drawn to mine.

He lifts a hand in greeting, and all I can give him is a simple nod in return. He smirks. I turn away. But I know he's still staring, hard and intent. I'm fairly certain his gaze is going to burn a hole in the side of my head soon enough.

This isn't how I wanted the night to go. It was supposed to be easy, fun, and straightforward. Now, I'm torn between the nice guy sitting beside me and this pull toward Hayes that's impossible to ignore.

Eventually, the need for a breather becomes too strong.

Excusing myself, I navigate through the crowd to the quiet hallway leading to the bathrooms. Of course, it's not long before Hayes finds me there.

"Hi," he says, casual and cool, leaning against the wall behind him.

I swallow something thick. "Hi."

"So, you're on a date?"

"Yep," I say, simple as that.

"With the QB?"

"Good observation skills."

His eyes narrow. "At Lucky's?"

"Is this an interrogation?"

He gives me a tight half-smile. "Lucky's is not a very date-worthy location."

"And you would know all about that, wouldn't you?"

He folds his arms over his broad chest, biceps bulging as he does. "Why Elliot?"

"Noah's a really nice guy."

"Oh, *Noah*, huh?" he asks in a mocking voice. "You're on a first-name basis?"

"With the guy I'm currently on a date with? Yes, I'd say we're very much on a first-name basis."

"Whatever." He waves me off. "Guy's a total dick."

I raise a brow. "West mentioned that you two were friends, actually."

"Acquaintances," he corrects, the corner of his lip twitching. "Okay, *fine*. I can't lie to you. He's a good guy. Love the guy, actually. One of the best."

I pat him on the chest. "Great, then I'm glad I'm on a date with him."

He stares at me for a long moment. "What do you say? You wanna get out of here?"

"Excuse me?"

"You should come home with me." He blows out a heated breath. "We can hang out. I haven't seen you since Saturday."

My eye twitches. "What part of 'I'm on a date' are you not understanding?"

"Oh, I'm understanding," he says. "I just don't like it very much."

"Don't do this, Hayes."

"Em, are we in a love triangle?"

I tilt my head in exasperation. "You and I are not together."

He tosses up both hands. "Apparently not anymore."

"We never were!"

"Again, sorry, I meant *not yet*."

"Stop messing around," I say firmly. "You can't agree to be friends, tell me you're never gonna date me because you'd screw it all up, and then act like I belong to you."

"Maybe I belong to *you*, then. Ever think about that?"

My lips form a flat line. "Stop it."

"Fine, I'll stop." He runs both hands through his hair, clenching the strands in his fists. "But just know you're making me feel things, Fuller."

I give him a long look. "I'm not leaving my date just because I make your dick hard."

His jaw drops, and he glances down to his crotch. "You leave him out of this."

"Speaking of leaving, I'm gone."

I turn to walk away and make it all of one step before he calls out, "Didn't you need to use the bathroom?"

"Leave me alone," I call back.

"Fine, enjoy your date," he murmurs, just loud enough for me to hear. "Maybe after it's over, he'll take you to see the stars."

I'm stewing inside as I head back to my booth, working to calm the irritation bubbling up inside me. Hayes has some nerve trying to ruin my date with his petty jealousy. It's misguided and severely misplaced.

I slide back into the vinyl seat across from Noah, pasting a smile on my face. That's it. There's no doubt about it. I'm going to enjoy the shit out of the rest of this date . . . whether or not I have to force it.

Chapter Ten

HAYES

THE BUZZ of Lucky's fades into the background as I blatantly stare over at Emmy. She's still on her little date with the quarterback. And I'm perched on a stool, nursing a drink, trying my best to look nonchalant.

But who am I kidding? Every laugh, every touch, every shared smile between her and Noah sets me even more on edge. And I'm not entirely sure why.

James nudges me. "Hey, you wanna head out?" he asks, voice laced with concern.

"Why would I wanna do that?"

"Because you're practically brooding over Emmy. You don't seem like you're having a very good time."

I casually dismiss him with a shrug. "Nah, we're just friends. I'm trying to look out for her, you know?"

He raises a disbelieving brow. "With Noah?"

"Yeah, can't trust the guy."

He snorts. "Come on, you know as well as I do that Noah's a stand-up guy."

"You ever heard the phrase, 'a friend to all is a friend to none'?"

"What about it?"

I poke him in the chest, half-joking, half-serious. "You're *my* best friend. So don't go siding with Noah fucking Elliot. The man doesn't need his balls licked by you."

He mimics a pout, dropping his voice to a whine. "But Daddy, I love him."

"Shut up, man."

He leans in closer. "Seriously, though. Do you wanna go? Or maybe hit up Liam? Heard his teammates are throwing something."

I let out a groan of resignation. "Fine, let's just head home."

"Good choice," he says, clapping me on the back.

I mutter under my breath, feeling like a little kid who can't hold his own. "It's like I just got grounded or something."

He grins. "No dessert for you tonight, big boy."

I roll my eyes, standing up. "Let's go."

We leave the dimly lit bar, and James drives us back home. Once we're there, at least the familiarity of our own place is a small comfort. I plop down on the couch, grabbing a tub of ice cream and a spoon, diving into COD with James to distract myself.

But no matter what I do, Emmy's still on my mind.

As if on cue, my phone buzzes on the coffee table. I pick it up, expecting disappointment but hoping like hell for the best.

EMMY

I'm blocking you

HAYES

home already? what a shame. Elliot's never been a very good closer

EMMY

you're annoying

I chuckle, my thumb hovering over the screen to type a response. But before I can, the phone rings in my hand. Emmy's name lights up the screen, and I can't help the smirk that tugs at my lips.

"I am so beyond irritated with you right now," she says as soon as I answer, her tone crackling with frustration.

I lean back against the couch. "You all worked up because your date went south?"

"Yeah, because of *you.*"

"Elaborate."

"Noah took me home," she says. "He told me that he had a nice time, but it seemed like I was hung up on somebody else. I tried to argue. But he said he understood because he's going through the *same thing.* Apparently, there's this girl called Steph. He still can't seem to get her out of his head."

"Ah, fuck, Em." A twinge of guilt forces my wince. "I'm sorry."

"No, you're not."

"Despite popular belief, I was still rooting for you tonight," I tell her. "And I certainly didn't want *him* to be the one opting out."

There's silence on the other end of the line. I catch the faint sound of her breathing and picture her processing my words.

"Yeah, well, now I feel shitty," she finally says, her voice softer now.

I sit up, a sudden urge to fix this surging through me. "Want me to come over?"

"Here? To Matty's?"

"Yeah, to your place. I can be there in less than twenty."

There's another long pause, the silence stretching between us. Then, "Yeah . . . Okay."

After we hang up, James gives me a sly grin, but I choose to ignore him as I run to grab my keys. I head toward the door, and he calls out, "Don't forget to use protection!"

I don't bother to respond, my mind already miles ahead, at Emmy's place.

The drive over is a blur. I'm half lost in thought, replaying the night's events, and half anxious about seeing Emmy again. I'm not even sure what I'm doing here in the first place. All I know is that I need to see her, want to see her, am dying to make sure she's okay.

Standing outside her door, I hesitate, my hand hovering there in limbo. It's a rare moment of nervousness for me, a feeling I'm not entirely comfortable with. Shaking off the uncertainty, I finally knock.

The door swings open, and there she is. Emmy, still in her date-night dress, her white-blonde hair cascading loosely around her shoulders. Absolutely fucking stunning. She looks weary, yet there's a glimmer of relief in her eyes.

"Hey," I say. "You alright?"

She steps aside, allowing me entrance. "Yeah, I'm okay. Just feeling a bit silly, I guess."

As I follow her into the living room, there's a lingering tension in the air, unspoken words hanging between us. We sit down on the couch, a comfortable distance apart.

"You know you have nothing to feel silly about," I say, meaning every word.

She offers a weak smile, her gaze drifting to the floor. "I thought the date was going well, but I guess Noah could tell my mind was elsewhere."

"Because of me," I say, rubbing the back of my neck. "I was being a dick."

She laughs dryly. "That didn't help, no."

"Do you want to talk about it more? Or just distract yourself?"

"I'd rather not think about another failed date," she says, pulling her legs up onto the couch. "Maybe we could just watch a movie or something?"

A thought strikes me, a way to bridge the gap between us. "Why don't you show me how to make those paper stars of yours?"

"Yeah?"

"Hell yeah."

She smiles, soft and sweet, and then heads to her room to grab the supplies. When she returns, she's wearing comfy clothes—a pair of sweats and an old cheer T-shirt. She sits cross-legged on the floor and pats the spot next to her. "Have a seat, buddy."

I chuckle and slide down beside her. She shows me the paper, already cut into strips and ready to be folded.

"It's easier than it looks," she says. "Just follow my lead."

Slowly and patiently, she guides me through the steps—folding the strip diagonally, then in half, creasing the edges and bringing opposite corners together. I fumble a bit, my big hands less nimble than hers, but eventually, I get the hang of it.

"Like this?" I hold up my lopsided star. Now that I'm seeing it up close and personal, it looks a whole lot worse than I thought.

Emmy grins. "That's terrible."

I toss it at her. "It's a good thing you don't want to be a teacher someday," I grumble. "'Cause you'd be awful at it."

Her laughter rings out, contagious in its warmth, drawing me in until I'm laughing along with her. The tension that hung between us dissolves into the air, leaving a lightness in its wake.

"Okay, okay, let's try this again," she says gently, scooting closer so our knees are touching.

She guides my hands through the folding steps once more, her fingers lightly brushing mine. I try to focus on the paper in front of me, but her proximity is distracting, and I think my breath fucking hitches as she leans in.

The scent of her—so sweet and clean—surrounds me, and I catch myself staring at the graceful slope of her neck. I've never thought much of necks before, but this one? Really fucking kissable.

Once Emmy deems my second star acceptable, she sets it aside and starts on another one herself. I watch her work, mesmerized by the delicate motions of her hands.

"Try on your own this time," she says, not bothering to meet my eyes.

So, I take a strip of paper and concentrate on replicating what she showed me. It's still a little messy, but better than my first attempt.

"That one's actually good," she says, delighted. "You want to add it to my jar or start your own?"

My brow lifts. "I can have my own jar?"

She tilts her head, muffling her smile. "Does that interest you?"

"Fuck yes, it does."

She chuckles. "Okay, let me go grab one."

She shuffles off to the kitchen, and when she returns, there's a small mason jar in her hands. She passes it over to me, beaming. Pride swells in my chest as I drop my star into it.

As she works, a peaceful quiet surrounds us, with only the faint sound of paper shuffling and our steady breaths breaking the stillness. Despite myself, a strong pull draws me toward her, my fingers itching to brush away a loose strand of hair from her face.

But as I lean in, my touch barely grazing her skin, she instinctively pulls back, setting an unspoken limit between us. "Matty will be home soon," she says, her voice steady but avoiding direct eye contact. "I should probably clean this up."

"Yeah?" I ask, curling my fingers into a loose fist. "He run a tight ship?"

She gathers the remaining strips of paper, tucking them into a neat little pile in her hands. "He's probably the cleanest and most organized guy I know."

"Good for him," I say.

She quietly takes the jars and the leftover supplies to her room, and I'm worried that this means our time together is over. So, when she comes back, I throw out a spontaneous suggestion. "Should we take this outside?"

"It's the middle of the night," she says, a hint of amusement in her voice.

"Yeah, but I want to look at the real stars with you."

"You really are big on the cosmos, aren't you?"

"Told you," I say. "Since before I was even born."

She lets out a disbelieving snort. "You know, Matty did

mention something about a rooftop patio on this building. I haven't been up there yet."

"See? It's kismet."

Together, we head through the maze of hallways and up a narrow stairwell, emerging onto the rooftop. The night air is cool and crisp against our skin, washing away the awkward moment from inside.

The patio is simple but charming, with a few benches and potted plants scattered around. Above, the night sky unfolds in a vast canvas of stars, each a tiny spark in the darkness.

There's something undeniably beautiful about the view from up here.

Drawn to the edge, I step closer to get a better look. It's thrilling, this sense of height and solitude, almost as if Emmy and I are the only ones left in the world. Leaning forward, I take in the view of the ground far below, shrouded in shadows.

"Hey, can you not?" Emmy's voice pulls me back, tinged with worry. "That makes me nervous."

"I'm a Division One shortstop," I say, turning back to face her. "I'm agile as shit."

"It still puts me on edge."

I flash her a smile, pushing it one step further. "Come on. Don't you trust me, Fuller?"

"Do I have a reason to?"

"Of course. I'm a trustworthy guy."

She purses her lips. "Don't know if I believe that."

I finally step away from the ledge, coming toward her. "Well, what do you believe, then?"

"What do you mean?"

I lift a brow. "When you think of me, what traits come to mind?"

She gives me a playful smirk. "Fishing for compliments?"

"Fishing for the truth," I say.

"Uh, well, you're cocky but in an endearing way." She laughs softly, dark blue eyes dancing with humor. "Funny to a fault. More thoughtful than I would have assumed. And . . . well, do you want me to be totally honest?"

"Always."

She hesitates for a moment, nibbling at her lower lip. "I don't know for sure, but I get this sense that you're a good person. A genuine friend who wouldn't intentionally hurt anyone. That's why it's hard for me to reconcile you smashing up a car in some midnight rage."

I fall silent, her words sinking in. It feels like an eternity passes before I find the courage to speak up. "Can I tell you a secret?" I finally ask.

Her expression shifts to one of curiosity. "Of course."

"And will you keep it?"

She grins. "Who would I tell?"

"I'm serious, Em." I gulp low in my throat. "You can't even tell Matty."

She motions over her chest and says, "Cross my heart."

"It wasn't me who destroyed the car that night."

Her eyes widen. "What?"

"It wasn't me." I shake my head, sidestepping her on the way to the lounge set. I take a seat, slumping against the cushions. "I took the fall for my little brother that night. He called me when you were in my shower. I showed up, and the cops were already out looking for him. I told him to run and to not look back."

She follows me, her movements tentative as she joins me, tucking her legs beneath her. "Why didn't you both run together?"

"We were cutting it too close. One of us was bound to be caught, and I couldn't let it be Sebastian." I drop my head back. "He had too much riding on it."

"And you didn't?"

"Not like him," I say. "I didn't have a signed contract with the fucking Blue Ridge Blazers. What kind of brother would I be if I let him lose that?"

It's something Bash worked for his entire life. A way to make a name for himself, to grow up, and step out from the bubble of our hometown. I spent years practically being more of a parent to Bash than a brother, guiding him through high school, ensuring he stayed on track, his eyes always fixed on that glimmering prize of a future in baseball.

To sit back and watch his dreams, his golden fucking ticket, potentially crumble to dust because of one reckless night? That was something I couldn't do.

His aspirations aren't just his alone; they became mine, in a way. His success is a testament to our collective struggle, our shared sacrifices. All those nights spent practicing until our hands were raw, the early morning drives to games, the weekends spent at tournaments instead of hanging out with friends.

His contract made everything worth it in the end. He needed this. We needed this. So when it all came to a head, how could I, in good conscience, jeopardize that?

She stares at me. "You are . . . incredibly selfless."

"No, I'm not." A bitter laugh escapes my lips. "I just really love Bash."

She looks down at her lap. "Wow."

"Yeah, so, that's my secret."

After a long while, she glances up, eyes meeting mine. "Who else knows?"

"Just my roommates," I admit. "My parents, coach, the rest of my teammates, they're all in the dark. That's how I intend to keep it."

She fiddles with her necklace. "Your parents . . . how did they react to all of this?"

"Angry at first," I say. "Indifference to follow. They didn't even stop to question why the hell I did it in the first place. If it was some misguided cry for help."

"Was it?"

"A cry for help?" I huff a laugh, gaze drifting off to the distant lights of campus. "No, it was a fucked-up initiation ritual with Bash's new team."

"Either way, your parents just didn't care?"

"I mean, they cared enough to set me up with our old family friend," I say. "He's the attorney who got me the plea deal. But that's where their efforts ended."

She tilts her head slightly, thoughtful. "This plea deal—if you follow through, does that mean your record will be cleared?"

"That's the intention," I say, plucking at a loose thread on the cushion.

"And you'll get to play in your final season?"

I glance at her again, offering a small, resigned smile. "I sure fucking hope so."

"I'm sorry, Hayes," she says softly.

"It is what it is, Em." I turn to face her more fully, my knee brushing against hers. "I've made my peace with it."

Her gaze is steady, searching. "Can I just ask you one more question?"

"Shoot."

"Out of everyone, why tell me?"

"Because . . . because I care about what you think of me," I admit, my voice low. "I don't want you to worry that something will set me off and that you won't see it coming. You're safe with me, Em."

She mulls it over for a beat. "I think I'm starting to realize that."

I lean back again, sling an arm around her shoulder. "Good," I say. "Then it's working."

Chapter Eleven

"You're telling me Grecco was here in our apartment last night?" Matty asks, leaning his elbows on the tiny kitchen table between us. "Alone with you, and *nothing* happened?"

I sigh for what feels like the thousandth time. "That's what I'm telling you."

"Damn, he's really giving this whole friend thing a try," he says. "Prison changed him."

I scowl. "He was never in *prison*."

"Face it," he says, leaning back in his chair, folding his arms over his chest. "Mama, you're in love with a criminal."

"Not a criminal, and I'm not in love!" I protest, maybe a little too vehemently. "In fact, I went on a date last night with someone else."

He lifts a brow. "I heard."

"From whom?"

He stretches his long legs out under the table, pushing mine to the side, a small smile playing on his lips. "I've been seeing someone myself. Another guy on the football team, but he's on the down-low. He mentioned your little thing with Noah."

"Really?"

He narrows his eyes. "Don't act so surprised."

"No, I just mean . . . *wow*. A football player, huh? What does he look like?"

"Handsome as fuck," he says with a smug grin. "But I'm not gonna describe him to you. He's still figuring things out."

"What's that like?" I ask. "Being with someone who's not out yet?"

"It's my first time," he admits, expression thoughtful. "And it's fine for now. Kind of fun trying to sidestep his teammates. But I can see how it might get old pretty fast. I like him, though, so I'm willing to see how it all plays out."

I give him an encouraging smile. "I'm happy for you."

"Thanks." He takes a long sip of his coffee. "Also, I've been meaning to ask you . . . there's this exhibition game coming up this weekend. It's at Coastal's campus. Would you want to come?"

"Definitely." I've only been to a handful of Matty's games during the regular season, and I've always wanted to visit Coastal U. Their campus is located right beside the beach, nestled in the cozy small town of Amber Isle. I can only imagine how beautiful it must be this time of year.

"I don't know if Grecco will show face."

"Oh, right. He won't be able to play, will he?" I ask calmly, though inside, my heart sinks at the thought. He'll be automatically excluded because of his suspension. Now that I know the truth behind it all, the situation makes me feel even worse.

He shakes his head, lips pressed in a thin line. "No, he won't. And it sucks, honestly. He's one of the best."

I fiddle with the handle of my mug, a surge of frustration and helplessness building inside me. "Have you . . . I mean, is there anything you can do? Any way to help him with lifting the suspension?"

He leans back, rubbing his forehead tiredly. "I've been talking to Coach about it, but he says it's out of his hands. At this point, it's solely the dean's decision. Trust me, I'm doing everything I can."

"It just feels so unfair."

"Yeah, it does," he agrees with a heavy sigh.

"I don't want to overstep, but maybe you should talk to Hayes himself. You know, just let him know you're still there for him, that you still believe in him. He hides behind humor a lot, but he might be struggling, feeling like he let the team down."

His green eyes widen. "Did he say something to you about it?"

"Not really," I say, shrugging it off. "But I relate, you know, with leaving the squad and all. I've only spoken to Shannon since then. The rest of the girls . . . I'm not sure they want to hear from me."

"Have any of them reached out to you?"

"No, and I've been giving them space. If they're upset with me for leaving, I don't want to push it."

His expression softens into one of understanding. "You know, they might be thinking the same thing—that you want space from *them.*"

I let out a heavy sigh, looking down at my hands as I twist my mug in circles on the table. "Right now, we're kind of in limbo, and I feel okay about it. But what if I reach out and they prove me right? What if they really don't want to hear from me?"

He flashes me a kind, reassuring smile. "If it falls apart, then I'll be here to pick up the pieces. And at least then you'll have closure."

"You're right," I say. "And . . . thank you. Don't know what I'd do without you, buddy."

"Suffer. Weep." His smirk splits into a wide grin. "Live on the streets."

"Have I mentioned today that you're infuriating?"

"Emmy loves me," he singsongs, "this I know."

I let out a laugh despite myself. "Regrettably."

As THE DAYS passed since Saturday, my mind's been caught up with thoughts of Hayes. But working at Lawson this afternoon provides a momentary escape. The bustling energy, the scent of freshly brewed coffee, it's almost enough to distract me from what's ahead.

I wonder if he'll show up this weekend, hiding in the stands to support his team, or if he'll avoid it altogether, the pain of not being able to play too much to bear. I want to bring it up, to offer some sort of comfort, but I'm unsure how he'll react.

Engrossed in my thoughts while I work, time slips by unnoticed. But as my shift nears its end, the door chimes, and it catches my attention. I glance up just in time to see the man in question stroll inside. He's wearing a backward cap, and the casual tilt of it does little to hide the confident glint in his eyes.

Our gazes meet, and he responds with that classic half-smirk of his. "Hey, Em," he greets, a casual ease in his step as he ambles up to the counter.

I narrow my eyes in playful suspicion. "How'd you know where I work?"

"I have my ways," he says with a wink.

"Creepy."

"I stopped by your place first." He gives a low chuckle. "Matty told me you'd be here."

"Wow, I'm surprised he gave up my location that easily."

His smile broadens, a hint of mischief in his eyes. "Apparently, he seems to trust me with you now."

"Bold assumption."

"Nah, we had a nice little chat back at the apartment. He gave me a hug, told me how much he missed me, said he doesn't resent me for the suspension." He slaps a hand down on the counter. "Suppose that was your doing?"

I busy myself, tucking a few old receipts into the trash can beneath the counter. "No clue what you mean."

He gives a derisive snort. "Right, well, since I'm here . . . can I get a small oat milk latte? Five pumps of vanilla with whipped cream on top."

I scrunch my nose in distaste. "You're kidding."

"Don't yuck my yum, Fuller."

"Well, sorry, but it's gross," I say, turning to make his drink anyway. While he waits, I work methodically—steaming the milk, adding the syrup, and topping it off with a generous dollop of whipped cream. When I hand the drink over, our fingers brush, and a little jolt of electricity sparks through my arm.

He beams. "Thanks, Em."

"You're welcome for the sugar bomb," I say, subtly shaking out my fingers. "You sticking around?"

"Yeah, if that's cool?" he asks. "Just finished trash duty before I popped by your apartment. Did my due diligence for the day." He looks a bit more tired than usual, the situational stress subtly etched into his expression.

I jerk my chin, motioning to an empty table. "Take a seat. I'm almost done with my shift."

While I work, I keep glancing over at Hayes every few minutes. It's like I can't help myself, drawn to whatever energy he's projecting over there. Engrossed in a sports journal, he flips through the pages with relaxed ease, standing out against the bustle of the shop.

Each time our eyes meet from behind my perch, warmth floods my cheeks. But despite the intrusion, time flies, and my shift quickly wraps up. As a little reward, I fix myself an iced coffee before sliding into the seat beside him.

"So, how's it going?" I ask, setting my drink down between us.

He glances up from his magazine, a grin spreading wide across his face. "Better now that you're here."

I rest my chin in my hands. "Wow, what a line."

"I have a few more. Do you wanna hear 'em?"

"Any of them actually work for you?"

"Of course," he says, his unmistakable confidence both irritating and charming in equal measure. "They always do."

I roll my eyes. "Right, should have known. You don't even need to work for it."

He leans in, elbows on the table, bringing us closer. "Well, there is *one girl* they don't particularly work on. But that's TBD."

"I don't know," I say. "Seems pretty conclusive to me."

His hazel eyes sparkle, amusement lighting him up. "What makes you think I'm talking about you, Em?"

I falter. "I—uh . . ."

He reaches across the table, lightly tapping my hand with a finger, his touch brief but intentional. "God, so full of yourself," he says with a chuckle. "All this time we're spending together is starting to rub off on you."

Shaking my head, I take a sip of my iced coffee, using the distraction to gather my thoughts. Then I set the cup down and meet his gaze squarely. "Can we talk about something serious for a minute?"

He leans back, his attention sharpening. "What is it?"

I fiddle with my straw. "This weekend . . . The exhibition game. Were you planning on going?"

"I'm still deciding." His gaze drops, revealing the conflict within—his longing to join the team wrestling with the reality of his suspension. "It's weird, you know? Being on the sidelines when I should be out there playing."

"Yeah, I can only imagine." I take another slow sip, swirl my straw around. "But, um, I'll be there. If it's any consolation."

He rubs his chin. "You're going?"

"Yeah, Matty invited me to watch. Thought it would be cool to check out Coastal, too."

His forehead wrinkles slightly, and he pauses, biting his lip, lost in thought. "Okay," he finally says.

"Okay?"

He offers a genuine smile, one that reaches his eyes, and for a moment, the weight of his troubles seems to lift. "Yeah, you just helped me make up my mind. Looks like we're both going to the coast this weekend."

An uncontrollable smile tugs at my own lips. "Yeah? You'll go?"

"I'll go." He eases further into his chair, stretching out his legs and letting out a slow breath. "Gotta support the boys. And besides, the thought of spending some more time with you, *my friend*, is a big plus."

I kick at his chair. "Why'd you say it like that?"

"Because, for whatever reason, everyone finds it so impossible to believe we can be friends."

"Maybe it has something to do with those pickup lines you mentioned earlier?"

"I'm not a wild animal, Em." His gaze rakes over me, slow and measured, and the intensity of it throws me off-balance. "I can control my urges, even if I'd love nothing more than to—"

"Okay!" I ball up a napkin and throw it at him. "Not the time or place, pal."

"Later, then?"

"No," I deadpan.

"Fine, fine." A soft chuckle escapes him. "But we should get dinner, though, right? Tomorrow night before we head out to the coast."

"You wanna go up a day early?"

"Of course. Gotta beat the traffic."

I peer at him, unconvinced. "And . . . you wanna drive there together?"

He takes one last sip of his coffee, tosses it toward the trash can a few feet away from us. It lands straight in the middle with a perfect clunk. "Well, neither of us can ride over with the team. And reducing emissions is always my top priority."

I gape at him. "Sure it is."

"I swear on everything that's true and noble," he says, crossing a hand over his heart. "I'm an environmentalist, first and foremost."

"I thought you were an astronomer?"

"That, too," he says.

I kiss the back of my teeth. "A man of many talents."

"Ain't that the truth, baby." He flashes another smirk, lets out a low whistle. "It's a Grecco thing."

Chapter Twelve

HAYES

I'M LEAVING MY CAR, about to head up to Emmy's apartment, when she bursts out of the building, jogging toward me in the parking lot. The sight of her stops me in my tracks, a mixture of surprise and something else—something much warmer—fluttering in my chest.

"I was gonna come up," I say with a slight frown.

"No need," she says briskly, her bright blonde hair bouncing as she moves. "Because this isn't a date."

"It's not?" I cock my head, feigning confusion, but inside, I'm all smiles. Emmy always calls me on my bullshit, and it's one of the many things I like about her. Almost as much as I like that plum-purple lipstick she wears.

She doesn't answer, just narrows her eyes at me, a silent challenge. I can't resist stepping closer, taking the opportunity to really look at her this time.

She's dressed casually, but there's something about the way she carries herself that always captivates me. The soft fabric of her shirt clings just right, and her jeans accentuate every curve. She's the epitome of effortless beauty, and it's damn hard not to notice.

A corner of my lip lifts, and I lower my voice deliberately. "You look good."

She groans, clearly flustered. "Don't do that."

"Do what?" I ask, innocence lacing my tone.

Her whole body shudders, and she wraps an arm protectively

over her chest. "Undress me with your eyes and pretend that it's just normal friend behavior."

"Sorry," I tease, "did you want me to undress you with my hands?"

That earns me a long, heavy sigh from her.

"Come on, honey bear," I say, trying to lighten the mood. I open the car door for her, sidestepping to let her in. As I lean over to buckle the seat belt, our eyes lock, and the intensity of the moment drills into me. "You really do look good tonight."

Her cheeks flush a soft shade of pink, a sight that sparks a glow of satisfaction. "So do you."

We drive to dinner, the car filled with a comfortable silence, the kind that speaks of an easy familiarity. We've grown close over the past month, and being with her now feels like being with someone I've known for years.

The restaurant we chose isn't anything fancy, just a nice place to grab food before hitting the road. Coastal is a couple of hours away, and the anticipation of the trip, of spending more time with Emmy, keeps my spirits high.

As we settle into our booth together, we briefly flip through the menus. I'm already scanning the burger section when our waitress approaches. She's got this air about her, like she knows she's attractive and isn't afraid to use it.

Normally, I'd be all about it. Tonight, I simply couldn't care less.

"Hey there, I'm Brooke," she says, her eyes locking onto mine, blatantly ignoring the woman sitting across from me. "Can I start you off with some drinks?"

"I'll have a chocolate milkshake," I say. "Thank you."

"And for you, ma'am?" She finally acknowledges Emmy, but her tone is flat, devoid of the warmth she just offered me.

Picking up on the awkward vibe, Emmy gives her a tight smile. "Iced tea, please."

"Okay," Brooke says, though her eyes never leave mine. She leans in a bit closer than necessary, letting her hand brush against my shoulder. "And have we decided on what we're having tonight, or do you need a few more minutes?"

Emmy's gaze locks on me, her face blending amusement with annoyance. It would be nice to reassure her, to smooth over the tension with a few well-chosen words. But I don't want to risk overstepping. Instead, all I say is, "We need a few more minutes."

Brooke lingers a moment longer, her smile a little too wide. "Sure thing. Just signal me when you're ready."

She saunters away, her attention still locked in, and I swear to God she even winks at me from across the bar. It's clear from her sly smirks and pointed glances that she's playing some kind of game here. And I'm entirely uninterested in being a part of it.

"So, that was a bit much," Emmy remarks, nibbling at her lower lip. "You gonna get her number?"

I scrunch up one side of my face. "Nah, she's not my type."

"Really? What is your type, then?"

"Sweethearts."

"*Sweethearts?*" she echoes in disbelief.

"Mhm," I say with a wide grin. "Anyone who's real nice to me."

She laughs, a soft sound. "You ever think about raising your standards?"

"Nope." I tap the top of my menu, my gaze fixed on her. "Have you?"

"I like to think my standards are fairly high already."

"I don't know about that," I say, giving her a knowing look. "I mean, you almost slept with *me*. Remember Showergate?"

"Momentary lapse in judgment."

I glance up at the ceiling, feigning exasperation. "And yet I continue to suffer for it."

She rolls her eyes. "Aside from that night, I can promise you that I do."

I hum in thought. "That reminds me . . . last weekend, you said you didn't want to think about another failed date. Is there a story there?"

"Not really," she says, leaning on the table, chin in her hand. "I hadn't been on a date since last spring. Another football player. It went . . . poorly, to say the least."

"Who was it?"

"Morgan Hughes."

"Yeah, that tracks." I give her a soft smile. "A killer tight end, but the guy's a total dipshit." Not that I know a single thing about him other than the position he plays. But if he fumbled Emmy, I can rightly assume.

She laughs. "Thanks."

"So, who else?"

"There was this short-term relationship the summer before that. He was part of the crew team, but he dumped me once the term started. Said he'd be too busy with practice and all that. Heard he was hooking up with some freshman two weeks later."

I frown. "Asshole."

"I know, right? So, that's why I'm not interested in the whole hookup thi—"

"Hey, you two," Brooke interrupts, returning with our drinks in hand.

As she leans over the table, her smile is forced, and her bright blue eyes linger on me much longer than necessary. Emmy, sensing the awkwardness, fidgets in her seat, her gaze bouncing uneasily between us.

"So, what can I get for you?" Brooke finally asks, voice dripping with a faux sweetness.

I request a burger and fries, maintaining a painfully neutral tone and offering only a polite glance in her direction. Emmy decides on the same. Brooke jots down our choices, her disappointment evident as she walks away.

Once she's out of earshot, I pivot toward Emmy, eager to redirect our conversation back to neutral ground. "You were saying something before," I prompt, leaning forward. "About your standards?"

Emmy gives me a half-smile, her guard back up. "Yeah, already forgot where I was going with that."

I chuckle. "Alright, I'll bite. Just fill me in later."

She quietly sips her iced tea, keeping her thoughts to herself. Meanwhile, I eagerly tackle my milkshake, making a point to enjoy the whipped cream topping. Noticing her intense gaze, I decide to entertain her a bit more.

Deliberately, I swipe a finger through the cream, giving it a taste, then triumphantly pop the cherry into my mouth. With a flick of my tongue, I tie the stem into a knot, showcasing my little party trick to Emmy like it's a trophy.

She watches without a word until I casually place the knotted stem on a napkin. Flashing a victorious smile, I lift my glass slightly in her direction. "You want some?"

"No, thanks," she says, nose scrunched. "But I am wondering— are you actually a child in a grown man's body?"

"No, and that would be wildly inappropriate on your part."

She rears back. "How so?"

"Because you were just ogling me."

"I absolutely was *not*."

"Baby, I love how you lie to yourself."

She's still laughing at me by the time our food arrives. Sadly, this round, Brooke's performance is even more over-the-top, almost theatrical in her attempts to flirt. She brings back napkins, refills my shake, and returns to our table about five more times before we've even had the chance to eat.

Throughout the whole charade, I pointedly focus on Emmy, giving her my full attention. Once Brooke seems to realize I'm not biting, we fall into our usual rhythm of teasing and laughter. It's comfortable, familiar, and for a moment, I can forget about everything else.

Later, when Brooke brings the check, she has the audacity to slip me her number along with it. I don't even glance at the note before crumpling it up in the palm of my hand.

As we stand to leave, I toss it in the trash can by the door and drape an arm casually around Emmy's shoulders. When I pull her in a bit closer, my lips easily find the side of her head, popping a protective little kiss just there.

She looks up at me, eyes wide with surprise. But then she smiles, a genuine, warm smile that makes me feel like I've done something right for once.

"We should get going," I say, Brooke's eyes burning into our backs. "Got a long drive ahead."

Walking to my car, I wrap my arm firmly around Emmy, and she leans into me—comfortable and close—tilting her head to rest against my side. I open the passenger door for her, and she slides in, tossing her bag at her feet.

After settling into the driver's seat, I glance over at her. "Ready to hit the road?"

She nods, a soft yawn escaping her lips. "Yeah, let's go."

The drive to Coastal unfolds in a quiet, contented silence. Emmy, clearly exhausted, rests her head against the window, her eyes fluttering shut. I turn on the radio to a low volume, allowing the soft music to fill the car. In the faint glow of the dashboard lights, I watch her, struck by how peaceful she looks—how serene.

I'm tempted to reach out and brush a strand of hair away from her face, but instead, I keep my hands firmly planted on the wheel.

The calm of our drive is disrupted by my car signaling an incoming call from Sebastian. Emmy, caught in a half-asleep daze, hardly reacts. I softly nudge her, asking, "You okay if I take this?"

She nods drowsily. "Go ahead, I'm fine."

I hit the speakerphone button. "Hey, Bashy, what's going on?"

"Just kicking back with the guys, you know, doing the whole team-bonding thing." His slurred words betray the fact that he's been drinking. "Kinda miss you, man."

"Miss you, too, buddy." I cock an amused brow. "Where are you all?"

"At some bar downtown. It's wild here tonight."

A wave of unease washes over me. "Bash, you know that's not a good idea, right? You're still underage."

He chuckles, carefree and light. "Come on, you and I have partied together before. It's no big deal."

"It may not seem like a big deal to you," I say, patience wearing thin, "but it's still illegal, Bash."

"You never seemed to care before," he says, defensive now.

"Yeah, well, things change," I say roughly, and even I hate the way it sounds. "If you get caught in public now, there could be serious consequences. An MIP, for one, which would make what I did last month completely worthless."

"I didn't think about it like that." His tone has shifted, guilt creeping into his voice.

"Just call me when you're sober," I say flatly. "We'll talk then."

"I'm sorry, Hayes," he mumbles.

I end the call, my mood officially soured. Emmy, more alert now, straightens in her seat, sensing my change in demeanor. "You okay?"

After pushing so hard for Bash to get to where he is now, to keep his spot on the team, he's still willing to put it all on the line for a night out. It's not just the legality that's eating at me—it's the fact that he doesn't even recognize when he's making a risky choice.

Yet, as my irritation simmers, a twinge of guilt gnaws at me, too. He's still young, entitled to his moments of fun and freedom, isn't he? The balance between caution and allowing him the space to grow is delicate, and I wonder if my harshness might push him further away rather than guide him.

"Not really."

She extends a hand over the center console, brushing her fingers across my upper arm. "Bash is out drinking?"

"Yep," I say tightly.

"Quite a risk after what you sacrificed."

"Exactly my point. I just . . . I want him to understand the stakes without feeling like I'm breathing down his neck," I mutter more to myself than to Emmy. "It's not like I'm oblivious to the fact that he'd want to party with his new team. Hell, I drank when I was fresh out of high school, too. And he's surrounded by a bunch of older guys now. It was bound to happen. But using a fake? Going to a bar in the town he plays in? It's a bold fucking move."

She squeezes my arm gently. "Hopefully, he'll take what you said to heart. He's really lucky to have someone that cares so much in his corner."

I glance over at her, meeting her earnest gaze. "Yeah. Thanks, Em. Sometimes I forget that he's just an eighteen-year-old kid. And then, on nights like tonight, I'm acutely aware of it."

I flip my palm over so I can link our fingers together, testing the waters. She just smiles, gives my hand a little shake, and lets me hold her.

"Siblings, right?"

"Yeah, do you have one?" I ask.

"Nope," she says softly. "And tonight, I think I'm even happier that I don't."

I chuckle softly, blow out a shuddery breath. "Man, I could really use a drink right now."

"Fight fire with fire," she says. "I like it."

"You think our hotel rooms have fully stocked minibars?"

She tilts her head against the window, staring out at the night sky, hand still linked with mine. "I think we're about to find out."

Chapter Thirteen

I TOSS my duffle on the rack in my hotel room, flopping down on the bed like it's my only salvation. My eyes slowly drift closed, and then a knock rackets against my wall. I glance up, startled.

But the sound isn't coming from the wall at all. It's coming from the adjoining door—the one I didn't bother to notice before.

"You decent?" shouts Hayes from the other side. "Either way, I'm coming in."

A second later, he bursts into the room like he owns the place, holding up two shooters in both hands like they're trophies.

I break into a grin. "Looks like your room was stocked after all."

"Just my luck," he says.

"Did you book us adjoining rooms on purpose?"

"Of course I did." He walks to the minifridge in the center of my room, kneeling down to rifle through the contents. "Oh, what the hell? Why do you get blue raspberry Smirnoff and Bailey's while I'm stuck with Jim Beam?"

"Discrimination?" I suggest with a laugh.

"Damn right." He pops up from his spot on the floor, tossing me some strawberry-flavored vodka. I fumble to catch it. "You want that one?"

"I'm not the one who needed a drink."

He scoffs. "I can't very well drink alone. That's just sad."

I debate for a moment, quickly deciding that a measly shot of vodka won't do much harm. The exhibition game's not until noon tomorrow, so we have plenty of time in the morning to rest and recuperate.

"Well, in the spirit of solidarity," I say, unscrewing the cap and bringing the tiny bottle to my lips. "Drink up."

We both tip back our respective shooters. Hayes swallows, smiles wide, and says, "Cheers, Em."

I grimace as the sickly sweet liquid slides down my throat, leaving a burning trail behind. Hayes doesn't seem bothered in the least by his electric-blue shot, simply scanning the contents of my minifridge once again.

"Ooh, Malibu rum," he says excitedly, grabbing the little bottle. "Let's do a round of these next."

I laugh, watching him eagerly unscrew the cap. "So much for one drink to take the edge off."

"Yeah, well, one leads to two, and now I'm committed. Might as well enjoy it." He comes closer, holds the rum out toward me. "To a night off from . . . everything?"

"I'll drink to that." I tip it back. This time, the coconut rum goes down much smoother.

Hayes claims a spot next to me on the bed, leaning back against the pillows. "So, Em, tell me something I don't know about you yet."

I raise an eyebrow. "Like what?"

"Anything and everything you're willing to share."

His words, combined with the earnest look on his face, make my heart skip a beat. I take a steadying breath. "Okay, let's see. I hate horror movies, I was raised by a single mother who's basically Superwoman incarnate, and . . . I'm kind of obsessed with retired crayons."

He grins. "*Crayons?*"

"Crayola, specifically. There are all these colors that they've retired over the years—Violet Blue, Magic Mint," I ramble, the alcohol loosening my tongue. "Most recently, the Dandelion crayon in 2017. It's this orangey-yellow color they replaced with one called Bluetiful. A *blue* crayon. Can you believe it?"

He gives a faux shudder. "I can hardly fathom the idea."

"Hey, you asked!"

"And I certainly received."

I shove him on the shoulder, and we both erupt in laughter. I bury my face in the pillows to muffle my giggles. Opening up to someone new has been a rarity for me lately, yet this feels effortless. Right. Eventually, our laughter subsides, and I look up into his warm hazel eyes, thinking I could get lost in them forever.

"Your turn," I say softly. "Tell me something."

He smiles, leaning in a little closer. "I've been really enjoying getting to know you. Not just right now . . . but ever since that first night we met."

I look down. "You mean Showergate?"

"Yeah."

"That wasn't the night we met."

His nose wrinkles in confusion. "It wasn't?"

"No, we met over a year ago, during your preseason training." I awkwardly fiddle with my fingers, letting the liquid courage pass right through me. "I was running late for practice one morning. Crashed right into you as you were leaving the locker room. All of our stuff went flying—water bottles, towel, your playbook. I was mortified, but you just laughed it off. Helped me gather everything up. You even made a little joke to help me relax. It was . . . really sweet, actually."

What I don't say aloud is that I'd already harbored a tiny crush on him from afar, one founded on glimpses of his practice sessions with Matty and the snippets of personality that shone through his public facade. That brief, chaotic encounter only served to fan the flames.

Since then, my mild infatuation continued to grow, nurtured by every shared glance and passing conversation. By the night of that party, I was already in deep.

"Damn," he says, scratching the back of his neck. "Can't believe I forgot."

"I saw you around a handful of times after that," I say softly. "Events with Matty, stuff like that. I figured you didn't remember me."

He stares up at the ceiling. "Em . . . I'm sorry. I should have."

"It's okay," I say. "I think, sometimes, I build up these interactions inside my head. Think they're more important, more life-changing than they really are. When, in reality, the other person completely forgets it ever happened in the first place. I don't know, maybe I'm just sort of . . . unmemorable?"

He shifts on the bed, turning on his side to face me. His fingers gently push the hair away from my forehead, and then he presses a tender knuckle to my cheek. "You're not unmemorable, Em. Now that I know you—*really* know you—there's not a shot in hell that I could ever forget."

"Hayes," I murmur, my voice a low whisper. "You're kind of confusing me."

"How so?"

"I just . . . when you touch me like this." I brush against his hand. "When you say things like that. I get this idea in my head that you . . . like me."

"I do like you."

"I mean that you like me as more than a friend." I give him a small smile, working to keep my tone light, teasing. "That you have a little crush on me or something."

"Oh, well, that's not true."

"Oh," I say, mortified.

"I have a *huge* fucking crush on you."

"Hayes."

"Emmy."

"How could I not?" He flips onto his back again, breaking eye contact. "You're my dream girl."

We're both quiet for a long while, the sound of our deep breathing and the smell of sweet alcohol filling the room. Eventually, I gather up the courage to ask, "*But?*"

"But," he continues. "I don't know if I'm in a place to give you what you're looking for. To promise you a future when mine has never been less clear."

My bravado deflates, leaving me empty and hollow inside. I knew he might say something like that. In fact, I expected it. But I still can't help the disappointment that creeps into my veins.

"I like you, too, Hayes. And honestly, I'd love to say to hell with it. Life is short, and we can just take things one step at a time. Have fun together. No pressure, no expectations. But I can't do that. I can't give up what I want just for the off chance that you might change your mind."

"I don't expect you to," he says, brow furrowed, jaw tight. "You shouldn't compromise for anyone, and especially not for me. You deserve your happy ending."

"Thank you for saying that," I murmur, racking my brain for a way to shift the conversation. This is too heavy, too real for a night of drinking before an exhibition game. "But I hope you realize that you owe me now."

"*Owe* you?"

"Yeah, you wasted your turn." I tap him on the nose. "I told you three real things about myself. All you've done is admit that you have a crush on me. But, sadly, I'm too good for you to follow through."

He laughs, low and deep this time. "Oh, is that right?"

"Mhm."

"Okay, let me think for a second." He rolls onto his stomach, propping himself up on both elbows. "Did you know that I fucking hate avocados? Can't stand the texture of them."

I let out a tiny giggle. "Well, you're wrong. But that's a start, I guess."

"Alright, you want something more serious?" he asks, and I nod my approval. "I told you before that my parents are pretty distant. Well, I never really minded because I was old enough to fend for myself. But Bash is nearly four years younger. He was still just a little kid when they stopped caring. I had to pick up the slack, and I've always felt like I didn't do that great of a job at it."

I give him a sad smile. "I'm sure that's not true."

"I don't know," he says. "Maybe my shoddy attempts are a big part of the reason he continues to get himself into trouble."

I place a comforting hand on his arm. "Hayes, you were just a kid yourself. I'm sure you did the best you could for Bash with the resources you had. Don't be so hard on yourself."

He lets out a long sigh, his shoulders sagging. "I know, rationally, you're right. But it's hard not to feel responsible."

"I get that." I curl my fingers around his bicep, rub my thumb along the thick band of muscle there. "But you can't change the past. All you can do is move forward, continue being the best brother you can be."

"Yeah," he says solemnly.

"Is that . . . part of why you took the fall for him?"

"I don't know. Maybe." He blows out a soft breath. "I just immediately snapped into protective mode that night. No thoughts up in this big head of mine." He taps a hand to his temple, grinning wide. "You know how they say mothers can, like, lift an entire car off their child in times of high stress? Well, that was me."

"Such a mama bear," I say, "I've always thought that about you."

He chuckles. "Hear me roar."

Laughing along with him, I roll onto my side and scooch off the bed, making my way to the minifridge. This time, I grab the Jim Beam, tossing one over to Hayes.

"To letting go of the past," I propose, unscrewing the cap and shooting him a hopeful smile.

"Cheers to that," he says, holding his tiny liquor bottle up in the air.

We both knock them back in one swift gulp, and I wince as the harsh whiskey burns its way down my throat. Even with the buffer from the previous two drinks, old Jim Beam has never tasted less sweet.

I rejoin him on the bed, cuddling up beside him, head resting on his chest. It's dangerous territory, but I can't seem to help myself.

"I hope you know," Hayes says after a while, "that even if we're not . . . together . . . I'll be there for you when you need me."

I look at him, taking in his messy bed hair and those soulful eyes that crinkle at the corners when he smiles. "And I you," I say softly.

Emotions surge inside me. It's an overwhelming mix of longing and regret, yet amidst all that, there's this faint glimmer of hope. A hope that someday, even though it won't be Hayes, I'll find someone who's perfect for me.

Someone who will give me exactly what I'm looking for, no questions asked.

Hayes breaks the silence, a soft thud as he places his now empty bottle on the nightstand. "God, my head's already spinning."

"I'm right there with you," I say, closing my eyes and letting out a slow breath. The alcohol takes effect, causing the room to sway softly around me.

Hayes shifts his body, an arm draping over me as he gives a contented sigh. "You're so pretty and warm," he says in a low voice. "And I'm *so* fucking tired." He yawns loudly, stretching his other arm out over his head before letting it fall back to the bed with a thump. "Do I have to get up?"

"No," I murmur, snuggling even closer. "Stay right here."

"Your wish . . . is my command," he says slowly, and then—fully clothed, alcohol warming our bellies—we drift off to sleep wrapped in each other's arms.

Chapter Fourteen

HAYES

THE NEXT MORNING, I wake up with a pounding headache and a raging hard-on. For a moment, I'm disoriented, unsure of where I am.

Then, the memories of last night come flooding back—the drinking, the confessions, the soft sound of Emmy's laughter mixing with the distant call of the ocean, falling asleep with her tangled up in my arms.

I open my eyes slowly, squinting against the bright sunlight streaming in through the curtains. I glance down to find her still curled against me, face peaceful in sleep. One arm is draped loosely over my waist, her white-blonde hair fanned out across my chest.

I know I should extract myself, but I can't force that to happen just yet. Having her this close feels too right. She's pressed against me in all of my favorite places. Too warm, too soft, too . . . real.

After a few more minutes of enjoyment, I reluctantly shift onto my side, tucking my erection into the waistband of my boxers. Emmy stirs, eyebrows drawing together as she reaches for me in her semiconscious state, looping an arm back around my waist.

Her eyes flutter open, and she gazes up at me through sleepy, delicate lashes. "What time is it?"

I glance at the alarm clock on the nightstand. "Almost eleven."

"Ugh." She drags a hand down her face. "That means the game's in two hours. I can't believe we slept this late."

"I can," I say with a chuckle. "We were sloshed after approximately three drinks."

Emmy rolls onto her back, stretching her arms over her head. The motion causes her shirt to ride up, exposing a strip of soft stomach that I try my hardest not to stare at.

Obviously, I fail.

"Yeah, I'm definitely feeling it this morning," she says. "My head is pounding."

"Mine, too."

"I think I have some ibuprofen in my bag," she says, slowly moving away from me. "And I can order us some room service. What do you want?"

"Uh . . . eggs and bacon?"

"Coming right up."

She shimmies out of bed and tiptoes to the bathroom, giving me a perfect view of her sweet backside. She's all soft curves and supple thighs, a vision in her rumpled clothes from yesterday. It's all I can do not to picture *everything* she has hiding beneath them.

Though I've never seen her fully naked, that night in my room is still burned into the back of my mind. Her flushed skin, those perfectly parted lips, the rosy nipples that poked through the wet fabric of her bra. Whether or not we're physically together, it seems to play on an endless loop.

So when I told her how I felt last night, alcohol loosening my lips, I wasn't lying.

Not only am I attracted to her, but there's something much deeper there that draws me in. She's funny, sweet, and kind. I like her brutal honesty and that distinct brand of charm she wears.

When I look at her, I can almost envision a future where she and I are . . . much more than what I can give her right now. A future where I'm the kind of man who knows exactly what he wants and isn't afraid to go after it.

Despite my previous commitment to one-night stands—to

spending time with girls I'll never see again—I'm not afraid to admit when I'm crushing. Sadly, a simple crush can't lay the foundation for a long-lasting relationship.

I'm carrying too much of my own baggage to add it to her load. She said it herself; she needs someone who can be *all in* from the beginning. Someone who can show her the love and care that she's been missing all this time.

I know I can't offer her that. I've never done it before, and I'm not even sure I know how to.

As Emmy emerges from the bathroom, I push these thoughts to the back of my mind. "Breakfast's on its way," she announces, her voice still rough with sleep. She passes off a couple of pills and a glass of water before crawling back into bed beside me.

This time, she avoids touching me altogether. Maybe it's a sign I should've moved while she was gone. Found my way back to my own room through that pesky adjoining door. But now, it's too little, too late.

"So," she says, nibbling on her lower lip, devoid of the usual plum lipstick she wears. "Last night . . ."

"We drank too much, talked too much, got just a little too close," I interject. "No big deal."

"Right," she says slowly, carefully. "And we probably shouldn't, like, make that a regular thing."

I scratch the back of my head. "Which part?"

"The cuddling bit."

I laugh. "But that was my favorite bit."

"Well, knowing that your love language is physical touch, I'm a little concerned about keeping it up. You might end up falling in love with me, and then we'd both be screwed."

I scoff, jaw dropping. "I don't know where you heard that, but that is *so* not my love language."

She lifts a brow. "Oh?"

"It's words of affirmation, thank you very much."

She tilts her head, gives me a thoughtful look. "So you're saying you have a praise kink?"

"*Madison Emilia Fuller*, that is extremely inappropriate."

She shudders. "Oh God, you just gave me flashbacks to being scolded by my mother."

"Smart woman."

She smiles, big and bright. "Don't be such a prude."

"What's yours, then?"

"My love language?"

"Yeah, let me guess . . . It's quality time, isn't it?"

"That's definitely up there," she says, a finger pressed to her chin. "But if I had to choose just one, I'd probably go with gift giving. Or, I guess, receiving in my case."

I kiss my teeth, chastising her with a simple shake of my head. "Always knew you were a bit of a gold digger."

"Not like that." She playfully hits my arm, and the simple touch sends a spark right through me. "It's just the little things that really get to me. Small, tangible gifts that show me how much you care."

She pulls her hand into her lap, and that brief touch echoes against my skin. I want to bring her into my arms, feel her body pressed against mine the same way it was when we first woke up. But I restrain myself.

"I should probably get back to my own room now. Get ready for the day," I say, sitting up. The pounding in my head intensifies. "Give me a knock when the food is here?"

"Sure," she says, her voice a little quieter now, the playful spark fading just a bit. "I'll let you know."

I swing my legs off the bed, standing and stretching, trying to shake off the remnants of last night. I head to the door that connects our rooms, and then I pause, glancing back at her. She's watching me, an unreadable expression on her face.

"Hey, Em?" I start, uncertain of where I'm going.

"Yeah?"

"Thanks for, you know, everything. For taking my mind off Bash. Last night was . . . it was really nice. Just talking and being with you."

Her smile returns, softer this time, more genuine. "Yeah, it was, wasn't it? Despite the ensuing hangover."

I nod, offering her a small smile before slipping into my own room. The cool, quiet space feels empty after the warmth of hers. I lean against the door for a moment, closing my eyes and taking a deep breath.

The truth is, being just friends with Emmy is . . . strange. It's simultaneously one of the easiest and most difficult things I've done so far.

Easy because she understands me in ways others don't, pushes back when I pull, and shares those quiet moments that feel like they could stretch on forever. Difficult because I want her, *really* want her, in ways that I've never quite wanted anyone before.

The whole thing is rife with complex emotions that I'm not ready—or willing—to navigate yet. It's like I'm walking on a tightrope without a safety net, balancing between what I want and what I can't allow myself to have.

I sink down onto the edge of my bed, head in my hands. Despite my frustration with Bash and confusion over Emmy, my thoughts are still consumed by the impending game—the game I *won't* be playing in today.

It's torture knowing my team is about to take the field while I sit uselessly on the sidelines. Everything in me longs to be out there with them. To feel the dirt beneath my cleats, the late-summer sun on my neck, the crack of the bat splitting the air.

Baseball isn't just a game to me—it's a passion, a purpose. A sport my little brother and I grew up loving, bonding over, forging a home inside. And the thought of sitting idle while the action unfolds before me is nothing short of torturous.

I shake it off and try to clear my head. I can't change what happened with Bash or the fact that I'm suspended in the first place. All I can do now is be there to support my team, even if it means hiding away in the stands.

A knock at the adjoining door startles me from my thoughts. "Room service is here," Emmy's voice calls out.

I stand up and smooth out my clothes, taking one more steadying breath before opening the door. I haven't bothered to shower or change yet, and Emmy is standing there—scrubbed clean and prepped for the day—balancing a tray loaded up with food.

"I ordered a little bit of everything," she says, holding the tray out to me.

"This looks great. Thanks, Em." I take the food from her and set it on the table near the window. We both take a seat and start dishing up.

"So, how are you feeling about today?" she asks.

I give a half-hearted shrug. "Excited to watch the game, I guess. It's been a while since I've been on this side of things."

"I can imagine it must be pretty tough for you."

"Yeah, well, it is what it is." I take a bite of the chocolate chip pancakes, savoring the sweetness, not meeting her gaze.

"You know, it's okay to admit that this really sucks," she says softly. "I know how important baseball is to you. I'm sure you were looking forward to all the preseason fun during your final year. And honestly, it's not fair that you have to sit out, especially for something that wasn't even your fault."

I meet her earnest gaze, swelling with gratitude for her empathy. "You're right. This does suck," I confess with a sigh, setting down my fork. "I'm trying to be positive, but not being able to play today is killing me."

She gives me a sympathetic nod. "I can understand that. I know it's quite different because it was my own decision, but I felt the same way when I quit the squad. It's just . . . really hard to lose something that's always been such a big part of your life." Her hand comes to rest on top of mine. "But you know, this doesn't change the fact that you're still an amazing player. A worthy team captain. This is just a bump in the road."

I gently rub my thumb along the back of her hand, tracing the lines and curves of her skin. "There she goes again," I say with a laugh. "My little fortune cookie."

A hush falls between us, the mood shifting. Her hand is soft and warm in mine, our eyes locked. If we were together, I might think about leaning in, brushing a soft kiss against those pouty lips.

But we're not, so I won't.

Clearing my throat, I reluctantly pull my hand back. "Anyway, you're right. Enough moping. I should probably jump in the shower and get ready to go."

I push up from the table and head into the bathroom, my heart pounding as erratically as it did after that final shot of whiskey.

"Hayes?"

I turn back, one hand propped on the doorframe. "Yeah?"

"Just think—once you're back out there again, you'll appreciate it even more," she says. "They say absence makes the heart grow fonder, right?"

"Yeah, they do. But I never really understood that." I run a hand through my hair, lips quirking into a teasing smile. "It's like saying 'being hungry makes the food taste better.' Sure, maybe, but it doesn't make the waiting any easier."

She lobs a throw pillow in my direction, and I catch it with practiced ease. "Can you take a bit of encouragement without turning it into a debate?"

"Hm, nope. But nice try." I chuckle, tossing the pillow right back. It lands with an obnoxious thud in the middle of her breakfast plate, and she glares at me.

"Go shower," she says, tipping her chin. "You really *stink*."

"Yeah, right," I say with a smirk. "That's why you were practically inhaling my skin before we woke up this morning. At one point, I even wondered if you were trying to crawl your way beneath it."

She flushes the brightest shade of pink, and my grin grows even wider. It's a sight I've already grown used to, one I doubt I'll ever grow tired of.

I toss her a quick wink and duck into the bathroom before she can respond, leaving her to stew in her own embarrassment. God, I think being "just friends" with this girl *just might* be the death of me.

Chapter Fifteen

Tucked away in the stands, we find ourselves a secluded spot cloaked in emerald green and gold. Hayes is beside me, his baseball cap drawn low in a makeshift attempt at disguise.

Surrounded by a sea of spectators, we're far enough from the Dayton student section to blend in, despite this being merely an exhibition game. It's still an official team event, which means Hayes' attendance is technically a violation of the rules.

Though, the likelihood of someone ratting him out is slim. And even if they did, the repercussions would be minimal since he's not actively participating.

Glancing at Hayes, I brace for signs of frustration or restlessness, expecting him to chafe at the sidelines. Instead, he's the epitome of enthusiasm, his face lit with genuine excitement.

It's this version of him, I think, that most draws people in. He's not merely the star player, the shortstop with a captain's title and highly impressive stats—but the heart and soul of the team. The man who radiates positivity even when faced with personal setbacks.

He embodies the essence of leadership, not by dominating the spotlight but by shining it on others, celebrating their successes as his own. It's a quality I admire, one that's difficult to emulate and impossible to ignore.

We're not waiting much longer before the game officially starts. Anticipation builds in the air, electric and contagious. The

Ospreys are the first up to bat, and Hayes is already on the edge of his seat.

At each pitch Matty throws, he's on his feet, a silent force of encouragement. Each swing of the bat, every strategic move by the Eagles, is met with his keen attention. The man is an integral part of the game, even from the stands.

When James, diving for a ball, makes a spectacular save, Hayes is the first to cheer, his voice ringing clear and proud. "That's how it's done, Donovan!" he bellows, a beacon of support. He glances over at me, eyes dancing. "This is still pretty damn fun, even from up here."

I laugh, shaking my head in amusement. Hayes is quick to find the silver lining, even in the gloomiest of clouds.

He continues to watch with rapt attention, but I'm studying his profile instead of the game. The strong line of his jaw, the curve of his smile, the crinkles at the corners of his eyes when he laughs. His soft brown hair and that little dimple in his left cheek.

He's more relaxed today than usual, his relentless energy now channeled into rallying the team. When he turns during a quick water break and catches me staring, I quickly look away, my cheeks burning.

"Enjoying the view?" he asks, a knowing smirk on his face.

"Oh, be quiet," I murmur, nudging him with my elbow, nodding toward the field. "Here comes the next batter."

He straightens in his seat, eyes locking onto the plate. It's the Ospreys up to bat again. Their power hitter, a menacing giant of a first baseman, lumbers into position.

"Come on, Brooks," Hayes mutters under his breath. "You got this."

Matty's curveball is deceptive, breaking at the last second and leaving the batter swinging at shadows. The crowd's reaction is a mix of awe and disappointment, a collective breath held and then released.

After two more perfect pitches, the umpire calls out the third strike, and Hayes is on his feet again, clapping. The next two players don't fare much better against my roommate's pitching. With three up and three down, the Eagles jog off the field.

As the game progresses, Dayton's lead widens. By the seventh-inning stretch, we're four runs up, and Hayes can't seem to wipe that beaming smile off his face.

"Not gonna lie," he says, leaning in close so only I can hear. "I kinda thought it'd just bum me out more to watch. But being here, feeling the energy again—it's reminding me why I love this sport so damn much."

I loop my arm through his and give it an affectionate squeeze. "I'm glad."

He turns to me, eyes softening. "And I'm really fucking glad you're here with me, Em."

My stomach flutters, but I'm at a loss for how to respond. As the final innings tick down, the tension on the field grows. Yet here in the stands, I'm caught in our little bubble of warmth, cozy and content.

The Ospreys rally, putting a couple of runs on the board and tightening the gap. Hayes leans forward, his earlier relaxation giving way to focused intensity. "Come on, Eagles, lock it down," he murmurs, almost as if he could will them to victory with his words alone.

His team responds in kind. In the top of the ninth, with the bases loaded, a Dayton batter cracks a line drive into the gap, clearing the bases and widening our lead once again. Hayes leaps up, cheering.

"That's the game right there!" he shouts, and I can't help but join in on his excitement, despite the stares from the opposing fans.

As the Eagles take the field for the last half of the inning, Matty returns to the mound, determination etched into every line of his body. He pitches with precision, closing out the game with a strikeout, a groundout, and a fly ball caught in deep left field.

The small group of Eagles fans erupts in cheers, and even though it's a simple preseason game, the joy is overwhelming. Hayes pulls me into a hug, spinning me around in a moment of pure happiness. "Did you see that? That's my fucking team, Em."

"Yeah, I saw," I say. "They killed it out there."

We stay a moment longer while the Eagles congratulate each other, their laughter and shouts reaching us from our distant perch. Hayes' arm remains around my shoulders, a comfortable weight that feels like it's always been there.

He leans in. "You up for going out with my team tonight?"

"Won't you get in trouble?"

"Nah, the Dayton-sanctioned part of the day is over," he says. "Nothing wrong with a little night out."

I hesitate, debating whether joining the team outing is a good idea, especially after last night's indulgence. My exhaustion weighs heavily on me. But a quick nap might just be enough to recharge. Given the long drive ahead, I take comfort in knowing Hayes wouldn't mind me catching some sleep on the ride.

Moreover, the joy he's radiating right now is nothing short of infectious. I can't bear to ruin his perfect day. "Alright, let's do it."

His grin widens. "Hell yeah," he says, then pulls out his phone to text the team, and our plans are set in motion.

AFTER DECOMPRESSING at home for a few short hours, Matty gives me a ride over to Lucky's. Hayes insisted on picking me up earlier, but I promised him he could drive me home instead. I wanted a little time alone with Matty to congratulate him. To connect with my friend after a busy week.

Not to mention, we are, in fact, all headed to the same location.

When Matty and I walk in, Hayes spots us the moment we

step through the door, waving us over with that easy grin of his. The one that somehow manages to make everyone around him feel included.

He engulfs me in a bear hug, and it knocks me off my feet. "You know I just spent the last two days with you, right?"

"Exactly. And now we've been apart for *hours*." He chuckles, keeping an arm slung around my shoulders as he guides us to the bar. "First round's on me. What are you having?"

"Something light," I say, settling onto a stool. Matty and James find their spots next to us, already launching into a recap of the game's highlights.

The bartender hands me a drink, and I quickly find out that Hayes ordered me a mojito. Light, refreshing, and slightly sweet. A much better drink than those mini shooters from last night. I take a sip, letting their conversation flow around me.

I've always enjoyed being part of the crowd rather than standing out in it. Like in cheer, I never yearned to be the star; being included was enough.

As the night progresses, I doze in and out of the chatter, sipping my drink as I people-watch. Hayes and his teammates are a sight to behold, their easy, teasing friendship on full display. I can see why they're such a force to be reckoned with on the field; they move with an effortless chemistry.

After a second mojito, this time courtesy of Matty, I make my way to the bathroom. There's a short line down the hallway tonight, so I pull out my phone to scroll while I wait.

"Hey," a deep voice says from behind, startling me. I glance up to find a tall man I don't recognize. He has dark hair and a blazing white smile, and he's giving me an expectant look.

"Hey?" I say cautiously. "Do we know each other?"

"Not yet."

My brows shoot up. "And you are?"

"Chase."

"Chase," I echo. "Do you often approach women in dark, secluded hallways?"

He laughs, gesturing to the short line in front of me. "We're hardly alone."

I tilt my head. "What's your last name, Chase?"

"Hadden," he says, a quirk to his lips. "You a Dayton student?"

"Mhm," I murmur. "You?"

"Uh-huh. If you've been to a soccer game, you might have seen me there? I'm a striker."

"Can't say I have."

He gives me a quick once-over. "Shame."

"You know, I think the men's restroom is open." I gesture to the other side of the hallway, noting that it is indeed free and clear. It's quite obvious the man is flirting with me, but I enjoy the push and pull of a good conversation. Besides, I'm not quite sure I'm willing to bite.

"But if I went in there, I might have missed my opportunity to talk to a pretty girl."

My cheeks heat a little. It's a simple compliment, but one that's always nice to hear. A random man at Lucky's called me pretty. Not sexy, not hot, but *pretty*. Good Lord, the bar is in hell, isn't it?

Just then, the line moves, and I'm next up for the bathroom. "Sorry," I say with a tight smile. "My turn."

By the time I'm done and I've made my way back to the hallway, Chase hasn't moved an inch. I walk right past him, silently waiting for him to make one last move. "Hey," he says smoothly. "Let me buy you a drink?"

"I, uh, I'm here with someone," I blurt out, not sure why I've said it at all. But the words are out there now, hanging between us like an unspoken challenge.

His brow crinkles. "Oh, is that so?"

I nod, playing along with my own white lie. While it's still *technically* the truth, it's not at all how I've made it sound. I'm here with Hayes, with Matty and the team. I may have told the former that I'd let him drive me home. But despite all that, I'm not beholden to anyone but myself.

"Well, I'm here with a few teammates. We're at the booth near the dance floor," he says, an undeniable sparkle in his eye. "Come say hi if you get bored."

I give him a tiny smile before making my way back to the bar, mulling over his invitation. A part of me is tempted—he's handsome, confident, interested. And yet, there's something that holds me back.

"There you are," Hayes says as I slide onto the stool beside him. "Another drink?"

I shake my head. "I'm good for now, thanks."

His eyes flit across my face, searching. "Everything okay?"

I slowly stir the ice in my glass. "Yeah, of course."

He leans in, his voice low. "Did that guy in the hallway give you trouble?"

My eyes snap up to meet his. "You saw that?"

"Hard not to. He was eyeing you from the second you got up." His jaw ticks. "Do you know him?"

"Barely. His name's Chase. Apparently, he plays soccer for Dayton."

He does some weird jerking motion with his head. "And he was flirting with you."

It's not a question, but I answer anyway. "He suggested I go say hi to his friends. No big deal."

"Right." His fingers drum against the bar top. "Emmy, look—I know we're not . . . you know. Whatever. But if some random guy is making you uncomfortable, just say the word. I'll take care of it."

A strange warmth blooms in my chest. "I'm okay, really. But thank you." I gently bump his shoulder with mine. "I can handle a few pickup lines from overly confident jocks."

He chuckles at that, the tension easing from his frame. "Clearly, you have plenty of experience in that arena."

"Oh, absolutely," I say wryly. "Expert level by this point."

Our eyes meet again, and his expression softens. He tucks a strand of hair behind my ear, his touch featherlight. "You deserve better than cheesy lines, Emmy. Someone who will really see you."

His words snag my breath. Before I can reply, Matty's voice slices through the air, and our moment fades. He gives my hand a quick squeeze, then pivots back to his friends, slipping back into their easy conversation.

I take a sip of my drink, attempting to quell the butterflies in my stomach. Better than cheesy lines, he claims. Yet, isn't *something* better than nothing at all?

Chapter Sixteen

Emmy's off talking to that loser again. After she came back from the bathroom, she sat with us for a while. And then, all of a sudden, she pushed up from her stool and sauntered right over to their booth, possessing the confidence of a woman on a mission.

I try to keep my eyes from drifting over to her, but it's a losing battle. She's leaning against their table now, back arched just so, head tossed lightly as she laughs at something one of them said.

Even from here, I can see the way that Chase guy looks at her—like she's a tall drink of water and he's dying of thirst.

"Who's Em talking to?" Matty asks, following my gaze.

I grit my teeth. "Just some soccer player. He was hitting on her earlier."

Matty raises a curious brow. "And you don't like that?"

"No, I don't," I say sharply. "Guy seems like a tool. Should we text Liam and find out if he's, like, some sort of low-key criminal?"

He snorts. "You're one to talk, jailbird."

I ignore him as Emmy slides into the booth next to Chase, tossing her hair over her shoulder, giving me an acute sense of déjà vu. This is the same feeling I had when I found her here with Noah Elliot, quarterback extraordinaire. Only this time, it's much, much worse.

Chase has a smug look on his face that makes my blood boil, draping his arm casually over the back of the booth behind her.

She's all smiles and laughs as she chats with the group, though I can't hear what they're saying over the noise of the bar.

"Stop glaring," Matty says, elbowing me in the ribs. "You're gonna bore holes into the back of that guy's head."

I force myself to look away, taking a big gulp of my water. If only I had some alcohol to wash down the frustration. But I was under the impression I'd be driving Emmy home tonight, so I didn't want to risk it, opting for water instead.

"I'm not glaring," I say. "Just keeping an eye on things."

Matty snorts. "Yeah, okay. And you're not jealous at all."

"Hardly," I insist through gritted teeth. But even as I say it, I know it's a lie. Emmy deserves better than some ball-kicking douchebag making moves on her all night. If he tries anything weird, so help me . . .

"Sure, man," James adds in from beside me. "Whatever you say."

Emmy throws her head back in laughter at something one of the guys says. Chase leans in close to whisper in her ear, and she playfully smacks his chest in response. An ugly, twisting feeling grips my gut.

Before I can think better of it, I'm sliding out of the booth and stalking across the bar toward them. When Emmy spots me approaching, she lifts a curious brow.

"Hey," I say brusquely. "Can we talk for a minute?"

Chase sizes me up, but I already know I'm taller, bigger, better, so it doesn't intimidate me in the slightest. "We're kind of in the middle of something here, man."

"I certainly wasn't asking *your* permission." I hold his gaze, refusing to back down. After a tense moment, he shrugs and removes his arm.

I gently take Emmy's hand, leading her away from the noise and chaos toward the back exit. The cool night air hits my face as we step outside. Emmy crosses her arms, waiting expectantly. "Are we really doing this again?"

I rake a hand through my hair. "Em, baby, come on. You know you can do way better than that guy."

She gives me a disappointed look. "You don't even know him."

Well, fuck, she's got me there.

For the first time in a long while, I'm actively panicking, and I have no clue what to do about it. But I suppose it's now or never. I rake a wary hand through my hair, taking a leap of faith. "I don't want you to go home with him tonight," I say, the words rushing out. "Or any other night. I know I have no right to ask that, but I'm asking anyway."

Her lips part, a short breath puffing out. "Hayes."

"Please?"

She closes her eyes. "This is silly. You know that, right?"

"I know. And I'm sorry for being so hot and cold. I'm sorry for keeping you at a distance."

She puts her head in her hands, impatient. "Why, then?"

"I think I've just been scared of needing someone this way. Even more so, of being the guy that *you* need." I step closer. "But I want to try, Emmy. For you, I can try."

Her eyes glisten in the dim light. "You are . . . the most confusing man on the planet."

"I don't want to be," I say. "I swear."

"I don't know if I can handle being your trial run." She gulps, folding her arms across her chest. "You're jealous now, and it's causing you to act irrationally. And believe me, Hayes, I get it. If I saw some girl trying to pick you up. I'd probably want to claw her eyes out. But that's . . . fleeting."

She takes a step back, and even though she's right in front of me, it feels like she's miles away. I had hoped, somehow, this conversation would bring us closer, but my words seem to have the opposite effect. She's putting up walls, convinced I'm just reacting on a whim, fueled by jealousy rather than genuine feelings.

"I care about you, Hayes. I really do," she says, her voice gentle, trying to soften the blow. "But I can't be your experiment while you figure things out. It's not fair to either of us."

Frustration courses through me, prompting my hand to rake through my hair once again. "I'm not trying to experiment here," I insist, my voice laced with desperation. "It's just . . . I fucking hate the way I feel when I see you with someone else. I want to be the only guy making you laugh, the one you lean on, share your life with. I want to be the one who gets to go home with you at the end of the night."

Her expression softens, but her resolve doesn't waver, those determined eyes telling me she's heard promises like mine before. "I know you believe that's true. But your actions say differently. You keep me at a distance until some imaginary threat shows up, then you stake your claim. That's not the foundation for a real relationship."

She sighs, wrapping her arms around herself in a self-protective hug, and it's like watching the door to her heart swing shut. "My feelings for you are real, Hayes. But until you figure out what you really want, this back-and-forth isn't good for either of us."

Her words hit me hard, a wake-up call I didn't know I needed. It's a painful realization—my indecision and jealousy have been sabotaging something that could be real, could be fucking amazing.

She's asking for something solid, and I'm standing here, struggling to offer her the certainty she deserves. "I haven't made a commitment to someone before because I'm scared of letting them down. Of not being enough," I tell her. "But with you . . . it feels different. I'm still scared, but I feel hopeful at the same time. Like maybe together we could take that leap."

She looks into my eyes, seeking some semblance of truth. "If you really want to give this—give us—a shot, then you have to show me. No more running hot and cold. I need to know you're actually *in this.*"

"I'm yours, Emmy. I swear to fucking God," I say with a wary chuckle. "You already know I'm good at everything I set my mind to. I can do this."

She doesn't laugh, but she gives me the tiniest, sweetest smile. "Yeah, okay, that last part is kind of true."

Taking a deep breath, I gather the courage to step closer. "Then give me a chance to prove it to you?"

We stand there, frozen in time, our hearts pounding in unison. "Okay," she says finally, her voice a quiet hush in the night air. "But you're on probation."

I give her an ear-splitting grin. "Well, that's certainly fitting."

"And our first kiss isn't gonna be in the alleyway behind Lucky's, that's for damn sure."

"Can I take you home, then?"

She gives a humorless snort. "Someone's eager."

"Well, I've been pretty fuckin' pissed off for the last half an hour." I rub my temples. "I need to channel that energy somewhere productive."

She laughs. "Then take me home, Grecco. Show me that you really mean it."

I quickly take her hand, leading her around the side of the building to where my car is parked, just around the corner—a quiet escape waiting. Opening the passenger door for her, I ensure she's safely inside, treating her with all the care of precious cargo.

But then she throws me a curveball. "Aren't you gonna tell your friends we're leaving first?"

I pause, hand on the door. "Fuck no, I'm not gonna waste another two minutes of my time. Why, you want me to go rub it in *Chase's* face that I'm taking you home?"

She gives me this look, sly and a bit challenging, her hand

moving to the buckle as if she's contemplating making a dash for it. "No, but I better go talk to him real qui—"

I place a gentle hand over hers, stopping her mid-motion. "Don't you dare." There's a plea in my voice, a desperate need for her to stay put, to choose me without any distractions.

Leaning over her to ensure the buckle clicks home, my proximity allows me the sweetness of her scent, the curve of her neck inviting a closeness I've been craving all night. I can't resist brushing my lips against the warm skin there, my breath skimming her ear before I give her a playful nip.

"If you get out of this car," I murmur, "then I won't show you what you've been missing all this time."

She folds her arms, an amused yet defiant tilt to her head. "I think that would be worse for you than it would for me."

"I'm irresistible, Fuller. It's about time you learned that."

Before she can launch another comeback, I close the passenger door firmly, sealing us into this moment, into the decision that tonight is where everything changes between us. I circle around to the driver's side, sliding in and meeting her gaze head-on. There's a spark there, a silent challenge.

And it's one I'm ready and willing to meet.

We're in my bedroom, and my palms are dripping with sweat. While Emmy's momentarily distracted, I discreetly wipe them down the front of my pants. I've never felt this nervous around anyone before.

She's talking about the stars again, something about a cosmic shift, and I hate to admit that I'm only half listening. All I can do is stare at her—animated, happy—bright blonde hair brushing against the rounded tops of her cheeks. It's like watching sunshine in motion.

She moves toward me, and I reach up to tuck a loose strand

behind her ear, my hand shaking. "You're so fucking pretty tonight," I say. "You always are."

Her response is laughter, surprising me into a frown. "Sorry, I'm not laughing at the compliment, I swear. I just . . . that guy from the bar earlier? He called me pretty, too, and I thought to myself how nice it was. *Pretty*, you know? It's such an innocent word."

I huff. "See, I knew you needed higher standards."

"You just said the exact same thing!"

I shake my head, arms folded as I puff up my chest. "It's different when it comes from me."

"Yeah?" She raises a challenging brow. "And why's that?"

I narrow the space between us, my voice dropping to a low murmur. "Because when I call you pretty, I don't just mean the way you look. I mean the way you light up a room when you walk in. The way your smile makes me feel like I'm staring into the goddamn sun. The way you seem to find the light in everything, even your tiny paper stars."

My fingertips glide across her collarbone, drawn to her in a way that makes it impossible not to touch. "When I say you're pretty, I mean you're the most captivating thing I've ever seen. That sometimes I can hardly breathe around you because it hits me all at once how you make me feel. How you make me want to be better, do better."

Her lips part, eyes searching mine, and I know I've rendered her speechless. It's a rare thing.

"Emmy," I say, and her name is like a prayer on my tongue. "Can I kiss you now?"

She answers by sliding her hands up my chest, fingers curling into the fabric of my shirt. Our mouths meet in a collision of heat and urgency, pent-up desire finally spilling over. I pull her against me, one hand tangled in her hair, the other splayed at the small of her back.

My tongue slips into her mouth, and I can taste a hint of mint and lingering sweetness from her mojito. She kisses me back eagerly, slanting her mouth against mine, her body melting into me. For once, my mind goes blissfully blank, overwhelmed by the feeling of her lips, her touch, her taste.

Nothing else matters.

My hand travels up her back, brushing her hair away, and I feel the chilling kiss of her necklace against my fingertips. I already know that the delicate chain bears her initials, and I'm reminded of that first night when we were here together.

We kiss until we're both gasping, her soft hands now fisted in my hair. When we finally break apart, her cheeks are flushed, eyes shining.

"I've wanted to do that all night," I confess, breathless.

"Yeah?" She nibbles at her lower lip. "What else have you been wanting to do?"

I curve a gentle hand around her neck, hauling her back against me. "You know, I think I'd really like to show you."

Chapter Seventeen

EMMY

Hayes effortlessly lifts me, his hands cradling the softness of my thighs as I secure my legs around his waist. He moves with a gentle assurance toward the bed. Since the moment he drew me into the secluded alleyway behind Lucky's, my heart has been a relentless drum in my chest, now threatening to leap from my chest with every beat.

I've wanted this for so long, dreamed about what it would feel like to kiss Hayes, to be wrapped up in his strong arms. But that was before I really knew him. Before I ever had the chance to. Now, here we are, tangled together, desperately seeking the other's touch.

His hand trails down my side, skimming along the curve of my hip before sliding under my shirt. I gasp against his lips as he cups my breast, his thumb brushing over the indent of my nipple through my bra.

"God, Emmy," he groans. "Do you know how often I've thought about these?"

I answer by grinding my hips against his, his arousal pressing into me. He lets out a shuddering breath, gripping my thigh and pulling it around his waist. We move together, wrapped up in each other, minds clouded with desire.

Tipping my head back to grant him better access, I grasp his shoulders as he plants fervent kisses down my neck. A gentle scrape of his teeth against my skin elicits a moan from me, igniting a fiery coil of heat within my belly.

"I want you so goddamn much," he says, voice rough. "Tell me if you need me to stop."

"Don't stop," I breathe.

And then his lips are everywhere: trailing fire down my jaw, sucking on the hollow of my collarbone, and then lower.

"Hayes," I whisper, aching with need.

He looks up at me through heavy lashes, his breathing ragged as he reaches for the button of my jeans. "I need you naked," he says.

I'm practically panting now, helping him undress me, tugging at our clothes until we're both bare and pressed together. Hayes is above me, all muscle and heat and need.

"See? So fucking pretty," he whispers, running a hand along my stomach before dipping lower. My hips jerk involuntarily as he slides a finger inside me, slow and deliberate.

I dig my nails into his back and bite down on my bottom lip to muffle my moan. No one's ever made me feel like this—so consumed by desire it's all I can think about. So focused on him that nothing could make me second-guess this moment.

"Look at me," he commands, thumb working circles against my clit while his other finger slides inside and out. "Don't hold back, baby."

I stare down at where he fills me, watching as he slowly pushes another thick finger inside. My gaze dips from my core to his strong hands and then all the way up to his biceps. His muscles flex, veins bulging as he works me over.

"God, I've dreamed about this for weeks," he mutters. "You, under me, begging for more."

I arch my hips, meeting his thrusts, and the tight coil of release builds in my core. He pushes his fingers inside me harder, tipping my hips upward as his lips move to my ear. "Will you come for me, Em?"

I clench around him, my back arching off the mattress. He groans, thrusting his hips against me, searching for his own friction. His mouth finds my breast, licking and sucking until I'm clawing at his back.

The man is a master at this—teasing me, bringing me to the edge, and then easing up just as I think I can't take any more.

"Do you want me to stop?" he teases, pausing for a moment.

"No!" I hiss. "God, no."

He listens, curling both fingers right up against my favorite place. The ensuing orgasm ripples through me like lightning, arching my body and tightening my muscles as a cry escapes. His thumb rubs circles against my clit while I tremble, and then he's kissing me again, swallowing the sounds spilling from my lips. I'm panting when it's over, heart pounding in time with his.

"You are—" I start to say, but he cuts me off with a searing kiss, pinning me to the mattress. His bare erection slides against my hip, and I know he must be dying for relief. So I slip a hand between us, curling my fingers around his thick shaft, giving him a light squeeze.

He groans into my neck, hips twitching against my touch. "Condom," he pants.

He instinctively grabs near the bedside table, fumbling with a foil package before sheathing himself in latex. Then he's back, kissing me with an intensity I didn't know possible. His lips are on mine, then my jaw, then down my neck.

God, he's everywhere except where I need him most.

"Hayes," I whimper, aching for more.

He smirks down at me. And then he's inside of me in one slow thrust, filling me so completely that I can't catch my breath. Heat pooling between my thighs, we rock together in a primal rhythm, our bodies slick with sweat and need.

"God, Emmy," he grunts out as he thrusts deep inside, grinding his hips against mine. "Feels so fucking good . . . just like that."

I can only nod, my eyes squeezing shut as I clench around him. He groans, picking up the pace, each push harder and deeper than the last. He cups my breast in one hand, squeezing gently before grazing his thumb across my nipple.

"Don't want to come yet," he says through gritted teeth.

"Then ease off."

He does as I ask, slowing his movements to a rhythm that's just shy of torture. Our eyes lock, and I know he's fighting for control. With his free hand, he reaches between us, stroking my clit in time with his thrusts.

"Want to see your face when you come again," he says, and those words are my undoing.

My second orgasm crashes over me, and I lose myself in the sensation, my body pulsing around him as I cry out his name. Hayes doesn't last long after that, groaning as he buries himself as deep inside of me as possible, shaking with the force of it.

His body weight presses into me as we both gasp for air, our chests heaving. Sweat mingles between us, hot and sticky, but I can't bring myself to care.

When he finally rolls off me, he rakes a hand through his hair and says, "Let's do that again in the shower, yeah? I want to take you from behind."

A smile forces its way onto my face as I roll over and straddle him, my wet core teasing his softening cock. "Did you not get enough?"

"When it comes to you," he says, "I doubt that's possible. Besides, I'd really love to relive that first night in my room. Except, this time, I'll stay."

He pinches off the condom from beneath me, and I move over to let him toss it away. As I lie there, still panting, I listen to the sounds of him moving around the room, then the faint click of the bathroom door. I'm still catching my breath when he calls out, "You coming, Fuller?"

"Thought I'd make you wait," I shout back.

His warm laughter mingles with the sound of the shower turning on, and I push myself up to join him. He's waiting for me with open arms, curtain pulled to the side, water cascading over the hard planes of his body.

"You don't know how hard that was," I say, eyes glued to his sculpted abs, his half-hard cock.

He fists a hand around the base, smirking. "What do you mean?"

"Not that," I say with a shake of my head. "I meant that I wanted to get dressed and ditch, but I knew you wouldn't take it as well as I did."

His grin widens. "That's right," he says. "Because nobody takes it as well as you."

"Oh, God." I roll my eyes as I step closer, sliding into the hot spray beside him. "Do you know how ridiculous you sound?"

"And yet, here you are," he counters, lathering up his hands with soap.

One finger crooks in my direction. I move closer, slowly inching toward him. Using both hands, he works the suds down my back, my stomach, and then between my legs, cupping me there.

"Oh," I breathe, leaning into his touch. "You know, you're really quite needy."

He rinses the soap from my hands, working a finger over my clit. "I fear the call is coming from inside the house."

"Shh," I murmur as I lean into his touch.

"I have another condom," he says, finger sinking into me. "You want to?"

I nod, unable to form a coherent thought. He grabs the tiny package from the ledge of the tub and sheaths himself before turning me around. I push both hands against the cool tile, bending at the waist and arching my hips for better access. Water dripping over us, he enters me slowly, so slowly that I whimper when he reaches the hilt.

Then he picks up the pace, thrusting into me from behind with enough force to make the wall shake. His grip on my hips tightens, his movements erratic.

"Fuck," he grunts. "Fuck, Emmy. This pussy's so fucking tight."

I glance behind me, desperate to see him. His hair is drenched now, sticking to his forehead in the sexiest way possible. He groans and pumps faster, quickly working me toward another orgasm.

"Touch yourself," he says in a low voice.

I do as he says, rubbing at my clit as he presses against it from behind, head spinning. "I'm going to," I gasp, bucking back against him.

"Me too," he grunts.

And with one final push, we both explode together, our cries muffled by the sound of the showerhead and our own thumping hearts. He collapses against my back, his chest heaving.

"God, yes," he pants in my ear. "I fucking knew it'd be like that between us."

A contented sigh slips out, but I'm too worn-out to say more. Instead, I nestle my head against his shoulder, drawing comfort from his warmth, his solid presence behind me. In the afterglow, a singular thought crosses my mind: sex with Hayes Grecco is something I could easily get used to.

It's the middle of the night, Hayes' arm is draped around my half-naked body, and I'm dying of thirst. I carefully shimmy out of his grasp, slipping from his bed without a sound.

The floor is cold beneath my bare feet as I tiptoe down the stairs. Once I've reached the kitchen, a light breeze from the open window grazes my thighs, Hayes' T-shirt barely covering the rest of me.

The refrigerator hums to life as I grab a bottle of water and twist off the cap. I'm about to take a sip when I'm startled by a loud sound. "Jesus!" I drop the bottle, water spilling over my feet as I whip around. "You scared me."

The younger Donovan brother, Liam, just stands there in front of me, arms folded over his chest, head tilted in confusion.

"I'm sorry," I say, tugging at the hemline of my T-shirt. "Did I wake you?"

He shrugs, leaning against the counter. "Nah, you're all good."

"Let me just clean this up," I murmur, grabbing a towel to mop up the spill.

"So, you and Hayes, then?"

"What about us?"

He shifts around me, grabbing his own bottle of water from the fridge. "You've been getting to know each other better."

"Um, is that a question or a statement?"

"Statement." His grin widens. "But here's a question—would you say, after tonight, Hayes knows you . . . inside and out?"

I wince, eyes squeezing shut as I push up from the floor. "You heard us, didn't you?"

"Hayes' en suite shares a wall with my bedroom."

My cheeks ignite. "Aw, fuck."

"Don't worry, it's nothing new."

I cringe internally, schooling my features. It's no secret that Hayes gets around—or used to, anyway—but it doesn't make the reality any less awkward to hear.

"Thanks for that, Liam."

"Ah, right." He gives me an appraising look. "You actually like him?"

"You could say that."

He leans back against the counter, folding his arms across his chest. "So, what are your intentions here?"

"Well, the two of us, we're . . . dating now."

His brows skyrocket, and he takes another long swig from his bottle. "Incredible."

"Yeah?"

Instead of answering, he returns to the fridge, pulling out a slice of what looks like chocolate cake in a to-go container. Turning his back on me, he rifles through a kitchen drawer.

"So, Emmy," he says absently as he grabs a fork. "You like chocolate?"

I stare at him, disconcerted. "Uh, yeah."

He passes over the container without another word. But before I can take a bite, my gaze catches on the scribbled words in the corner. *Happy Birthday, Liam.*

"It's your birthday?"

"No."

I wait for him to elaborate, and when he doesn't make another sound, I ask, "Then what's this all about?"

"Birthday perks," he says. "Most companies have them. I sign up for accounts with a new date of birth each time. That way, I can spread the wealth. I have a spreadsheet and everything."

"Of course you do."

He shoots me a sideways smile. "I'm up to one hundred and thirteen days now. The goal is to find something new to fill every slot, excluding major holidays and about two weeks of vacation. Give or take."

I blink in astonishment. "A full-time job with benefits."

"That's the idea."

I snort a laugh before shoveling a small bite into my mouth. Though the circumstances may be strange, who am I to deny free cake? Besides, it's fucking delicious, and chocolate just so happens to be my favorite.

I pass the container back to him. "Thanks," I say. "It's really good. But I'm, uh, I'm gonna go back to bed now."

"Good night." He pushes himself up onto the ledge of the counter, starting in on the cake himself. When I turn on my heel, he adds, "Oh, and tell Hayes I'm proud of him for locking it down."

I roll my eyes, not bothering to look back. "Good night, Liam."

Chapter Eighteen
HAYES

I ROLL ONTO MY SIDE, reaching out across the sheets until I come into contact with . . . nothing. My eyes fly open, blinking against the harsh rays of sunlight. The space next to me in bed is empty, the sheets cool to the touch.

Sitting up, I scan the room but find no signs of Emmy. The cell phone on my nightstand reads just after nine o'clock in the morning. I rub the sleep from my eyes and slide out of bed, pulling on a pair of sweatpants.

Padding down to the kitchen, I find it empty except for Liam, who's seated at the counter, shoveling cereal into his mouth. He glances up at me through sleepy eyes and mumbles a "good morning" around his mouthful of Frosted Flakes.

"Morning," I say. "Have you seen Emmy?"

He shakes his head, swallowing loudly. "Not after last night."

My brow furrows. "Last night?"

"Yeah, we had cake around . . . 1:00 a.m.?"

"Cake?" I frown, a nervous pit forming in my stomach. "Why?"

"Because I had some in the fridge."

"From that birthday shit you do?"

"Mhm."

He continues eating, and my mind is whirling. She came downstairs and ate a piece of cake with my roommate in the middle of the night. That's something that a person who's feeling restless, someone who can't seem to find peace enough to sleep, might do.

And now, she's left my house without so much as a word.

Did I do something wrong last night? Say something to upset her, something that made her want to leave?

I grab my phone from the counter, scrolling through to her name. My thumb hovers over it for a moment before I shove the phone in my pocket, shaking my head. No need to come across as desperate. If she wants space for whatever reason, I suppose it's best to give it to her.

"You good?" Liam asks, eyeing me over his cereal bowl.

"Yeah," I mutter. "I'm sure she just had something to take care of. Where's James?"

"Hell if I know." He shrugs, turning his attention back to his sugary breakfast. Meanwhile, I busy myself making coffee, but my mind keeps wandering back to the same fruitless questions.

Did I move too fast last night?

I thought she wanted it as much as I did, but maybe I misread the signals. Maybe she needed more space than I realized. Maybe she needed time alone, a moment to collect her thoughts and feelings, away from it all. My concentration wavers, the coffee grounds spilling slightly over the edge of the filter.

What if she regrets being with me? What if she thinks I just want her for sex?

That couldn't be further from the truth. I've never wanted someone in the way that I want Emmy. It's not just her body, though God knows I'm drawn to her like the tide to the moon.

It's her spirit, her laughter, the way she sees the world. I've never met anyone like her, and now the thought of her sneaking out in the morning, possibly regretting what happened between us, is tearing me apart inside.

Past hookups hold no torch to what I'm feeling now, faces and names blurring together in a parade of meaninglessness. None of them sparked the same sort of fire inside me.

I used to roll out of bed, indifferent to the space left cold. Now, those empty sheets feel a whole lot like a personal failure. It's a startling revelation—the depth of my feelings for her—and it scares me as much as it exhilarates me.

I'm standing in the middle of the kitchen, lost in thought, when the coffee maker sputters to a stop. Pouring myself a cup, I try to shake off the unease settling in my chest.

By midmorning, I'm back in my room, wallowing. Yes, *wallowing* in self-pity. There's no other word for it. I'm sprawled across my bed, staring at the ceiling, trying to make sense of everything. And then, without really thinking about it, I find myself pulling out my phone and typing into the search bar, "What to do if the girl you like sneaks out after sex?"

The results are a mix of forum posts, dubious advice columns, and one particularly eye-catching article titled "5 Ways to Tell If She's Into You or If It's Just a One-Night Stand."

I scoff, rejecting the idea altogether. That isn't us. We agreed to try dating, didn't we? Another thought strikes me, and I quickly type out, "What happens if we agree to date and then have sex right away?"

As I scroll through the responses, none seem to fit the complexity of our situation. It's unhelpful, confusing, and my frustration continues to build until I come across a different type of article: "Top 10 Presents to Give Your Girlfriend."

That finally catches my attention. *A gift.* Something to show Emmy that she's not just another name, another face, another night of frivolous sex. She's become my focal point, the person who's turned my world upside down and made me want to be someone better.

One suggestion on the list jumps out at me. It's perfect. Personal, thoughtful, something she can wrap herself up in when I'm not there to do it myself. Before I can second-guess myself, I'm grabbing my keys and heading out the door.

The drive to Joann Fabrics is short, buzzing with energy and a dash of nerves. I'm usually not the crafty type, but today, I'm driven by a purpose.

The store is a maze of colors and textures, but I don't let it distract me from the mission. I select a soft fleece in a dark shade of plum, one that matches her lipstick, and all the other supplies I'll need. It only takes me about fifteen minutes and a quick consultation with the cashier before I'm satisfied with my purchase.

Back at home, I spread everything out on the living room floor, determined to make the best damn fleece tie blanket Emmy Fuller has ever seen. I'm nearly halfway through cutting the fringe when the front door opens. James walks in, stopping short at the sight of me surrounded by fabric, scissors in hand.

"Hayes, buddy," he says, "what the fuck are you doing?"

"Boyfriend shit," I answer without looking up, focused on getting each tie just right.

He chuckles. "Never thought I'd see the day."

"Yeah, well, the lengths I'll go to for this girl."

"So, you're finally admitting it?"

I nod, pausing my work to glance up at him. "Yeah, I am. We're giving it the good old college try this time."

"No shit?"

I give him a little smirk. "Yeah, you proud of me?"

"That I am," he says. "A moment that will go down in history."

His astonishment coaxes out a smile. James knows me better than almost anyone, and if he's surprised by my domestic endeavor, it only reinforces how far I'm willing to go to prove myself.

An hour later, when I finally lay the finished blanket out in front of me, pride swells in my chest. It's not perfect, but it's a tangible symbol of my feelings for Emmy—something warm and comforting she can hold on to.

I hustle up to my room to fetch a bottle of my cologne, the final touch to my plan. A light spray of my favorite scent on the corner of the blanket, I hope, will remind her of me whenever she uses it.

Folding it up with care, it strikes me how cheesy this gesture might seem, yet it feels right at the same time. I stuff the gift into a bag, not wasting another second, and dash out the front door.

The drive to her place is a blur of anticipation. I practice my speech, turning phrases over in my mind, attempting to perfect my words. Yet, as soon as I pull into the driveway, all my rehearsed lines evaporate, leaving a bundle of nerves in their wake.

I find myself at the doorstep, the gift bag waiting in my hands. The moment Emmy opens the door, the sight of her, pretty as ever, somehow intensifies my anxiety instead of easing it.

"Hayes, hi!" she greets me, visibly delighted, though doubt still plagues me.

"Hey, Em."

"What do you have there?" she asks.

I open my mouth to answer, but the words get stuck somewhere between my brain and my lips. Instead, I find myself frowning. "The real question is why'd you sneak out on me?"

She gives me an amused smile, the kind that always manages to disarm me. "I didn't *sneak.*"

I scoff, incredulous. "You left without saying anything."

"No, I left you a note," she says. "On your bathroom counter. Told you I needed to get some schoolwork done, but to stop by my house later if you wanted."

My hand instinctively goes to the back of my neck, scratching awkwardly. "Oh."

She tilts her head, studying me with those piercing eyes. "Did you think I was just . . . what? Running away?"

I shrug, suddenly feeling foolish. This gift is more like an anchor than a buoy now, a physical manifestation of my overthinking. "I guess I just . . . I don't know. I didn't see the note."

She steps aside, gesturing for me to come in. The interior of her apartment is warm, inviting, a stark contrast to the turmoil in my head. I step inside, still clutching the bag tightly to my chest.

She closes the door behind me and turns, her gaze falling back to my hands. "So, what did you bring me, then?"

I awkwardly hand it over, my heart in my throat. "It's . . . well, it's kind of ridiculous, actually. But I made you something."

Her eyes light up as she pulls out the blanket, unfolding it to reveal the purple fleece pattern. A soft "wow" escapes her, and she wraps it around her shoulders, my cologne filling the air between us.

"It's not much, just . . . I wanted you to have something to keep you warm when I can't be there to do it myself."

Her smile softens, and she draws closer, the blanket wrapped around her like a cocoon. "Aw, you got me a sex present."

I snort. "It's not a *sex* present, per se. Just a . . . *I want to show you that I'm trying* present."

"Hayes, this is the sweetest sex present anyone's ever given me."

I laugh, but an acute sense relief floods through my body. She likes it. She really likes it.

"Yeah?" I manage, a goofy grin spreading across my face.

"Yes." She reaches up, pulling my head down to hers, and presses her lips to mine in a tender kiss. When we break apart, she's smiling. "You're really committed to this whole thing, aren't you?"

"To *you?*" I chuckle, wrapping my arms around her. "Yeah, I really am."

AFTER THE HIGH of spending an unforgettable weekend with Emmy, I'm walking into Dr. Vargas' office for my fourth anger management session. By now, I feel less like a caged animal paying for someone else's crimes and more like . . . well, a slightly less agitated caged animal.

Dr. Vargas greets me with her usual serene smile, which I'm

convinced is permanently etched onto her face through years of therapy sessions. "Good afternoon, Hayes. How are you feeling today?"

"Just grand," I say, slumping into the familiar plush chair across from her. "I had a good weekend."

"That's wonderful to hear," she says, her tone genuine. "Does this 'good weekend' have anything to do with someone special?" Her knowing look tells me she's already pieced together more than I've explicitly shared.

I don't bother to suppress my grin. "Might have something to do with a girl, yeah."

Dr. Vargas nods, jotting something down in her notes. "I'm glad. It's important to have positive relationships in your life."

The conversation quickly shifts, as it always does, to the deeper stuff. The stuff I'm less keen on unpacking. The stuff that perhaps Sebastian should be in this room discussing for himself.

"So, you've mentioned your relationship with your parents a few times now. Could you elaborate on that for me?"

"Well, they're very talented people," I say, a hint of sarcasm sneaking into my tone.

"What is it that they do?"

"For one, they made Bash and me from scratch." I chuckle, but the laughter doesn't quite reach my eyes. Dr. Vargas doesn't humor me. Instead, she simply waits for me to continue, her expression neutral and patient. "They're just . . . they've always been more interested in their business ventures than in being parents. They run a local barbecue chain in our hometown, and it's always sucked up all their time."

"I see," she says, attention wholly focused on me. "And what about their relationship to each other?"

"They rarely got along, but I think they've stayed together all this time to protect what they've built. It was hard . . . hearing them fight so much over the years. But like I told you before, Bash and I learned to fend for ourselves early on."

"That sounds like it could be quite lonely," she observes softly.

I shrug, uncomfortable with the direction this is heading. "We had each other. And we turned out fine, other than a little blip here and there."

"Perhaps," she concedes. "Do you feel this dynamic may have affected certain views on trust and reliance on others? Maybe even on how you view romantic relationships?"

That hits closer to home than I'd like. I've always been the type to keep things light in that arena, never letting anyone get too close. Until Emmy. It's not that I don't trust myself in a relationship; it's more so that I never saw the point in getting too attached. Not when everything eventually ends up in turmoil.

"I guess I've never really seen the point in going there," I confess. "Seemed like a surefire way to end up disappointed. Or, to end up disappointing someone yourself."

"And yet, you're here talking about a woman who's changed your mind."

"Yeah." I run a hand through my hair, feeling suddenly exposed. "With Emmy . . . it feels different. I don't want to screw it up with my usual bullshit."

"That's a step in the right direction, Hayes. Recognizing that you want something more is the first step toward change."

Change. By now, it's a concept that I know all too well. There's been an overwhelming amount of change for me already this year. From my arrest, to probation, to suspension. To wanting things I've never let myself want before.

A real relationship. A potential future with Emmy.

"Old habits die hard," I say. "I don't exactly have the best track record when it comes to that kind of commitment."

She regards me steadily. "Tell me more about that. Other than fear of disappointment, why do you feel you struggle in that area?"

I drag my fingers along my jawline and sigh. "I guess I just don't know how. My parents were never role models when it came to being in a stable relationship. Bash and me, well, the girls just always seem to come and go . . ." I trail off, frowning.

"Do you see your inability to commit as a way to protect yourself?" she asks. "A method of maintaining control over your relationships?"

I chew the inside of my cheek. As much as I hate to admit it, she may have nailed me there. I always just thought I enjoyed sex, craved the momentary distraction, but maybe there's a little more to it.

"Maybe," I say quietly.

"That's very common. But the good news is, you can learn new patterns. Healthier ways of relating, just like with your anger." She pauses, studying me. "But you should know that change takes time and conscious effort."

"Where do I even start?" I ask.

Her face brightens with a tender smile. "By continuing to show up. Both here and with this Emmy of yours."

"Okay," I say softly, earnestly. "I can do that."

Chapter Nineteen

OTHER THAN A QUICK meet-up between classes, I haven't seen Hayes much since Sunday. It's been a whirlwind of assignments and late-night study sessions, bolstered by my tiny paper stars.

Matty's been my rock through it all, keeping me fueled with an endless supply of coffee and moral support. But Thursday morning brings a surprise. There's a knock at our door, and when I pull it open, there's Hayes, leaning against the frame with that lopsided grin that does funny things to my heart.

"Just came by for a good-morning kiss," he says, stepping into my space like he belongs there.

Without waiting for a response, he leans down, capturing my lips in a kiss that's lingering and just a little bit lazy, like the slow rise of the morning sun. It's a perfect, peaceful moment, a bubble of calm before the day's chaos ensues.

"Oh, and I brought you this," he says when we break apart. With one hand behind his back, he slowly brings it around to reveal what he's been hiding.

It's a bunch of mixed fruit, the kind with little skewered pieces, chocolate-dipped, and arranged like a bouquet. I can't help but laugh, both at the gesture and the absurdity of it all. "An . . . edible arrangement? Hayes, you know you don't have to bring me, like, biweekly gifts, right?"

"It's more of a *regift*," he admits, scratching the back of his neck. "Bash sent it to me as an apology for last weekend. I already ate most of the strawberries."

"Oh, so this is you giving me your leftovers?"

He grins, unapologetic. "Hey, I left you all the fruit flowers. So it's the thought that counts, right?"

"I'll go with it. Thank you, Hayes." I set the fruit down on the entryway table. "Do you want to come in for a sec?"

"I can't, baby," he says sweetly. "Gotta head to class. I just wanted to see you before we got swallowed up by the day."

"Well, thank you for coming by. And again, for the half-eaten fruit." He wraps his arms around me once more, pulling me close. "You have community service this afternoon, right?"

"That's right."

"Do you . . . maybe want some company?"

He pulls back, strong hands still wrapped around my shoulders, arms extended. "You want to hang out with me during trash duty?"

I tilt my head as I grab hold of his wrists. "When you put it that way, who could possibly resist?"

"You know I'd love your company, Em," he says. "Don't even need to ask."

"Good. Then I'll be there," I say, and then he presses one final, tender kiss to my forehead before spinning away, off to conquer his day.

THE REST of the morning drags on until finally, it's time to meet Hayes on the quad. I spot him from a distance, donned in an emerald-green Dayton U vest that's too big, wielding a grabber and a trash bag like he was always made for the job. I stifle a laugh as I approach.

"Wow, look at you, saving the planet one candy wrapper at a time," I tease, falling into step beside him.

He glances over, feigning offense. "I'll have you know this is very serious business, Fuller."

I snort. "Okay, Captain Planet."

He chuckles, bending to pick up a soda can. "You know, they say volunteering increases your attractiveness by seventy-five percent."

"Who's 'they'?" I ask, picking up a stray piece of paper and tossing it in his bag.

"Science people. Very official."

"Does it count if you're only doing it because of your plea bargain?"

He scoffs. "Come on, give me a little credit here. At this point, it's safe to say I'm going above and beyond. I already served my time, got the scars to prove it and everything."

"Yeah, and what scars are those?" I playfully bump his shoulder as we continue walking. "Did your cellmate carve his initials into your thigh?"

"Nah, I'm saving that spot for you."

I snort a laugh. "Into branding, are you?"

He flashes a cheeky grin my way. "All I'm saying is that my motives are pure. I'm just trying to do my part to beautify our campus."

"Uh-huh." I roll my eyes in amusement. "So you're telling me you'd be out here picking up trash if you didn't have to?"

"Absolutely," he says, punctuating it with a decisive nod. "In fact, I was going to suggest organizing a campus cleanup with the team before all this happened."

My lips curl into a soft smile. "Sure you were."

He winks before bending down to pick up another piece of litter. Crumpling it in his gloved hand, he flicks it in my direction. I dodge it, laughing, and the game is on.

He chases me, merely a step behind, lobbing little balls of paper and discarded wrappers my way. I dart around a bench, giggling as I try to escape his playful assault. "You know you're just making more work for yourself," I call over my shoulder, narrowly avoiding another paper missile.

"Yeah, but it's worth it."

I feint left, then sprint right, but Hayes is quick, managing to tag me with a softly balled-up napkin.

"Ew, okay. That one actually got me," I say, nose scrunched. "I'm calling for a truce."

He steps closer. "And what do I get if I agree?"

"What do you want?"

His gaze locks with mine, hazel eyes glimmering in the sunlight. Slowly, he reaches out with his clean hand and tucks a strand of hair behind my ear. "How about dinner tomorrow night? Just you and me."

My breath hitches. "Like a real date?"

"You mean, you don't consider *this* a real date?" One corner of his mouth ticks up, and I frown. "Kidding," he says. "Yeah, I mean like a real date."

Warmth spreads through my chest. After years of pining after him, the idea of going on an actual date with Hayes feels almost surreal. But knowing he's committed to making an effort—to taking steps outside of his usual comfort zone—reassures me that I made the right choice.

I bite my lip, holding back a giddy smile. "I'd love to, but I promised Shannon and Jade I'd see them tomorrow."

His face falls, but he recovers quickly. "No problem. Rain check for Saturday?"

"Sounds like a plan."

We continue walking, Hayes scooping up litter while I trail beside him. "You know," he says after a while, slinging an arm around me. "I haven't agreed to the truce yet."

I stop in my tracks. "If you throw another piece of trash, I'm canceling our date."

"Tell you what," he says, voice low. "How about you kiss me to seal the deal, and we'll call it even?"

"Hmm." I feign contemplation for half a second. Then, meeting his demand, I push onto my tiptoes and close the distance between us.

Our mouths slant together, his lips soft yet firm against mine. I loop my arms around his neck, pressed tight to his solid chest as our kiss deepens. His free hand cups my cheek, fingers tangling in my hair, and I eagerly drink him in.

It's a kiss that whispers of mornings yet to come, of laughter shared and quiet moments between the chaos of days. The world seems to pause just for the two of us. When we break apart, his grin grows wide.

"Yeah, I'd say that seals it," he murmurs.

Reluctantly, I step back, smoothing my rumpled shirt. "Alright, let's finish this so you can get out of here."

He gives a mock salute. "Yes, ma'am."

THE NEXT NIGHT finds me collapsed on Shannon's bed, the three of us girls huddled together in a semblance of a sleepover. The air in the room is thick with the scent of popcorn and nail polish, and before long, we're delving into murky territory.

That is, a conversation about the squad I've carefully evaded until now.

"You know the girls miss you, Em," Shannon says, her voice soft, tentative. "They keep asking me how you're doing."

My heart sinks a little. It's nice of her to say, but deep down, I still wonder if it's just a platitude. "That's nice," I manage, forcing a smile. "You can tell them I'm doing well."

The truth is, I already reached out after my conversation with Matty. Once he convinced me that the girls were just giving me space, I decided to shoot them a quick text. There were a few of us in a group chat last year, so it felt like the perfect opportunity to test the waters.

All I received back was crickets.

I've been trying not to take it to heart. At the same time, it's hard not to feel forgotten, a shadow of the girl who once believed the squad was her whole world. But at least I still have Shannon.

"It's well enough that you left," she adds. "Practice has been brutal with Cass in charge."

"I'm sure," I murmur. "She was always quite the pusher."

Shannon continues to chat about the team—cautious not to overstep—and I deflect until the topic shifts, inevitably, to boys. Jade brings up my ill-fated date with Noah, and the memory alone is enough to make me wince.

"I'm still sorry about that, Em," she says earnestly. "I honestly thought he was getting over Steph. I wouldn't have encouraged it if I'd known."

"It's no biggie," I assure her. "It's hardly your fault."

Part of me wonders if things would've been different had Hayes not . . . well, been *Hayes* that night. He wouldn't have shown up at my place afterward, and the two of us may not have ended up together in the first place.

"Yeah, it all worked out for the best," Jade says. "How are things going with you two, by the way?"

"Good," I murmur with a smile. "Hayes has been really sweet. Showing up for me. Putting his whole back into this dating thing so far."

"Sounds like West after he met Jade," Shannon says softly.

I turn my attention to her. She's been unusually quiet about her own love life, and I'm curious if there's a reason. "What about you, Shan?"

She twirls a strand of honey-red hair between her fingers. "What about me?"

"Anyone you're interested in lately?"

"Well, I mentioned it to Jade already, but there was this guy—this *man*—I met at camp over the summer. An older counselor. We hit it off right away." She hesitates, worrying over her bottom lip. "But in the end, we decided long distance was a no go. I thought I knew what I wanted, but now . . ."

"To be fair, last year was weird for you," Jade chimes in. "You know, after Ace and all."

A hint of old tension surfaces. Ace, otherwise known as Mica Jennings, is Jade's older brother. He's a pro football player for the Bobcats, and he and Shannon ended up sleeping together on a whim last spring.

The whole situation drove a wedge between them. But they were able to work through it, and now it all feels like a distant memory.

Shannon nods, a wry smile on her lips. "Swore off athletes, then fell for a sweetheart. No matter what I do, nothing seems to work out how I'd hoped. Now, I'm just . . . open to whatever comes my way, I guess."

Jade smiles, and there's a spark in her dark brown eyes. "What about a *triple* date? I can set you up this time. Now that I've got Theo."

Shannon's nose wrinkles. "Maybe not a football player, though. Being around them all season is enough."

"Hayes might know someone," I suggest instead. "One of his friends or teammates?"

Shannon shrugs, indifferent, so I pull out my phone to text him.

EMMY

do you know anyone who might be a good match for shannon? the girls want to do a group date

HAYES

Liam's available. young and ripe for the picking

I stifle a giggle. "He suggested his roommate Liam," I tell the girls. "He's on the soccer team, but I think he's only nineteen."

Shannon's expression shifts. "Oh, God," she says. "A whole child."

EMMY

Liam's a bit too young for her. and at the same, too much lol. what about James?

HAYES

he's not really into the whole dating scene. but I'll see if he's interested.

EMMY

no, no. we need someone who's excited to be there

HAYES

okay, got someone else in mind. Matty can vouch too. I'll set it up.

EMMY

perfect

HAYES

miss u

EMMY

miss you too

With an uncontrollable smile, I pocket my phone, catching the girls exchanging one of those looks. The kind that says they're about to dive into a topic I'm wholly unprepared for.

I reach over and tug at a curl of Jade's hair. "Would you stop looking at me like that?"

Her grin widens, mischief sparkling in her eyes. "You looove him," she teases, dragging out the word like it's some grand proclamation.

My cheeks flame. "I don't *love* him. We're just . . . seeing how the dating thing goes."

"Oh, come on, Em. That's a 'more-than-just-seeing' smile," Shannon says.

I put my cheek in my hand, conceding. "He's new to all this. I'm trying to relieve some of the pressure for both of us. Keep him off the pedestal for a while."

"Yeah, that's probably smart," Shannon says. "Because if there's one thing that's certain about men, it's that they're bound to fuck up eventually."

Jade gives a long, dramatic sigh, flopping onto her back as we laugh. "I, for one, am willing to bet on Hayes Grecco."

"Yeah," I say with a chuckle. "Me too."

<h1 style="text-align:center">Chapter Twenty</h1>

HAYES

I'm preparing for a date that feels a helluva lot like my first, although it's far from it. Emmy and I have had our moments, but this? This is our first official night out together—a real fucking date —and I'll be damned if I don't make it perfect.

I stand in front of my closet, flicking through hangers with a frown. Everything seems either too casual or too try-hard. It's ridiculous, really. Emmy doesn't give a shit what I wear. Yet, here I am, contemplating my wardrobe like she'll leave me if I don't choose the right pair of slacks.

From the doorway, Liam watches, amused. "Dude, why are you so worked up? She knows what you look like."

James pushes past his brother, brazenly entering my room, a smirk playing on his lips. "Yeah, we know she's already seen the goods. What's with the fashion show?"

I shoot them both a look, cockiness masking my internal panic. "Gentlemen, it's all about presentation. We know I'm devilishly handsome, but sometimes there's more to it than that."

Liam snorts. "Oh yeah? I'd give you an 8.6 on a good day."

James chimes in with a dry, "7.6, but only because I'm feeling generous."

"7.6?" I echo, mock outrage lacing my tone. "And what about you two? If we're throwing numbers around."

Liam, ever confident, doesn't hesitate. "8.9, obviously."

James and I exchange a look, both our brows shooting up. "What in the world gives you that extra 0.3?" I ask, astounded.

Liam puffs out his chest, a grin spreading across his face. "Physical prowess, my friends. I'm the strongest, and you know it. Could take both of you down easy."

His challenge hangs in the air, and for a moment, we're all grinning, the tension of my impending date falling by the wayside. "Is that so?" James muses. "Because last time I checked, technique beats strength."

And that's all it takes. The room transforms into a makeshift wrestling ring. Clothes and textbooks become collateral as we dive into a bout of mock wrestling. Liam's all bravado, James is technique, and I'm caught in the middle, trying not to laugh too hard or break anything.

Too late for that, though. A poorly aimed tackle from Liam sends us crashing into my study chair. There's a crack, a moment of silence, then the realization that the leg has snapped clean off.

"Well, shit," I mutter, surveying the damage. Our laughter fades as we try, and fail, to piece it back together. But it's a lost cause.

Liam grins, sheepish. "Told you I was really fucking strong."

"Yeah, a real brute," I mutter.

James pats my back. "We'll fix it, buddy. Or find you a new one."

I glance at the mess—my pre-date catastrophe. Clothes everywhere, a broken chair, and the two dipshit brothers I call my friends. What a way to start off the night.

"Alright, get the fuck out of my room," I say, laughter in my voice. "If I don't show up on time, I'm gonna be even more pissed at myself."

My friends chuckle but take the hint, clearing out to let me get ready. Once I'm alone, I take a deep breath and try to gather my thoughts. *It's just Emmy.* Sweet, kind, beautiful Emmy, who makes me feel at ease even during my most chaotic moments.

So why the hell am I so nervous?

Maybe because this night needs to be perfect. Because she deserves perfect. Because I desperately want to prove that I can be the guy she needs me to be, the one who has his shit together and treats her the way she should be treated—like she's the most important person in the world.

I shake my head and get back to the task at hand. I need to find an outfit that strikes the right balance between a dinner date and a nightcap at Lucky's with her friends.

After agonizing over it, I finally settle on dark-wash jeans and a hunter green button-up that brings out the gold flecks in my eyes. I style my hair just so, spritz on some cologne, and check myself in the mirror.

Yeah, I clean up alright. But beyond the surface level, there's a simmering anticipation in my veins that shines on through. I've been waiting for this chance, and there's no way I'm letting it slip through my fingers.

This girl who snuck past my defenses, capturing my attention when I least expected it. Her smile, her compassion, the way she sees through my bullshit to the real me—it knocks me sideways.

Grabbing my wallet and keys, I head downstairs for the door, dodging more teasing from my roommates. It's time to show Emmy, officially, that I'm not just here to play around. Not anymore. When I set my mind on something, I follow through.

And I've set my mind on her.

I'M WAITING for Emmy to answer the door, ready and eager to pull her in for a kiss. Instead, Matty's handsome face is the one that greets me. His arms are folded over his chest, and a faux scowl wrinkles his brow.

"So, young man, I hear that you're trying to date my daughter," he says, sizing me up with his eyes. "Is that right?"

"Yes, sir," I say with a half-assed salute. "That's correct."

"And what is it you bring to the table?"

"As you can tell, I'm a very punctual man. Responsible." I lean in closer, whispering conspiratorially. "And I've also got a huge d—"

"Woah, woah." He holds up both hands, glancing down to my crotch. "You expect us to just take your word for it?"

I snort. "I know you've seen it, Matty baby. Those long showers after a bone-chilling practice."

"I would never disrespect you by looking there."

A scoff rings out from behind him. "Do you two need a ruler or something?"

Emmy pops up, and my grin widens at the sight of her. She's wearing a little black dress, her hair cascading over her shoulders in these tiny waves that I want to run my fingers through.

"Hi," I say, my voice softening as I take her in. "You look super fucking pretty tonight."

"Thanks, so do you." A playful smile dances on her lips. "Are you guys done, though? Because we have a date to get to, and I'd hate to miss our reservation over a fake pissing contest."

Matty chuckles, stepping aside to let her pass. "Just looking out for you, Em. Make sure he treats you right, or he'll have me to answer to."

"I'm sure he's well aware," Emmy says, looping her arm through mine. "Aren't you, Hayes?"

"Absolutely," I assure, giving Matty a nod. "I've got nothing but the utmost respect for you, Daddy."

Matty grins like a cat who got the cream. "Good to hear, bud. You two have fun tonight."

"We will," Emmy says and then slams the door behind her. I

can't resist the urge any longer. I lean down, capturing her lips in a kiss that I hope conveys all my anticipation.

It's soft, sweet, and all too brief, but it sets the tone for the evening ahead. As I pull back, an eager smile takes over my face. "Ready for the best fucking date of your life?"

She laughs, her eyes sparkling with something tender, something that makes my heartbeat just a little faster. "Lead the way."

The drive to the neighboring town is quicker than I expected. We arrive at our destination, and I park under a canopy of twinkling streetlights. Rushing to the passenger side, I pull open Emmy's door, and we head over to the restaurant hand in hand.

The hostess leads us to a table under the open sky, where the first stars begin to make their shy appearance. It's a perfect setup— just secluded enough for intimacy but open enough to feel the pulse of the city around us.

Emmy looks across the table, navy eyes gleaming. "This is amazing. I didn't even know they did outdoor dining."

I lean back, watching her with a mixture of pride and nerves. "Yeah, they close the street after eight. It's the last weekend of the year."

"I love it."

As we settle into our seats, the initial excitement gives way to an easy conversation. Emmy chats about her friends, her classes, her excitement over the gruyere mac 'n' cheese she just ordered. But when I bring the topic back around to school, there's a slight stiffness in her posture that I immediately question.

"What?" I ask. "You don't like your major?

"No, I really do like marketing." She leans forward, elbow propped on the table, chin in her hand. "But I have this . . . guilt inside me that I'm not interested in more of a caretaking role. That I'm not doing something more impactful, something life-changing. My mom's this superstar of a nurse. She constantly works her ass off for her patients, whereas I'm just, like, hoping to help people sell shit."

"Don't downplay it. You're gonna change lives no matter what you do, Em," I say softly. "You've got this fire in you. It's one of the many things I like about you."

A soft blush heats her cheeks, and she gives a shy smile. "Thank you for saying that. So is that what drew you to kinesiology, then? *Fire?*"

"No." I breathe an easy laugh. "It just seemed fitting with what we already learn at practice. I thought maybe I could coach or take up personal training after college."

"You never wanted to play baseball professionally?"

I give a careless shrug. "That was always more of Bash's thing."

She frowns, a cute little wrinkle between her brows. "But you're an incredible player."

"Yeah, well, who knows if I'll even get to play this season."

"I'm sure you will." She reaches across the table, taking my hand in hers. "I have faith."

A helpless, crooked smile parts my lips. "There's my vote of positivity for the day."

"What can I say?" She beams. "You're born to be a leader. It's the Leo in you."

"You're telling me you actually believe in all that astrology stuff?"

She laughs again, and a familiar warmth spreads through my chest. "And you don't, Mr. Cosmos?"

"If you're a believer, I'm a believer." My mouth twists into a smirk. "What's your sign?"

"My birthday's in the beginning of December."

I lean back in my chair, eyes playfully narrowed. "Yeah, that tells me absolutely nothing."

"I'm a Sagittarius."

"And what does that say about you? Are you a leader, too?"

She shakes her head. "No, I'm an idealist."

"Ah, so when you give me your little fortune cookie phrases, you're actually just full of shit?"

Her jaw slackens. "*Positive* shit, thank you."

"Well, at least there's that," I say, and our shared laughter bursts out, loud and genuine. Being here with her like this, so comfortable and close beneath the stars, fills me with a sense of peace. It urges me to open up the floodgates, to share those parts of myself I'm still piecing together.

"Speaking of positivity," I say, "you know my anger management sessions?"

"Yeah." Curiosity colors her expression. This is a new topic of conversation for us, and I can tell she's dying to know more. "With Dr. Vargas, right?"

"The woman, the myth, the legend." I crack a tentative smile. "I know it's just part of the plea bargain. That I'm meant to be bullshitting my way through it. But she's actually been helping me see things . . . about my parents, my view on relationships. Stuff I never really faced before."

"That sounds like it could be really healthy," she says gently.

"Yeah, I think it might be kind of good for me." I work through a heavy swallow. "I think it could be really good for Bash, though."

"Maybe you could suggest he try a few sessions? He could find someone close by the complex."

"Yeah, maybe I will. I just . . . I don't want the kid to feel like I think something's wrong with him. Because I don't. I just know he's got his own shit to work through."

Bash has always been the more hopeful one of the two of us. He gives our parents the benefit of the doubt, and he has this tendency to see the silver lining, even when it's more dark cloud than anything else.

It's like he's wired to find the good, to make excuses for them, to laugh off the bad stuff. Maybe it's because, growing up, I was always there, shielding him from the worst of it, picking up the slack where our folks dropped the ball. I took on the role of protector, of provider, and in doing so, maybe I sheltered him too much from the reality of our situation.

To Bash, this kind of support was just how things were supposed to be. He never saw it as me stepping in where our parents checked out. It's probably why he feels letdowns more acutely than I do. He hasn't built up the same kind of walls.

When things go south, it hits him harder, slices through the optimism he clings to. I'm sure it has a lot to do with why he acts out, seeking attention in ways that aren't always the best. Because deep down, he still holds on to hope—hope that things will change, that people will live up to the expectations he sets for them.

It's a double-edged sword, really. On one hand, his ability to see the best in our folks, in the world, it's enviable. It's something pure, something I've seen erode in myself over the years. On the other, it sets him up for a fall, time and time again. He's buoyed by this belief that, maybe this time, it'll be different. And when it's not, it's not just disappointment he feels; it's disillusionment.

I didn't have the heart to tell him the hard truths about our parents when we were kids. I thought I was protecting him, but maybe in some ways, I was also doing him a disservice. Maybe if he'd seen a bit more of the reality, he wouldn't swing so wildly between hope and despair.

But then, that's Bash. He's always been the more emotional one, wearing his heart on his sleeve, while I learned to guard mine behind a veneer of indifference, of humor.

"Yeah, I suppose we all do," she says, giving me a comforting smile.

"Is that right?" I ask, deflecting. "You want to tell me more about the shit you've got?"

She tilts her head, scrunches up one side of her face. "Well, there's this guy I kinda like . . . but he can be cocky, overbearing. He also used to be a *huge* player."

"Wow, baby, he sounds like a fucking catch."

A wide grin stretches across her rosy cheeks. "Yeah," she says, "he really is."

Chapter Twenty-One

EMMY

DINNER under the stars was nothing short of magical, and now we're headed inside Lucky's to round out the night with our group date. Hayes told his buddy to meet us all here, a second baseman he's known for years. Apparently, he was stoked for the opportunity to meet Shannon, so I can only hope the match is a success.

As we head inside the bar, Hayes leads the way, his hand warm in mine. We carefully weave through the crowd, and I spot my friends at a high table in the back. The trio waves us over, and we make our way to join them. When we approach, Shannon's laughing at something West just said, and Jade's dark eyes light up.

"Hey, you two!" she greets, scooting over to make room for us at the table. "Dinner was good?"

"Amazing," I say, sliding into the seat next to her. Hayes takes the spot beside me, his leg brushing against mine under the table. "And the company? Can't beat it."

Shannon raises her brows, a playful grin on her face. "Sounds like someone's smitten."

I make a poor attempt to hide my blush, even as Hayes squeezes my hand under the table. "Damn right, I am," he says, earning a round of teasing "awws" from the girls.

West leans forward, resting his elbows on the table. "So, Hayes, I hear you're wingmanning for Shan tonight?"

Hayes nods, a smirk playing at the corner of his mouth. "Yeah, he should be here any minute. Alex is a great guy; I think you'll like him, Shannon."

Before she can respond, the door to Lucky's opens again, and in walks a man with dark, sandy hair, a bit lanky but undeniably handsome. He scans the room, his gaze landing on our group.

"Speak of the devil," Hayes says, standing to greet him. "Hey, man, over here!"

He approaches us with a confident stride, a wide smile spreading across his face as he reaches our table. "Hayes, good to see you, bud." His gaze flicks to the gorgeous redhead beside me. "And you must be Shannon. Heard a lot about you."

She smiles. "All good things, I hope."

"Nothing but," Alex assures her, pulling her in for a quick side hug.

His presence sparks a new wave of conversation at the table. Jade and West pop in, claiming to recognize Alex from parties at the Cathouse, a place where the football players often congregate. And, of course, Hayes introduces me in a way that has me flushing like a tomato.

"And this is Emmy Fuller," he says, "my dream girl."

Before long, everyone's hit it off, chatting easily, swapping stories about their time at Dayton. Shannon leans closer to Alex as they talk, and it seems she's genuinely interested in what he has to say.

"Looks like they're getting along," Hayes whispers in a low voice.

A smile tugs at my lips. "Yeah, it does. I guess you're a good matchmaker."

He chuckles, his breath warm against my neck. "Only the best for my girl."

"You know, I kinda like the sound of that."

He nudges my cheek with his nose. "Knew you would."

I lean into him, savoring the feeling of his body pressed against mine. Across the table, Shannon laughs at something Alex said, lightly touching his arm. While Jade and West practically make out across the table, the other two seem enthralled in their own little world.

"Want to play some pool?" Hayes asks me, snorting at the sight in front of us.

I grin and turn to face him. "You asking because you want to spend more time alone with me or because you're hoping to cop a feel?"

He winks, taking my hand. "Can't it be both?"

We each select a pool cue and approach the only available table, setting up for our game. With a sharp crack, I initiate the break, sending the colorful array of balls careening across the green. Hayes leans back casually against the wall, his gaze following my movements with an intensity that sends a thrill through me.

"Your turn, hotshot," I tease, stepping aside to give him room.

With a light laugh, he circles the table, positioning himself. The fabric of his T-shirt stretches over his muscles as he bends forward, aiming with precision. I catch myself biting my lower lip, my eyes drawn to the display of strength and focus.

His first shot is a masterstroke, pocketing two stripes with ease. Straightening, he turns to me, a knowing smirk playing on his lips. "Seems like someone's distracted, huh?"

I let out a playful snort. "Just evaluating your approach, that's all."

As I circle the table, searching for my next move, his gaze tracks my every step. When I position myself for the shot, he closes the distance, his hand lightly brushing my hip, and my breath catches in my throat.

"Could use a hand?" he asks, his voice a soft murmur in my ear.

"No, I've got it," I say, attempting to maintain concentration while his thumb draws lazy circles on my hip. I execute my shot, missing the pocket by a hair.

"Tough luck," he tuts sympathetically.

His touch lingers, sliding up my side as he steps around for his turn, leaving a trail of goose bumps in its wake. My heart races, but I'm not one to let go without a fight.

I edge closer as he prepares his shot, my fingers skimming his lower back. He tenses, a subtle reaction to my caress. Undeterred, I slip my hand beneath his shirt, fingertips dancing across the skin of his lower abdomen, sketching aimless patterns.

He glances at me over his shoulder, eyes darkening. "Trying to throw me off, Em?"

"Would I do that?" I ask, inching to the waistband of his jeans.

He sucks in a sharp breath, his own shot going wide. The cue ball ricochets off the side, scattering the balls haphazardly across the table. In one smooth motion, he turns and cages me with his arms. His body presses against mine, and when he speaks, his voice is low and rough in a way that makes my knees weak.

"That wasn't very nice of you, Madison."

"Well, fair is fair," I say, heat flooding my cheeks.

His eyes drop to my lips. "Mm, do you want me to show you fair?"

He closes the scant distance between us, mouth slotting over mine in a searing kiss. My fingers curl into his shirt, pulling him tighter against me, the chatter of the bar fading away. When we finally break for air, his forehead rests against mine, both of us panting.

"Maybe we should take this game somewhere more private," he suggests.

I bite my lip and nod, desire burning through my veins as he leads us down the hallway toward the restrooms. But there's a fucking line again tonight, so we shift course and head out to his car. It's probably for the better, anyway. More sanitary, more private, less risk of being permanently banned from our favorite bar.

He yanks open the back door of his car, and I'm gently pushed inside. It's cramped, but there's just enough room for me to crawl onto his lap. In the dim light, his eyes roam over my body, his hands trembling as they skim up my legs, lifting my dress until it's pooled around my waist.

"You're everything, Em," he whispers, tracing a finger along my thigh-high stocking, reaching to cup me through my underwear.

I moan into his mouth as he uses his other hand to unbutton his jeans. "Hayes," I gasp, head spinning as he slips his boxers down far enough to free his erection. "What about . . .?"

He shakes his head, a hungry look in his eyes. "We're good. I've got a condom."

Relief floods me as he fishes in his wallet, sliding the latex over himself, lifting me until we're perfectly aligned, my panties pushed to the side. I know I'm wet enough already, but the lack of preparation has me tensing.

"Tell me if it's too fast," he mutters, slowly easing into me.

"Hayes," I breathe, nails digging into his shoulders as he fills me completely. Heat unravels in my stomach.

"God, Emmy," he groans, burying his face in my neck as he grinds his hips into mine from below. "You're really fucking wet tonight, you know that?"

"Mhm."

"Does it turn you on?" he murmurs, hips picking up speed. "Fucking me in public where anyone might see us?"

My head tips back, eyes fluttering closed. "No."

"No?" He chuckles, cupping my ass cheeks, pumping me up and down against his length. "You don't want them to see the way your pussy stretches around my cock? The way your perfect tits look pushed up inside this tiny dress?"

"No, I only want . . . you . . . to see me."

"So, this is all for me, huh?"

"Mhmm," I pant, my legs tightening around his waist as I try to keep my rhythm.

"Yeah, I know you're mine." He groans, and the movement of his hips grows more erratic. "I really fucking like you, Emmy."

"I really like . . . you, too, Hayes." His name sounds so good on my lips, the words wrapping around my tongue like silk.

"Do you?" He grunts as I bounce on my knees, working the little amount of leverage I have left. "Tell me again, baby."

"I really, really like you," I gasp, the sensation building between my legs. "Hayes, I think . . . I'm going to . . ."

"That's it, Em," he growls, fingers digging into my hips as I sink down to the hilt one last time. It's sweaty, fast, and perfect. And then we both come together, shuddering.

Once we're spent, I carefully slide off him and into the next seat over. He glances at me, grinning wide. "You know . . . I fantasized about this the first time I ever saw you here at Lucky's."

I give a humorless snort, tugging my dress and panties back into place. "Yeah, well, *you're lucky* I'm easy."

He leans over, swipes a finger across my bottom lip. "Far from it, babe."

"Do you think if we go back in there, they're gonna know right away that we had sex?"

"No shot," he says, pinching off the condom. He grabs a tissue from the center console and wipes himself off. "They're too wrapped up in each other to care, anyway."

"Right." I laugh nervously, smoothing my hair down before snagging my purse from the floorboard. He tucks himself away—casual, nonchalant—as if we hadn't just finished having sex in the back of his car ten seconds ago.

"You good?" he asks, a crease between his brows as he studies me.

"Yeah, sorry." I scoot closer, quickly peck him on the lips.

"That was just a new one for me."

"Sex in a parking lot?"

"Yes, that and . . . *etcetera*."

He laughs. "Did you like it, though?"

With an eye roll, I nudge him aside and grab the car door handle. "Sorry, I'm not stroking your ego anymore tonight."

"But Em, I love it when you stroke me."

I don't attempt to humor him. Instead, I simply say, "Get out of the car, Hayes."

Without another word, he tumbles out, and I follow suit. Then we're both standing there, alone beneath a blanket of stars. He loops an arm around my waist, pulling me in tight, no semblance of space left between us.

His eyes reflect tiny specks of golden starlight as he gazes down at me, and there's a softness there I haven't seen before. It's a look filled with more than just the afterglow of sex; it's layered with affection, adoration, maybe something more.

"I know I'm always joking around," he says, his voice low and sincere. "But I would like to know. Did you really enjoy it? Did you . . . want me as badly as I wanted you?"

The earnestness in his question makes me pause, and for a moment, I'm lost in his gaze, in the firm resolve that's replaced his usual playfulness. I smile, leaning my head against his chest, listening to the steady beat of his heart.

"Yes. Being with you is . . . exciting. Different, but in the best possible way."

There's an acute sense of relief in the way his body relaxes. "Good, because that's all I want. To make you happy, to give you new experiences, to be with you in any way that I can. In any way that you want me to be."

His words wrap around me, warming me from the inside out. It's a declaration, simple yet profound, and it fills me with a sense of rightness, of being deeply understood and cared for.

"You are . . . different than I thought."

"Different how?" he asks.

"You're more . . . considerate, more open than I anticipated. You've been surprising me lately."

It's not that I expected him to be shallow or self-centered, but from a distance, Hayes always seemed so carefree, so untroubled. I've always thought of him as kind, lighthearted, and undeniably sweet, observations gathered from afar and through the filter of Matty's unwavering respect.

Matty, who's never had a bad word to say about anyone, especially Hayes.

Yet, there was this nagging doubt, a whisper of uncertainty—could the real Hayes ever reach the pedestal I'd placed him on inside my mind? The place where he was safe, untouchable, and idealized.

But as we've grown closer, he hasn't just lived up to it; he's surpassed it. Hayes Grecco is more than the sum of my distant observations. He's a complex, thoughtful person, and his warmth isn't just surface-level charm. It's a genuine, undeniable truth.

A soft chuckle escapes him, and he looks away for a second, almost shy. "Yeah?" he asks, locking eyes with me once more. "I'm surprising myself, to be honest." He gives an awkward laugh. "Never thought I'd be the guy getting all deep and emotional after . . . well, you know."

"Fucking me in the back of your car?"

"Emmy Fuller," he mock scolds, slapping me lightly on the ass. "Behave."

"Well, either way, I like this side of you," I say sincerely. "A lot."

He gives me a lopsided grin. "That's good, baby, 'cause you're kinda stuck with me."

"Yeah," I say, "I figured."

Chapter Twenty-Two

HAYES

I ROLL over in Emmy's cozy bed, tucking her fluffy duvet beneath my chin and pushing a thigh between both of hers. She's so soft, sweet, perfect, warm—the best fucking thing a guy could ever wake up to in the morning.

I already want to fuck her again. Kiss her, hold her, talk about the goddamn stars with her. By this point, it's starting to feel a lot like an illness.

Emmy stirs beside me, her eyes fluttering open, and she greets me with that sleepy, content smile that punches straight through my chest every damn time. "Morning," she murmurs, her voice rough with sleep.

"Morning," I say, unable to resist leaning in for a quick, soft kiss. It's nothing like last night's fervor—just a gentle press of lips—but it speaks volumes about how I feel without diving back into the depths.

She snuggles closer, her head finding the crook of my arm while one hand lies flat over my chest, fingers absently drawing patterns over my skin. It's a quiet, peaceful moment—the kind you wish could last forever because everything just feels so fucking right.

Then, breaking the silence, her phone dings loudly from the nightstand. She lets out a soft groan but reaches for it, curiosity winning her over.

I watch her, half-amused, half-annoyed at the intrusion, until her expression shifts from sleepy interest to amusement. She bursts into laughter, the sound so infectious I can't help but smile despite not knowing the joke.

"What's so funny?" I ask, propping myself up on one elbow to get a better look at her face.

She turns the screen toward me, still giggling. "It's a message from Shannon. You're not going to believe this."

I squint at the text, and then, as the words register, I laugh, too.

SHANNON

got a kiss last night! but he was all teeth :(my lip was bleeding for twenty minutes after. blech.

"Good God, Alex fumbled it. Just like him, too."

Her laughter subsides into a soft sigh. "Didn't you say he'd be a good match for her?"

"I did. But Alex . . . he's been single for ages, and he's been dying for a girlfriend. I guess now it's starting to make sense why."

She nudges me gently, a mischievous glint in her eyes. "Chomping at the bit, huh?"

I wince. "Might need more practice before he sends some poor girl to the ER."

"Aw, maybe she'll give him another chance. First kisses are always awkward."

"Not ours," I say without thinking. But it's true—our first kiss was fucking perfect.

A pretty blush blooms on her cheeks. "You're right, ours was . . ."

I brush my thumb over her lip. "Incredible. Earth-shattering. One that should have happened way fucking sooner."

She laughs, leaning into my touch. Her dark eyes are warm, affectionate, and I'm about to replay that moment for us when my phone buzzes with a message. I debate ignoring it, but Alex's name flashing on the screen has me curious.

ALEX

dude, I fucked up. chomped down on Shannon's lip last night. there was blood EVERYWHERE. now she won't answer my texts. help! what do I do??

I groan, showing the text to Emmy. She presses a hand to her mouth, stifling more giggles. "Poor Alex," she says. "And poor Shan!"

"I know." I sit up, and her duvet slips to my lap. "I'd better call him, see if I can offer any advice."

She tugs me back down, pouting playfully. "Do you have to do that right this very second?"

I press a kiss to those perfect, unbloodied lips of hers. "I guess he can suffer a little longer."

I toss my phone back on the nightstand, unable to resist Emmy's sweet pout and the feel of her soft body pressed against mine. Alex's love life woes can wait—right now, I just want to savor this perfect morning with the girl I'm falling for.

I trail kisses along her jaw as she hums contentedly, arching into my touch. My hands wander her curves, relearning the feel of her, and I'm already growing hard against her thigh. Last night was incredible, but it only left me wanting more.

She giggles as I nip just below her jawline, her fingers threading into my hair to keep me close. Then I move back to her lips and deepen the kiss, tasting every sweet corner of her mouth.

"Hayes," she breathes, and God do I love the way my name sounds on her lips.

I kiss lower, over the swells of her breasts through the T-shirt she stole from me to sleep in. Together, we lift the fabric over her head, and I eagerly resume my position, taking a pert nipple into my mouth. She gasps, fingers tightening in my hair.

I continue downward, peppering her stomach with kisses until

I reach the apex of her thighs. I kiss her there, too, earning another sweet moan. "Yes, please," she whispers.

I grin up at her, pleased to see the want reflected in her eyes. "Say it again," I tease, running a finger over the damp heat of her panties.

"Hayes, please . . . I want it."

That's all I need to hear. I slip her panties down her legs and gently part her folds with my fingers, admiring the sight of her. "Look at this pretty pussy," I say. "So desperate for me."

I press a long, lingering kiss to her core, drawing her into my mouth. She tastes like honeyed wine, and I'm instantly drunk on it.

Her nails dig into the mattress as she arches into me. Groaning my approval, I work at teasing her with my tongue and thumbs, zeroing in on her sweet spot. Her breathless moans spur me on, so I pick up the pace, working her closer to the edge before backing off again.

"Hayes!" she whines in protest, but I'm already moving up her body until we're lip-to-lip again.

"You got me so worked up last night . . . thought I'd give you a taste of your own medicine," I say against her swollen lips.

She smacks my chest. "You're . . . *mean*."

"Oh, that really hurts me, babe." I grin back, brushing a stray hair behind her ear. "How about we make it up to each other instead?"

She gives me an eager nod, so I reach for the condoms on her nightstand, carefully sliding one on. Her hips lift off the bed, searching for mine. And when I push inside of her, the stars align.

By the end of Sunday night, Emmy and I have officially spent more than twenty-four hours straight together. I've added a few more paper stars to my jar, we've had two takeout meals each, and

I've watched her fight with Matty over how to properly load the dishwasher.

Matty was right, of course, but I had to side with my girl on principle.

It's nearing nine o'clock when I finally decide to extricate myself from the premises. Or, rather, Emmy decides to kick me out. She says she needs to get some quality sleep before another full week of classes, and I don't blame her.

I press one last lingering kiss to her forehead at the front door. "I'll call you tomorrow," I promise, voice thick with something I can't quite name.

"Okay," she whispers back.

Reluctantly, I pull away and make my exit. The brisk breeze tugs at my clothes with each step, offering a stark contrast to the cozy warmth I've left behind. It isn't until I'm by my car, enveloped in the evening's quiet, that I notice the absence of my hat—an old baseball cap my uncle gave me, unremarkable to most, but it's still my favorite.

I jog back up the stairs, two at a time, and knock on the front door. No answer. She and Matty must have retreated to their rooms already. Not wanting to intrude further, I quietly head in— the dead bolt unlocked—and head directly to Emmy's room, planning to grab my hat and leave without disturbing her.

But as I approach her door, the sound of her voice, light and bubbly, floats through the slight crack. She's on the phone, and although it's only her side of the conversation I can hear, it's clear she's talking to Shannon.

"Alex seems nice, though," she says. "Maybe a bit . . . awkward. But Hayes mentioned he's been single for a long time, and he's looking for something serious."

Emmy's quiet for a long moment before she laughs, long and hard. I lean in closer, my hand frozen on the doorknob. "Hayes is *not* my boyfriend. We're still seeing how the dating thing goes, remember?" she says, and a jolt of pain slices through my chest, as if I've been physically struck.

The warmth of the last two days, the closeness we shared, suddenly feels miles away. I stand motionless, my heart pounding in my ears. I'm . . . gutted, but I'm not even sure I have a reason to be. As I step away from her door, letting my hand fall from the knob, the thought of retrieving my once-favorite hat no longer seems worth the interruption.

Silently, I head back down the stairs, each step heavier than the last. The night air hits me again, this time carrying a chill that seeps deep into my bones. I climb into my car, and as I start the engine, a part of me wants to call her, to listen to her voice again, to pretend I didn't hear what I just did.

But I can't shake off this haunting feeling, this sense of disillusionment. In a split second, I went from an utter sense of contentment to being on the outside looking in. *Is this what dating is supposed to feel like? This uncertainty, this fear of not being enough?* Because if so, I'm not sure I'm cut out for it.

The drive home is a blur, my mind a mess of doubts and insecurities. When I pull up to our house, everything is quiet, so I brace myself for the solitude of my room.

But the moment I whip open the front door, the silence is shattered by the rapid gunfire of COD blaring from the living room. And there, in all his glory, is Liam—boxers, a day's worth of stubble, and a concentration so intense it's as if the fate of the free world rests on his next kill streak.

"Dude, you're back," he says without taking his eyes off the screen. "Thought you'd be tied up in Emmy-land forever."

I toss my keys on the counter. "Change of plans," I mutter, trying to keep the disappointment from my voice.

He pauses the game, turning to look at me with a furrowed brow. "You good?"

"Yeah, just . . . tired, I guess." I force a laugh, but even I know it sounds hollow. "You know, long weekend."

He nods, accepting the explanation, and a devilish grin spreads across his face. "Hey, since you're here, wanna see if we can beat the high score on Zombies? James bailed to 'meditate,'" he says, using air quotes so sarcastically it's a miracle they don't leave marks in the air.

I hesitate for a moment, the night's weight still bearing down. But then, a defiant thought crosses my mind: *fuck it.* Right now, a distraction is exactly what I need, something to drag me out of my own head.

"Sure, why not?" I say, dropping onto the couch beside him. "But if we're doing this, we're going all in. No half-assing."

His response is to restart the game, a determined gleam in his eye. "Let's kick some undead ass, then."

And for the next few hours, that's exactly what we do. It's the perfect distraction, pulling me out of the spiral of thoughts about Emmy, about us, or the lack thereof. For a while, I manage to forget.

As we finally wrap up, our score embarrassingly low, Liam turns off the console and stretches. He glances at me, his eyes narrowing as if he's about to delve into territories we usually avoid. "So, you gonna tell me the reason you're acting so fucking constipated?"

"Mind your business, Donovan," I say. I'm not in the mood to dissect my feelings, especially not with Liam, who's about as subtle as a sledgehammer.

"You are my business," he retorts, undeterred by my scowl. "Something's off with you."

I sigh, rubbing a hand over my face. Part of me wants to confide in him, to spill everything. Perhaps I'll find some solace in his likely blunt but well-meaning advice. But another part wants to keep it all locked up, to pretend like everything's fine.

"I heard Emmy tell someone that I'm not her boyfriend," I finally admit, the words tasting bitter on my tongue.

I've never been someone's boyfriend before, never had the urge or intention to, either. It's daunting, isn't it? To be the man someone else depends on for love, for support, to plan a future with. Yet, somewhere along the line, I found myself drifting toward that role with Emmy, as if it were the most natural path for us both.

I've spent so much time not knowing or caring where I stood with other women, but this time, everything felt different. Clear. And just when I thought I had a handle on it, everything I thought I knew, everything I felt, has unraveled at the seams.

He raises a brow. "Well, *are you* her boyfriend?"

"I . . . I don't know," I confess. "We're hanging out all the time, going on dates, swapping secrets, *fucking*. I thought . . . doesn't that make me . . ."

"Aw, buddy, no." He shakes his head, amused. "You can't just assume these things."

My shoulders slump. "You think she doesn't want me to be her boyfriend?"

"I think she needs you to *ask*."

"Ask?" I drop my head into my hands. "Fuck, why is this shit so confusing?"

"Love is confusing," he says. "That's why I don't do it."

"Yeah, well, I didn't, either. Before Emmy."

"So you admit it, then? You're in love with her?"

"I—I mean, I . . . you know what? Go to bed, Liam."

He shoots me a knowing look; the kind that says he's scored a point in a game I didn't even know we were playing. "Admitting it is the first step, Hayes. Next step, actually telling her."

I glare at him, but it's half-hearted. "Shut up."

He stands, stretching his limbs with exaggerated care. "Well, if you're not going to spill your guts to me, might as well get some sleep. God knows you look like you need it."

"I do not—"

"Look like a lovesick puppy? Yeah, you kinda do." He claps me on the shoulder, a solid, grounding gesture. "But hey, it's not the worst thing. Means you're human after all."

I swat his hand away, but the ghost of a smile tugs at my lips. "Get out of here, man."

He laughs, heading for his room as he throws a few parting words over his shoulder, "Remember that free choice is an illusion, pookie. We have no choice but to accept our destiny."

I give a humorless snort, rubbing at my temples. Well, fuck, maybe he's right. Not about the destiny bullshit but the rest of it. Maybe it's time to make my intentions crystal clear, to lay it all on the line once and for all.

The thought scares me. But the thought of losing Emmy because I didn't speak up? Well, that's fucking unbearable.

Chapter Twenty-Three

I'VE BEEN ACTING LIKE A . . . *man* scorned since that night at Emmy's, wallowing in my own baseless assumptions. I even opened up to Dr. Vargas about it the next day in therapy. She agreed with Liam's assessment, which is, frankly, a terrifying thought in and of itself.

So, it's been a few days of bare-bones conversations, and I know I need to talk to her. To man up and tell her that I want to make things official. That I may not know what I'm doing, but that I'm desperate to be doing it with her.

The thought of putting myself out there, of being vulnerable, makes me want to crawl out of my own skin. Still, I can't go on like this, stewing in uncertainty and letting miscommunication drive a wedge between us.

I'll set the stage for us this weekend. It'll be casual, nothing too dramatic—just a moment between us, intimate and real. But before I make any moves, I need a solid game plan, or at the very least, I need to practice my speech.

And who better to practice on than James, the least romantic person I know?

Wednesday morning finds me in the kitchen, James sitting across from me with a bowl of cereal, looking like he'd rather be anywhere else. "Come on, it'll be quick," I plead, trying to keep the desperation out of my voice.

He sighs, setting his spoon down with exaggerated patience. "Fine, but make it fast. And I swear, Hayes, if you try to fucking kiss me . . ."

I roll my eyes. "Oh, you could only be so lucky." Then, clearing my throat, I start, "Emmy, *baby*, this past month with you has been nothing short of—"

He interrupts me with a snort. "Try sounding a little less . . . gross."

I scowl. "Helpful feedback, thanks. Let me finish."

Taking a deep breath, I try again, this time trying to sound more like myself and less like a script. "Em, you know I'm not good at this stuff, but being with you feels different. It feels right. And I know we haven't talked labels or made anything official yet . . ." I trail off, the words catching in my throat.

"Man, just get right into it. No frills." James sets down his spoon, scratching at his jaw. "Something like, 'Hey, I like you a lot. Wanna make this official?'"

"Yeah, that's simple. I like it."

He grins. "Of course you do. Now, about the—"

The sound of my phone ringing cuts him off, and I glance at the screen to see an unknown number flashing. "Hold that thought," I say, stepping away to answer. "Hello?"

The voice on the other end is unfamiliar, clinical. "Hello, is this Hayes Grecco?"

"Yeah, speaking." I frown, confusion setting in. "Who's this?"

"You're listed as the emergency contact for Sebastian Grecco. He's being transferred from the emergency department at Mercy Hospital in Blue Ridge."

My heart stops. "What? Is he okay? What happened?"

The rest of the call is hazy, the voice on the other line delivering information with a detached professionalism that makes my stomach churn. "There was an accident," they say. "He's stable now. We're moving him to the ICU to monitor his concussion."

My hands tremble, the phone nearly slipping through my fingers as those words echo in my head. The room spins, my heart slamming against my chest as if trying to break free from the sudden grip of fear.

Images flash through my mind—Bash, laughing, shouting, the annoying little brother with too much energy and not enough caution. Now, lying in a hospital bed, hurt, unconscious, *alone.*

Reality slams into me with the force of a freight train. Every other thought, every minor worry about my relationship with Emmy, about what we are or aren't, evaporates into insignificance.

"I can be there in a couple of hours," I hear myself say, though my voice sounds distant, as if coming from someone else. I'm already moving, action overtaking thought, driven by a primal need to be there, to fix, to protect.

James' voice, filled with concern, barely registers as I grab my keys and jacket, my mind a whirlwind of fear and urgency. "It's Bash," I choke out, the words sticking in my throat like thorns. "He's . . . I just, *goddammit,* I have to go—now."

I'm out the door before I fully comprehend my own movements, propelled by a singular focus. The fall air hits me, but my every sense is homed in on the road ahead, on the miles I need to cover to reach my brother.

The drive is blurry, my mind overwhelmed with thoughts, with memories, with a gnawing fear for Bash. The brotherly squabbles, the shared laughs, even the times I wanted to throttle him for his reckless behavior—all of it coalesces into a sharp ache in my chest, a desperate hope that he's okay.

Right now, nothing else matters. My baby brother needs me, and I'll be damned if I let him down.

I'm sitting at Bash's bedside while he drifts in and out of sleep. His face is pale, a frightening blend against the stark white of the hospital sheets. There's a bandage wrapped tightly around his head. Every so often, he winces or mumbles something incoherent, and my heart clenches with the sound.

He was conscious by the time I arrived, but fits of sleep have kept him occupied. The story of what happened has come out in bits and pieces, from the doctors and Bash himself when he's been coherent enough to talk.

It was a rooftop stunt gone wrong—a misguided attempt to jump into the pool from the third story of his teammate's house, egged on by a mix of adrenaline and peer pressure. Apparently, one of them made the jump before, and all was well.

Only when Bash attempted the same feat, he missed the water. Instead of a safe landing, his body hit the edge of the pool, resulting in a moderate concussion and a fractured leg.

Sitting here as he battles through the pain, a part of me wants to scream, to rage against the recklessness, the sheer lack of responsibility. But anger won't undo what's done. It won't heal his wounds or turn back time. So, I swallow it down, focusing instead on being here for him, on offering whatever comfort I can.

"Try to get some rest," I say softly, squeezing his hand. "You're gonna be okay. We'll get through this."

He nods, eyelids fluttering as sleep pulls at him once more. "Stay . . .?"

"I'm not going anywhere, Bashy," I assure him, settling in. The chair beside his bed is uncomfortable, the room either too hot or too cold, but none of that matters. I'm here for Bash, just like I always promised I'd be.

After the day I've had—the roller coaster of emotions I've experienced over the last few hours—it doesn't take too long for me to doze off myself. When I wake up an hour later, it's to the sounds of my brother flirting with his nurse, winking as she hands him another cup of ice chips.

Even laid up in a hospital bed with a concussion, he still has that same playful spark in his eyes. "You know, I think I need some more pillows," he says, giving the nurse his most winning smile. "Would you mind helping fluff them for me?"

She obliges, carefully adjusting the pillows behind his head. "There, is that better?"

"Much better, thank you," Bash says. "With such great care, I'll be back on my feet in no time."

The nurse ducks her head, hiding her grin. "Just focus on resting for now. I'll come check on you later."

As she leaves the room, Bash sighs loudly. "Man, the nurses here are something else."

I snort and shake my head. "Even with a head injury, you're still trying to work your magic. Un-fucking-believable."

He laughs, then winces. "Hey, I wasn't kidding about the pillows. My head is killing me."

My amusement fades. "Do you need me to call the nurse back?"

"Nah, I'll survive. Besides, I've got you, don't I?"

A swell of emotion wells up in my chest. Bash has always looked up to me, relied on me. And I've always tried my best to be there for him when it counted. But there's only so much of this I can handle on my own.

"I'm not going anywhere," I say. "Once the doctor clears it, we'll get you home so you can really start healing up."

Some of the playfulness leaves his eyes. "Thanks for coming all this way. I know I screwed up, but I'm glad you're here."

"Nowhere else I'd rather be." I blow out a strained breath. "But Bash, I just—*fuck*, never mind. We'll talk about it when you get discharged."

"I know," he says. There's a thick swallow, and then, "I'm so fucking sorry, by the way. I don't know what's wrong with me, why I keep doing this."

Now isn't the time to reprimand him, to give him a lecture on responsibility and recklessness. Yet, the urge is there, pressing against the inside of my skull. It's a conversation we need to have, a reality he needs to face. I've always been there to catch him when he falls, but it's getting harder.

Bash needs to understand that his actions have consequences, not just for him but for those around him, too. It's not just about being there for each other anymore; it's about being responsible for our own paths. I can't keep fixing things for him, not if it means neglecting my own life, my own future.

Caring for someone who doesn't seem to care for themselves is draining, and I'm starting to feel the wear. It's a bitter realization, but I have to protect my own well-being, too. I need Bash to see that—to start taking steps on his own, to find his balance without leaning so heavily on me.

It's a tough-love kind of thought, one I'm not entirely comfortable with. But love isn't just about showing up; it's about teaching each other how to stand alone.

We sit in tense silence for a few more moments. But soon, his eyes begin to droop again, his body craving rest to recover. Before he drifts off entirely, he mumbles, "Love you, Hayes."

I lean forward, gently ruffle his hair. "Love you, too, Bashy. Sleep well."

Once he's out, I leave the room to do something I've been putting off since I got the initial call. I dial the familiar number, my stomach churning. It rings three times before my mom picks up, her voice chipper and oblivious to the storm brewing inside me. "Hayes! To what do we owe this rare pleasure?"

"Mom," I start, my voice tight, "it's Bash. He's in the hospital."

There's a pause on the line, a hitch in her breath. "Oh my goodness, what happened? Is he okay?"

I explain the situation as calmly as I can manage, though every word feels like it's being dragged from a well of frustration. "He tried to jump into a pool from a rooftop. Missed and hit the edge. He's got a concussion and a fractured leg."

"Oh, that boy." She sighs, the sound carrying a mixture of concern and exasperation. "He's always been too daring for his own good."

"Yeah, well, he needs you now," I say, the words heavy. "Can you and Dad come see him? He was asking for you earlier."

There's another pause, longer this time, and when my mom speaks again, her voice is apologetic but firm. "Honey, you know this weekend is the annual Sizzle Fest. We've been planning for months. Your father and I can't just leave."

Anger simmers in my veins, a bitter taste in my mouth. "So, a fucking *barbecue* festival is more important than your son lying in a hospital bed?"

"It's not that, Hayes," she says, and I can almost hear the pursing of her lips. "It's just that we have responsibilities here. Can't this be something you boys handle on your own? Sebastian will be sent home soon, won't he?"

"Yeah, he will," I reply, my voice cold, hollow. "Don't worry about it. We'll handle it. Like always."

"I'm so sorry, sweetheart. We really are. Give Sebastian our love, and tell him we'll call soon."

"Sure."

We say our goodbyes, but as I hang up, the phone feels like lead in my hand. The conversation confirms what I've always known deep down—when it comes to being there for Bash and me, my parents will always fall short.

I lean against the cold, sterile wall of the hospital corridor, closing my eyes as I try to rein in the emotions threatening to consume me. Anger, disappointment, resignation—they all swirl together.

But dwelling on it won't change anything. It won't make my

parents suddenly prioritize us over their business, won't erase the years of missed moments and absent support. All I can do is be there for Bash, to be the family he needs, even if it means doing it alone.

Chapter Twenty-Four
HAYES

Bash is home, all safe and sound, carefully tucked into his bed. We were discharged with instructions for him to rest, and the Blazers have already created a support structure for his return to play. Per the doctors, his tibial plateau fracture should heal up within a few weeks or so.

It's a stroke of luck, and possibly some benevolent force from the universe, that this one event won't completely hinder his progression.

Personally, I'm still reeling from the last two days. I haven't spoken to anyone other than my brother and his doctors all day. And now that he's back home, I feel like I can finally breathe again.

I need to call a few people, talk to someone about the community service I missed today. But I think I'll have a word with Bash's roommates first. He adamantly begged me not to confront them, said that it wouldn't do either of us any good. Unfortunately for Bash, I don't often do what I'm told.

I find his roommates, Ozzie and Jordan, in the kitchen, beers in hand as they cook up burgers on the stovetop. They pause when I enter, twin looks of guilt on their faces.

"Hey, how's Sebastian doing?" Jordan asks tentatively.

"He's resting," I say, leaning against the counter and fixing them both with a hard look. "He was lucky, you know? Could've been a helluva lot worse."

Ozzie flips a burger, not quite meeting my eyes. "Yeah, man. We feel awful about what happened."

I cross my arms. "Do you? Because I heard that you two dipshits were there encouraging him to jump."

"We were just having a bit of fun," Jordan mumbles under his breath.

"Fun?" I repeat incredulously. "He ended up in the fucking hospital. You think that's fun?"

"No, of course not—"

"Did you stop to think for even one second how risky it was?" I plow on, heat rising in my chest. "How badly he could've been hurt? What it might do to his career?"

Jordan pales a little, shrinking back. "We didn't think—"

"That's right, you didn't think," I snap. "You didn't look out for him. Some teammates you are."

Jordan's face flashes with guilt before hardening. "Hey, don't put this all on us. Sebastian's a big boy. He can make his own choices."

"Can he?" I shoot back. "Or did you pressure him into it because you knew he'd cave? Bash tries to please everyone. And you and the rest of the team continue to take advantage of that."

They exchange uneasy glances, and I know I've hit the mark.

"Look," I say, trying to rein in my anger. "I know my brother can be reckless. But he looks up to you. As his teammates—as his only family out here—you should have his back. Not egg him on."

My words seem to land heavily on them. They both look properly chastised.

"You're right," Ozzie says quietly. "We messed up. We'll do better."

Jordan nods. "It won't happen again. We promise."

I hold their gazes for a long moment. "Good. He's gonna need your support while he recovers."

I turn to leave, and as I do, Ozzie calls out, "Hey, you want a burger?"

I pause, then shake my head with a wry quirk of my lips. "I'm good. You knuckleheads enjoy."

I head upstairs, feeling slightly better. Bash has good guys in his corner, even if they are a bit misguided at times. They're all young, fresh, and new to the scene. As long as they learn from this, as long as they start looking out for each other more, that's what matters.

After making a quick phone call to my attorney—pleading my case—I slip back into Bash's room to check on him. He's sleeping soundly, leg propped up on two pillows. In the soft glow of his night-light, he looks years younger, and my heart clenches at the sight.

No matter how old Sebastian gets, he'll always be my baby brother.

I grab a blanket and spread it out on the floor beside his bed. Curling up, I close my eyes, willing my mind to settle. I'm bone-tired but too fucking wired to sleep. After a few minutes of fruitless tossing and turning, I give up.

Snagging my phone from the floor, I open up my messages. My finger hovers over Emmy's name. It's been less than forty-eight hours, and she's already sent me a string of texts asking what's going on. Of course, I want to confide in her, but right now, it just feels like more pressure.

It's like I'm walking through a minefield, where every step carries the risk of making a mistake. My head's a mess, tangled with concerns about Bash, our parents' apathy, and where Emmy and I stand. As far as I'm concerned, we're still in limbo, neither here nor there, and the last thing I want is to burden her with my chaos.

I draft a message, delete it, then start over, struggling to find the right balance. I don't want to come across as too distant or too clingy, too casual or too serious. It's a ridiculous dance, trying to calibrate my tone.

In the end, I opt for simplicity, a straightforward message that lays out the facts.

HAYES

> Bash had an emergency, I'm in Blue Ridge for a few more days. talk soon

It's basic, almost clinical, but it's all I can manage without unraveling at the seams.

EMMY

> let me know if you need anything. thinking of you both <3

I want to say more, to open up about the fear, the frustration, the longing for comfort. But I hold back, recognizing the need to focus on the immediate crisis, to be there for Bash and navigate the aftermath of all this.

HAYES

> thanks, Em

I set the phone aside, a sense of resolve settling over me. Now isn't the time for declarations or decisions about our future. Now is the time for family, for healing. So, I lie back down—the soft breathing of my brother a constant in the quiet room—and I let myself drift.

By Sunday, Bash is well on his way to recuperating, and it's time for me to head back to Dayton. My attorney managed to excuse me from missing my trash duty last week, but if I skip my session with Dr. Vargas tomorrow, I doubt they'd be as lenient.

Bash, propped up on a mountain of pillows, gives me a weak thumbs-up as I pack my bag. "You sure you're gonna be okay without me?" I ask, not for the first time.

He rolls his eyes, the action slow and a bit strained. "I survived a jump from the top of a building, Hayes. I think I can handle a few days on my own."

I give a worried huff of a chuckle. "Just . . . try not to hurt yourself again, okay? You're not fuckin' invincible."

He grins, that devilish spark still present despite the circumstances. "Scout's honor."

I zip up my bag and sling it over my shoulder, pausing at the door to look back at him. "Call me if you need anything. And I mean anything, Bash."

"I will," he says, and there's a distinct sincerity in his voice—one that eases a fraction of the worry knotting my chest.

The drive back is a mix of relief and apprehension. On one hand, I'm happy that Bash is on the mend, but I'm also concerned about what waits for me back at Dayton. The weight of responsibility sits heavy on my shoulders, a burden I'm not sure I can carry alone.

Once I'm finally back home, all I want to do is lie in bed for the rest of the day. To sink under the covers and shut out the rest of the world. So, I proceed to drag myself up the stairs to my room.

I'm barely through the door when I hear it—Liam's voice, calling out from his own room beside me. "Hayes!" he shouts. "You all good, buddy?"

I'm not in the mood to talk, not even close, but I poke my head into his doorway. Liam's sprawled on his bed, laptop perched in front of him, a mess of snack wrappers littered around him.

"Yeah, I'm back," I confirm, my voice flat.

He closes his screen, eyes narrowing as he takes in my expression. "What's with the long face? James told me that Bash was doing okay."

I tense. "He's fine. Healing."

"Bet he learned his lesson about flying, huh?"

That's it—the comment, meant as a joke, hits a nerve I didn't realize was so raw. "You think that's funny?" I snap, stepping fully into his room. "My brother could've died. And you're making jokes about it?"

He sits up, his grin fading. "Hey, man, I was just—"

"No," I cut him off, anger boiling over. "I'm really not in the mood, Liam."

His face drops, his usual cockiness replaced by a rare seriousness. "Sorry, I didn't—"

But I'm not interested in what else he has to say, not right now. I need space, a moment to collect my thoughts without the noise, a moment to myself for once.

"We'll talk later," I say, turning on my heel and slinking back to my room.

I shut the door behind me, the sound echoing loudly in the silence. Alone, I let out a heavy sigh, running a hand through my hair. The anger slowly ebbs away, leaving behind a hollow exhaustion.

I don't even have enough time to settle into bed before my phone rings in my hand. I'd love nothing more than to press Ignore, but it's my coach, and the sight of his name immediately puts me on edge.

When I answer, he asks, "Grecco, you got a minute?" His tone is void of its usual emotion, and I can already tell this isn't just a courtesy call.

"Yeah, Coach, what's up?" I ask, bracing myself.

"It's about your missed assignments, the community service from last week. The dean's pretty upset with you. Says that this is strike two. Step out of line one more time, and you'll officially be ineligible to play this spring."

Anger flares up inside me, hot and sharp. "It was an *emergency* situation, Coach. I didn't just skip out for the hell of it. My little brother was in the hospital."

"I understand that, and I'm on your side, but they're taking a hard line. Says it's about setting a precedent."

A precedent. The words feel like a slap in the face. Since when did handling a family emergency equate to being a hardened criminal? The unfairness of it all, the way my efforts to juggle everything are being disregarded, it's infuriating.

"Thanks for letting me know, Coach," I manage to say through gritted teeth, trying to keep my composure.

"We'll figure this out. Just . . . try to keep your head down for now, alright?"

"Sure," I say, but as soon as I hang up, the frustration boils over. I toss my phone onto my bed, utterly defeated.

This isn't how things were supposed to go. I was meant to be getting my act together, proving to everyone—Emmy, my team, myself—that I could handle my shit. That covering for Bash was just a momentary blip. But now, with every step forward, it feels like I'm taking two steps back.

I sink down onto the edge of my mattress, my head in my hands. Between the plea bargain, Bash's accident, my parents' absence, and now the repeated threats from the dean, it's all too much.

I close my eyes, trying to quell the rising panic. There's this acute sense of being trapped in a cycle I can't break. The conversation with Emmy, the one I'd been steeling myself for, now seems like just another hurdle in a long line that never ends.

No matter what I do, I can't shake the feeling that I'm on the edge of an unending precipice. One wrong move and everything will come crashing down.

Chapter Twenty-Five

FOR THE PAST SIX DAYS, I've been consumed by worry, but now I'm eager to spend time with the man who's always on my mind.

After his session with Dr. Vargas, Hayes arrives at my apartment with a weary smile. It's obvious he's still raw, the emotional toll of the past week written all over his face. He greets me with a kiss that's a bit too desperate, too hungry, as if he's trying to drown out the world.

I gently pull back, searching his warm hazel eyes. "Hey," I say softly, brushing my thumb over his cheek. "Talk to me. What's going on in that head of yours?"

He lets out a shaky breath, his shoulders slumping. "I just . . . I don't really want to talk right now. I'm so damn tired of talking. Can we just . . . be here together? Please?"

"Of course."

He lets out a shaky breath, leaning into my touch. "I just—I need to not think right now, Em. I need . . ."

His voice trails off, but I understand. After bearing his soul in therapy, he's seeking an escape, some way to numb the ache.

"You want me to make you feel better?" I ask.

A ghost of a smile crosses his lips. "You always do."

I nod, the heat of his admission swirling through me. Taking his hand, I lead him to my room, where we fall together onto the bed. He pulls me into his arms, and I slowly undress him, one button at a time.

When he's stripped down to only his boxers, he helps me out of my clothes, his fingers scorching as they graze over me. We lie skin to skin, and the tension is still thrumming through his body.

"I've got you," I whisper, running my hands up and down his back in soothing motions.

He buries his face in the crook of my neck, his arms around me as though he's drowning and I'm his lifeline. I hold him, stroking his hair, trying to communicate in the only way I know how that I'm here for him, for as long as he needs me.

He lifts his head, gaze searching. "I'm sorry for being MIA."

"It's okay," I say, brushing a stray hair off his forehead. "You've been dealing with a lot."

He frowns, a shadow of doubt clouding his face. "I don't want to push you away, Em. I just . . . I just need to figure this shit out on my own first."

I sit up, my naked body pressing against his side. He pulls me back down against him, resting his chin on top of my head.

"Okay," I say softly.

He presses a hard kiss to my neck, lips trailing up to my ear. "And you want to help me forget, don't you?"

"I do."

His hand slips between my legs, his fingers warm and sure as they push inside of me. My back arches, and a moan escapes my lips. Hayes has always had this way of knowing how to make me lose control—of my body, my thoughts, *everything*.

I press my thighs together, urging him deeper. He obliges, two fingers curling against my walls as his thumb circles my clit. His cock is hard, pressing into my hip. So, I squeeze him through the fabric, eliciting a groan from both of us.

"Need you so bad," he murmurs.

My hand dips inside, and I eagerly swipe my thumb across the bead of precum pooling on his tip. "Yeah?" I tease, nipping his earlobe. "You and me both."

With a growl, he flips me onto my stomach, and I arch my back, offering myself up to him. He pulls down his boxers, revealing his throbbing erection. Pushing my panties down, he enters me with one slow thrust.

White-hot pleasure bursts through every nerve ending. Gripping the sheets, I moan as he picks up the pace, the rhythm of his hips matching my own desperate grind against the mattress.

His movements are fevered, desperate, like he's trying to outrun his demons along with our joined bodies. And while part of me wants to slow him down, to remind him that I'm here for him no matter what, another part of me understands.

Sometimes actions do speak louder than words.

So I let go, losing myself in the sensation of him inside me, his hands gripping my hips as he drives deeper and deeper. One finger slowly circles my other hole, just barely nudging the entrance.

My hips jut off the bed at the sensation, and he asks me in a low voice, "You want this, baby?"

"Mhmm," is all I can say.

He pops his thumb into his mouth, wetting it, and then returns it to that same tender spot. As I moan, he gently pushes his way inside, and I'm so unbelievably full. I've never felt this close to anyone before—mind, body, and soul.

Hayes is claiming every inch of me, and it feels better, sweeter, than I could've ever imagined. My orgasm builds quickly, coiling low in my stomach before exploding outward in bursts of pleasure that leave me breathless. He follows close behind, collapsing on top of me with a shuddering sigh.

"Never get enough of you," he mumbles against my neck.

"Me neither."

He carefully slides off me, tugs me close as we catch our breath. I'm still reeling from it all—my core pulsing, fluttering around nothing—when I realize that his cum is dripping out of me.

"*Fuck*," I say, panicking.

He sits up. "What is it? Did I hurt you?"

"No," I mutter. "We didn't use a condom, Hayes."

A look of horror washes over his face. "Fuck, I'm so sorry. I wasn't thinking. I just needed—"

I shake my head, gently pressing my finger to his lips. "It's okay, I think. I'm on birth control."

He exhales a sigh of relief. "I get tested regularly. I'm all clear."

"So am I."

He swallows, hard and heavy. "So . . . we're good, then?"

"Yeah, we are."

He falls onto his back and hugs me tight. "I don't want to be reckless with you, Em. I just . . ."

"I know," I interrupt, my voice soft. "No worries. Now we know for next time."

"Yeah, next time," he echoes, but there's a hesitance in his voice that wasn't there before.

In just a matter of minutes, the mood shifts. He disentangles himself from the sheets and stands up, his movements quick and decisive. A knot forms in my stomach as he retrieves his clothes from the floor, dressing with a speed that feels like he's running from something.

My brow furrows. "Are you leaving already?"

"Yeah." He avoids my gaze, scratching at the back of his neck. "Sorry, I just—I think I need to be alone tonight. Sleep in my own bed, you know?"

"Oh."

He hesitates, a clear struggle playing across his features. "Do you want me to stay?"

Of course I want him to stay. Moreover, I want him to *want* to stay. But if he truly needs the time to himself, then I'll respect that.

Hayes hasn't been in a relationship before. He might not fully grasp how important it is for him to share his thoughts and burdens with me, how a genuine, thriving relationship is built on the foundation of mutual support.

Yet, this moment isn't the right time for a discussion like that—his mind cluttered, his emotions a mess. It wouldn't be fair to either of us to delve into the topic when he's barely holding on to his composure.

A quick hit it and quit it doesn't sit well with me, but laying it all out now, demanding answers or changes, won't lead to a genuine resolution.

"I—um, no, if you need to be alone, then you should . . . do that."

He nods his agreement, and it feels like a small betrayal, the space between us widening with each passing second. "Okay, yeah." He gives me a small smile, one that doesn't quite reach his eyes. "I'll grab a towel so you can clean up."

I stiffen. "I've got it."

"Ah, okay." His gaze darts around my face, and I shutter what must be a hurt expression. "I'll see you later, then?"

"You want me to come hang out with you again on Thursday?"

He waves me off. "Nah, I wouldn't bother. I'm doing double time since I missed last week."

"Oh, okay. This weekend, then?"

"Yeah, baby," he says, "this weekend."

Once he's dressed, he leans over me to press one final kiss to my forehead. Then he leaves, the click of the door behind him echoing like the final note in a song. And now, I'm all alone.

I FOLD my eighteenth paper star of the night, my books and laptop scattered around me on the living room floor. I have a marketing midterm tomorrow, my first of the year, and I'm struggling to stay awake long enough to study.

But it's not just the exam that's weighing down on me—it's everything with Hayes, too.

Ever since he walked out Monday night, things have felt . . . off. He's barely texted, and every attempt I've made to reach out, to understand what's going on inside his head, has been met with silence or short replies.

When we had sex, I wanted to be there for him in whatever way he needed. But the way he left, it just felt wrong. He needed space, and I get that. Of course I do. But my empathy for him doesn't stop the worry, the self-doubt, from creeping in.

That night, after the door clicked shut behind him, I curled up with the fleece blanket he made me, trying to hold back tears. It's silly, but I've kept the thing close ever since, a small piece of comfort to tide me over. It smells like him, like us, and some nights, it's the only thing that can calm the storm inside my head.

It's been a little over a week now since the accident, and I'm already wishing for those sweet moments back. For that feeling of being utterly connected, not just physically but emotionally, too. We were headed in the right direction—so unbelievably happy together—when the universe threw a wrench in it.

I suppose that's life, though, unpredictable and unfair at the best of times. Still, the uncertainty of where we stand has been gnawing at me, leaving me confused and isolated. Maybe even more so than when I first left the squad.

I wrap the tie blanket over my shoulders, curling in on myself, when the front door swings wide open. Matty strides in, breaking the silence of my concentration—or lack thereof. He's holding a bizarre kitchen gadget that looks like a cross between a blender and a weapon from a sci-fi movie.

"Em, guess what I just bought?" he asks with a grin that could light up the room.

I glance up, the corners of my mouth twitching despite my exhaustion. "The latest in alien defense technology?"

"Nah, it's supposed to be used to make zucchini noodles. But I swear it looks like it's a torture device or something." He sets it on the counter with exaggerated care, turning to me with a more serious expression. "You look like you're about to pass out. What's going on?"

My attempted smile fades as quickly as it appeared. "Just tired. And overwhelmed, I guess." I gesture vaguely to the chaos of my study materials.

He plops down, the couch dipping under his weight. "You've been saying you're 'just tired' for weeks now. And you look like that monster robot from *Power Rangers* we used to watch. What was its name? SleepyZord?"

A laugh escapes me, short and surprised. "It was SleepoTron, and I do not."

"Could've fooled me." His tone softens. "Seriously, Em, is there something more going on here?"

I sigh, a sound heavy with weariness. "It's just . . . everything. I'm still so sleepy all the time, my brain feels hazy, and now I'm worried about Hayes, too. He's going through so much, and I can already see him pulling away. Just when I thought we were getting somewhere."

"Honestly, I feel like this isn't a normal baseline for you. Or for most other healthy people our age. I mean, God, Em, you're only twenty-one years old. You shouldn't be so exhausted from simple everyday tasks." His brows knit together in concern. "Do you . . . would you consider going back to the doctor? Getting a second opinion?"

I nod slowly, the idea having circled my mind more than once. "I have, but . . . I don't know. It feels like a dead end, like they'll never listen to my concerns. Never take me seriously."

He huffs. "Come on. You know your own body, and you gotta take care of yourself. Keep pushing it."

His words, simple and straightforward, cut through the fog of my indecision. "Yeah, you're right. I'll make an appointment at the Dayton health center. Maybe a university provider would be better suited for me, more understanding of what we go through."

"Good. Glad we had this talk." He stands, stretching. "Now I'm gonna go see if I can make some zoodles without creating a wormhole."

I laugh. "Thank you, Matty."

"I got you, Em," he says. "Always."

Chapter Twenty-Six

I KICK my legs off the side of the exam table, tucking my hands beneath my thighs to resist the urge to pick. My cuticles are aching, and I'm one wrong move away from creating the hangnail of the century.

The paper beneath me crinkles with every slight movement, a constant, grating reminder that I'm once again sitting in a doctor's office. This one is different, though; it's not the sterile, stark white I've grown accustomed to, but softer, with gentle blues that coat the walls and little paintings of cows. Small touches that somehow make the clinical setting less daunting.

It's a wonder I was able to get an appointment here so quickly, but I suppose student cancellations are inevitable. My new provider, Dr. Patel, had greeted me earlier with a warmth that felt genuine, a rarity in the revolving door of doctors I've encountered over the past year.

As she enters the room again, her smile is reassuring. She's been thorough during our appointment, more so than any other doctor I've met thus far. We've gone over my exhaustive history of symptoms, the relentless fatigue that clings to my bones, the headaches, and the muscle pain.

And then, there were the blood tests, another round in what feels like an endless series.

Dr. Patel sits across from me now, her hands clasped together on her lap, and there's a softness in her eyes that prepares me before she even speaks. "Emmy, based on everything we've discussed and the results of your earlier tests, I believe what you're experiencing may be chronic fatigue syndrome."

The words hang in the air, a diagnosis that feels both like a weight holding me down and a rope pulling me up. *Chronic fatigue syndrome.* An answer to the riddle my body has become, a name to the invisible force that's hijacked my life for the last year. It's strange, the relief I'm experiencing. This knowledge that at least it hasn't all been in my head, a mere figment of my imagination.

Dr. Patel explains the condition, the methods to relieve symptoms. It's a lot to take in, but her voice is steady, a guiding light in the fog that's enveloped my life. As the appointment wraps up, she hands me a few pamphlets, and then I'm out the door.

Before I can make it back to my car, my phone rings in my pocket, the word *Mom* flashing on the screen. "Emmy, honey, how did it go?" she asks as soon as I pick up. Her voice is a warm hug, concern laced through every word.

"Um, good, I guess? They think it's something called chronic fatigue syndrome."

"Aw, honey." There's a long pause, and then, "You know, I have quite a few patients with that diagnosis, all living very different lifestyles. I know it will be hard, I know it's already been hard. But from my understanding, it can be quite manageable if you know your limits."

I wrinkle my nose. "Yeah, so I've heard."

"Are you okay?"

"Yeah, I . . . I'm still processing." I run a hand through my hair, my emotions a tangled mess. "Honestly, it's just nice to have an answer, you know?"

"I do," she says gently. "Did your doctor mention anything about treatments?"

"She just suggested pain meds. Said we'll maybe look into anti-depressants to help with sleep stuff. We also talked a bit about pacing, but it was all just preliminary. I'm gonna go back in a few weeks to be seen again."

"That's a good start. And I'm here for you every step of the way." There's another pause, and I envision her nodding to herself, deciding whether to broach whatever thought is on her mind. "Is there . . . anything else you might want to talk about?"

I stiffen. "What do you mean?"

"Just . . . anything," she says suspiciously. "About school, friends, *boys*."

"Boys?" My brows shoot up. "Oh God. Matty spilled the beans, didn't he?"

She laughs, unbridled. "I'm not sure what you're referring to, dear."

"Mom, I know Matty tells Jolene everything."

"His mother may have mentioned that you and Matty were both seeing new people. Just in passing conversation. We didn't make a thing of it."

"Yeah, somehow I still don't believe you." I roll my eyes but decide to fess up anyway. "If I'm being honest, there is . . . *someone*. His name is Hayes."

"Oh?" There's a noticeable shift in her tone, a mix of surprise and curiosity. "And who is this Hayes of yours?"

I laugh, a nervous, fluttering sound. "Someone I've been seeing. A Dayton baseball player. It's still new, but I really like him. It's just . . . he's going through a lot right now. And I'm worried he might pull away. For good. He's already been . . . pretty distant lately."

Her response is immediate, protective. "Madison, you know you can't let a man walk all over you, especially with everything else on your plate."

I sigh. "I know that, Mom. And I won't. I'm trying to work through things with Hayes, but I'm also aware of my limits. In the end, I know when to stay and when to walk away."

Silence stretches between us, a bridge of unspoken words and shared understanding. My mind drifts to my father, a man who was never a part of my life. My mom walked away from him when she was pregnant with me, determined to carve out a life for us.

She never had anyone to rely on other than herself, never complained about it, either. She's the epitome of strength and independence, a beacon I've always tried to emulate.

Yet, here I am, yearning for love and family, a desire as deep-rooted as the lessons she's instilled in me. I'm proud of her, of us, but I also want more. I want to believe in the possibility of love, of letting someone in without losing myself in the process.

"Em, honey, are you still there?"

"Yeah, Mom, I'm here." My voice is steadier than I feel. "I just . . . I want to find that balance, you know? Between wanting love and not compromising my self-worth."

Her voice softens, a tender note. "I can understand that. You're strong, and you deserve someone who respects and loves you for who you are. Never settle for less."

"I won't," I say. "I promise."

By the time night falls, I still haven't heard from Hayes. He said we'd see each other this weekend, so I've been clinging to that promise, giving him the space he so obviously needed. But now it's Friday night, and I'll be damned if I'm gonna sit alone in my bedroom, staring at my phone while I wait for him to call.

My fingers hover over his name, an internal debate raging within me. I don't want to seem needy, but the silence between us has grown too loud, too heavy. Finally, with a deep breath that does little to steady my racing heart, I type out a message.

EMMY

> hey, are we still on for this weekend? I was
> hoping we could see each other tonight, actually

I hit Send before I can talk myself out of it, and the waiting game begins. Each minute stretches longer than the last, my anxiety twisting into a tight knot. After what feels like an eternity, my phone finally vibrates.

HAYES

> hey baby. yeah, I was actually gonna text you.
> there's a party at a teammate's house tonight.
> was planning to invite you. we can meet there in
> an hour?

A party. The last thing I want tonight is to drown in a sea of strangers, with loud music numbing my senses. Plus, it will be nearly impossible to have the conversation I wanted to have. I was hoping for quiet, intimacy, a space where I could open up to Hayes, tell him about my diagnosis.

But maybe this is just what we need—a chance to break the ice after days of silence, to reconnect in the easy atmosphere that a social setting can provide.

EMMY

> yeah, okay. send me the address?

The location pops up on my screen moments later, and a flurry of nerves invades my stomach. This isn't how I imagined tonight unfolding, but at least it's something. An opportunity to reconnect with Hayes, to gauge where we stand.

I had hoped to have Matty by my side for support, but he opted for a night out with his boyfriend—the football player he's yet to open up about. I understand, though. Matty's walking a tightrope, juggling his relationship in secret, away from prying eyes. It's a tricky situation, balancing his personal happiness against his partner's fear of judgment. And while he's keeping me in the dark, too, I can't fault him for it.

When I arrive at the party, the night is already in full swing. I knock on the door, but there's no response amidst the thumping bass drifting from within. Steeling my nerves, I turn the handle and let myself inside.

The air is thick with heat and the stale smell of beer. People are packed shoulder to shoulder in the living room, swaying and bouncing to the music. I weave my way through the crowd, scanning faces, but there's no sign of Hayes yet.

In the kitchen, I seek out the cooler of drinks and help myself to a bottled water. Leaning against the counter, I take a few sips, trying to gather my wits. My eyes dart around, searching, hoping. And then, just as I'm about to take another sip, I find him standing there across the room.

He's easy enough to find, the life of the party as always, surrounded by a group of people hanging on his every word. His hazel eyes light up when he sees me, and for a moment, it's like nothing has changed. He's the Hayes I first fell for—goofy, charming, and irresistibly magnetic.

"Emmy, baby, you're here!" He breaks out from the crowd of people, stalking toward me, and it's all I can do not to beam up at him.

His familiar scent envelops me as he pulls me in for a hug. "Hey," I say. "It's good to see you."

He pulls back, his hands lingering on my arms. "You look so fucking good. I'm really glad you came."

I offer a small smile in return, unsure how to navigate the sudden intimacy after days of distance. "Can I get you a drink?" he asks, but before I can respond, he plucks the water bottle from my hand, replacing it with a Solo cup. "Here, you can have mine."

I eye the cup warily. "What's in it?"

"Oh, just my special recipe." He winks. "Don't worry, it's not too strong."

I take a tentative sip, the mixture of fruit and alcohol tickling my tongue. "This is really good, actually. Thanks."

He grins, clearly pleased. "Come on, let's go sit down. I want to hear all about your week."

He leads me to a quieter corner of the house, an oversized armchair just big enough for two. I nestle into the crook of his arm, the drink and his warmth relaxing me.

For a while, we fall back into our familiar rapport, the conversation flowing easily. He asks about my classes and my marketing exam. He fills me in on the latest drama with James and Liam. It almost feels normal again.

But there's still an elephant in the room, and we can't outrun it forever. I know we need to talk about what's been going on with him—with baseball, with Bash. And I need to tell him about my diagnosis, about what it might mean for me, for us.

I take a deep, bracing breath and open my mouth to speak. But before I can form the words, a pretty brunette plops down on the arm of Hayes' chair, draping herself over his shoulders.

"There you are!" she exclaims, her words slightly slurred. "I've been looking everywhere for you."

Hayes shifts, his body language screaming discomfort. But his tone remains light. "Oh, hey, Luce. Emmy, this is Lucy. She's an old friend of mine."

Lucy ignores me completely, focusing her giggly attention on Hayes. As she babbles in his ear, his eyes meet mine, silently apologizing. Finally, with an awkward laugh, Hayes manages to disentangle himself from her grasp.

Lucy huffs, clearly annoyed, and stomps off into the crowd, leaving an awkward tension in her wake.

I tilt my head. "What the hell was that about?"

He loops an arm around me. "Not sure. She's probably just

upset because we used to hook up . . . for a while, back in the summer."

"Um, okay," I say, shocked by his cavalier attitude.

I know he's been drinking, but there's a look in his eyes that I don't recognize despite that fact. A sort of emptiness that belies a hard edge.

He's never flaunted his past hookups in front of me or made a spectacle of them. It's out of character, and I wonder if this is his way of dealing with the pressures he's facing or if there's something deeper going on.

The way he just talked about being with Lucy, so blatantly indifferent to how it might affect me, stings more than I'd like to admit. It's a side of him I've never been exposed to, and I'm struggling to grapple with it.

I've always been fairly levelheaded when it comes to jealousy, to understanding that we had separate lives before each other. But this feels different, like a disregard for the respect and understanding we've built between us. It feels like a provocation, like he wants to test boundaries without concern for the fallout.

I'm torn between wanting to confront him and wanting to keep the peace, to not add to the pile of things he's already dealing with. But it's clear we're at a crossroads, and how we handle it could shape the direction of our relationship.

I try to stand, to detach myself from this conversation that's veered into uncomfortable territory, but he gently pulls me back down. He places a soft, apologetic kiss to my temple, but I'm still stiff, unresponsive to his advances.

Eventually, he pulls away, brows knitting in confusion. "What's wrong?"

"What's wrong?" I echo, my voice rising slightly. "Don't you think that was a weird thing to say to me just now?"

He looks genuinely bewildered. "The truth is weird to you?"

"Hayes, come on."

"What?" He gives a noncommittal shrug. "I was just saying that we used to hook up. We don't anymore. So, what's the problem?"

I scoff, disbelief clouding my thoughts. "Right, Mr. Jealousy. You don't see a problem with it all. Telling me that, acting so casual about an ex-hookup draping herself over you."

He gives a humorless snort. "Whatever. I mean, it's not like I'm your boyfriend, right?"

Hurt lodges in my throat, a bitter lump that refuses to be swallowed down. "I—Hayes, that's not fair. You know how I feel about you."

He abruptly stands, creating a physical distance to match the emotional one. "Em, I just don't know what you want from me. I've done nothing but follow your lead, and now I'm just trying to be honest here."

Honesty is one thing, but this feels like something else entirely —carelessness, maybe, or a last-ditch effort to push me away. A challenge to test my reaction. The party around us fades into a dull roar, and all I can do is shake my head.

I'm at a complete loss for words. The only thing I can think about is the pain in my chest, the realization that maybe Hayes and I aren't on the same page after all. Maybe we never will be.

"*Honest?* I don't think you're being honest with me or with yourself," I say quietly. "I care about you, Hayes. A lot. But I already told you I won't be strung along, used as a distraction, while you figure your shit out."

His expression flashes—guilt, hurt, and then a shuttered look as if closing the doors to his soul, locking away the vulnerability that had briefly shown through. "Okay," he says, the word falling carelessly from his lips. "Then you're done?"

The question is like a slap in the face, the final blow in a fight I hadn't even realized we were having. After everything, I'm shocked that he'd dismiss my feelings so easily, brush off our connection as if it were nothing more than a minor inconvenience to his evening.

"Yeah," I say, "I'm done."

And when I walk out of the house a few minutes later, tears welling in my eyes, he doesn't bother to follow.

Chapter Twenty-Seven

My head is pounding, my heart is aching, and I know, undoubtedly, that I fucked up last night. I fucked up so badly that Emmy dumped me. She left without so much as looking back.

I press my cheek into the cool surface of the breakfast counter, replaying our conversation from last night. Over and over and over again. All I want is for the world to swallow me up, to spit me back out to a time where I could still make things right with my girl. Where I can tell her how much she means to me, how much her walking away scared me, how the thought of not having her in my life anymore makes me severely unwell.

But wishes are for fairy tales, and I'm stuck in a harsh reality where my actions have consequences. I knew I was playing with fire last night, and maybe, for a moment, I wanted to watch the world burn. But replaying the hurt in her eyes now, it's haunting me.

A throat clears from behind, startling me, so much so that I nearly fall from my stool. When I look up, James is standing there, one brow raised, a look of pure amusement on his face. "So, you gonna bang your head against that counter?" he asks, "or can I sit over here without worrying about your safety?"

I straighten up, giving a half-hearted shrug. "Yeah, sure. Sit down. I'm fine."

He doesn't seem convinced, but he takes a seat anyway, his

gaze sharp and assessing. "You don't look fine. You look like shit, actually. Want to talk about it?"

I groan. "God, you sound like your brother."

"I'm much smarter than Liam."

"You're not."

He fixes me with a harsh glare, arms folded across his chest. "*Anyway*, what do you have to say for yourself, young man?"

I frown. "What do you mean?"

"Word on the street is that Emmy left the Garda party in tears."

I toss my head back, wincing at the fresh pang in my temples. "*Shit.*"

"What did you do, Hayes?"

"I . . . don't know." I toss my hands up. "She's the one who broke up with me."

He gives me an incredulous snort. "Right. You *don't know.*"

"I was tipsy. Drunk, maybe. And overwhelmed, I guess. All I know is that I was trying my best to act normal, and maybe I was being a little callous. Some stuff I said came out the wrong way."

"*Some stuff you said,*" he mocks.

"Are you just gonna repeat me?"

"No," he says, "I'm gonna repeat you with *emphasis.*"

I squeeze my eyes shut, groaning. "I'm tired, James, and I don't have time for this."

"So, you're just done with Emmy, then? You're not even gonna try to apologize?"

"No," I say gruffly. "I'm gonna tell her I'm sorry, but I'm not so sure that it's gonna get me anywhere. I heard what she said last night loud and clear. She's not willing to wait around while I deal with all my bullshit."

"Then stop with the bullshit."

I scoff. "Like it's my choice!"

"There's been a lot of bad shit that's been out of your control, sure. But it's been your choice all along in how to deal with it. It's been your choice whether or not you wanted to confide in your girlfriend. *You* chose to push her away."

"She's not my girlfriend," I mumble.

"Yeah, 'cause she dumped your sorry ass."

My spine straightens. "No, I mean, she was never my girlfriend. The accident happened, and I never got around to asking her."

"*Hayes.*"

"What?"

He stares at me, unblinking. "Is that what your fight was about last night?"

"No." I blow out a breath, run a ragged hand through my hair, reassess the meaning of life. "I mean . . . not really. I guess, kind of?"

"Spell out the actual words you used, please."

I wave him off. "There's no fucking point, man. It doesn't matter."

"Oh, it matters." He gives a dubious chuckle. "It really fucking matters because clearly, you don't have your head screwed on right. I'm not gonna sit here and watch while you make one of the biggest mistakes of your life."

A muscle in my jaw ticks. "Fine, *fuck*, I'll tell you. Everything started off fine when she got to the party. She was happy to see me, we were talking, and then . . . Lucy showed up."

His face scrunches. "Who the hell is Lucy?"

"It's honestly beside the point."

"Clearly, it's not."

"She's just some girl I used to . . . *you know.*"

His brow furrows. "So, she and Emmy talked?"

"No, I brushed Lucy off. She was pissed. Then I mentioned to Emmy that we used to hook up and—"

"Well, there's your first mistake."

"Right, I know." I worry over my bottom lip. "Em wasn't very happy with me."

"And then?"

I press my fingertips together, forming a steeple at my temple. "And then I brought up the fact that I wasn't even her boyfriend, and it all went downhill from there."

"Hayes, you are the biggest fucking dipshit I've ever had the displeasure of being friends with."

I push away from the counter. "Well aware, thanks."

"You imploded your own relationship before you even had the chance to make things official."

I work through a hard swallow. "Yeah, I should've known I wasn't cut out for all this from the get-go."

Relationships are difficult. They can be messy, heartbreaking, and confusing, a fact my parents taught with their constant arguments and cold silences. They showed me how easy it is to let someone down, how quickly love can turn into disappointment.

It's wild how you can live under the same roof, share a life, and still manage to break each other down, piece by piece. I can't shake off the feeling that I might end up doing the same to someone I care about. Someone like Emmy, who deserves so much more.

"Oh, stop that."

"Stop what?" I snap.

"Stop acting like you're the victim here," he fires back, his voice laced with frustration. "You're not. You made a mess, sure, but you're also the only one who can clean it up. Emmy's good for you, and she really fucking cares about you. More than you realize, obviously."

The truth in his words stings, a reminder of what I've lost, what I pushed away with my own hands. "And if she doesn't want to hear it? What then?"

"You make her listen," he insists. "You show her that you're serious. Actions speak louder than words, Grecco. It's time you started using them."

I mull over his advice, the simplicity of it. Maybe he's right. Maybe there's still a chance to fix things, to show Emmy that I'm not the guy she walked away from last night. That I can still be better, for her. That relationships might be tough, but they're also worth fighting for.

Emmy's shown me what it means to truly care for someone, to consider their feelings alongside my own. It's a lesson I'm still learning, and if she's willing to stand by me, I owe it to both of us to try. To try and be the partner she deserves, the one who doesn't run at the first sign of conflict or bury his head in the sand when things get hard.

"How?"

He leans back, his expression softening. "Start with the truth. Tell her everything—how you feel, why you've been acting like a jerk. Apologize, genuinely. And then? Give her space to process. Be there for her, but don't push. It's her call, ultimately."

"I don't even know where to begin," I admit.

"Begin at the beginning," he says, standing up. "But you should go to her. Now. Before it's too late."

Standing from my stool, I give him a nod, a semblance of gratitude mixed with a heavy dose of resignation. "Thanks, man. It's . . . weird, you know, getting relationship advice from you. Since you don't even believe in them yourself."

He shrugs, a half-smile playing on his lips. "I don't think you quite get it. It's not that I don't *believe* in relationships. It's just that I don't want one for myself. I don't have any desire to pursue them."

The room falls into a thoughtful silence, his words hanging between us like a delicate thread. One I hadn't fully grasped until now. It's a rare moment where I see beyond his sarcastic veneer, to the truth of who he is.

"So, you're . . ."

"I don't know." He waves me off with a casual flick of his wrist. "Labels aren't my thing. But, yeah, the whole romance thing? Doesn't apply to me. I can see why it's important to others, why it's worth fighting for. Just like I can see how messed up you are without Emmy."

His straight talk opens up a whole new level of respect between us. It's like a nudge, reminding me that understanding someone isn't about walking in their shoes but about being willing to see things from their point of view.

"I get it," I say, and I truly do. "And you're right, James. Thanks for the kick in the ass and for the perspective. I've been a coward about this whole thing. It's time I showed Emmy—and myself—what I'm really made of."

"Don't mention it," he says, pushing away from the counter. "Just go fix things with your girl. And don't screw it up this time. Because as much as I enjoy our little chats, I'd rather not have to play therapist again. Especially not for a situation you could've avoided."

"Yeah, bud." A chuckle escapes me, bitter yet tinged with hope. "I'll do my fuckin' best. Just for you."

"Atta boy."

I'm standing outside of Emmy's apartment without a clear plan in mind. Maybe I'll end up on my knees, literally begging for forgiveness. Or maybe she'll take one look into my eyes and know exactly how I'm feeling, no words needed.

Yeah fucking right. A man can dream.

I'm still busy contemplating my existence, poised to knock when the door swings open in my face. It's Matty, of course, because only I could be so lucky.

He gives me nothing but a cursory glance. "Yeah, fuck no. You're not coming inside."

"I just want to talk to her, buddy."

"Right now, you're not my *buddy*. Em's my buddy, and you're the shit stain on my shoe."

"*Matt.*"

"I'm serious, Hayes. I know we're always joking around, but when I told you not to hurt her, I meant it. And now look what happened."

"I know I made a mistake." My brow knits into a frown. "But I think I can still fix it. At least, I want to try."

He gives me a long, hard look—assessing, scrutinizing, burning a red-hot laser beam straight through my forehead. And then he sighs. "Fine. But if you screw up again, I'm telling Coach that you . . . fucking smashed up another car or something. You'll never play again."

I clap him on the shoulder. "Thanks, man. You can trust me."

His gaze lingers a moment longer, skepticism etched deep within his expression. But he steps aside, allowing me passage. "She's in her room. And Hayes?"

I pause at the threshold, turning back to face him. "Yeah?"

"Don't make me regret this."

I nod, swallowing the lump in my throat. "You got it."

As I walk down the familiar hallway, the weight of the situation bears down on me even more. Slowly, I push open the door to find her sitting propped up on her bed, wrapped in the fleece blanket I made for her. Her eyes are fixed on some forgotten show playing on her laptop. And the sight of her, so vulnerable yet so distant, sends a pang of guilt through my heart.

"Emmy," I murmur.

She looks up, her expression guarded, a hint of surprise flickering in her eyes before it's quickly masked by indifference. "So, he let you in, huh?"

I take a cautious step closer, but not too close. "He did. Can we talk?"

She considers this for a moment, her gaze shifting away from mine, then back again. "Okay. Talk."

I gulp down air, gathering my thoughts. This is it, my chance to make things right—or at least to start the process. "First off, I'm sorry. Truly, deeply sorry. What I said, how I've been acting . . . it's inexcusable. I was a coward, and I hurt you, which is the last thing I ever wanted to do."

Her expression's unreadable. "Go on."

"I've been doing a lot of thinking—about us, about me. And I've realized that I've been pushing you away because . . . because I'm scared. Scared of everything going on in my life. Scared of how much I need you, how much I want this—us—to work. And even more so, of us failing. I've been so focused on my own issues that I lost sight of what really matters."

Her eyes soften slightly, but she remains silent, prompting me to continue.

"I don't expect forgiveness, not right away. But I'm asking, begging, for a chance to prove that I can be better. That we can be better, together. I know actions speak louder than words, so let me show you. Please."

"Hayes, I appreciate your apology, and I can see that you're trying right now. But words are easy." She shifts onto crossed legs, pushing her laptop to the side. "I know that we can't plan for every curveball life throws, but you told me you were willing to try. When everything was going fine, you were putting *your all* into this relationship. Yet, the second things got tough, you stopped. You pulled away. You broke your promise."

"I know, and I'm sorry. I freaked out when I heard you on the phone before Bash's accident. You—you were telling Shannon that I wasn't your boyfriend. And, I don't know, I guess I took it the wrong way. I got in my head about it because I thought—I assumed

—that I didn't even need to ask. The guys helped me figure my shit out, and I was planning on asking you to make things official, but then . . ."

"Then Bash jumped off a building and wound up in the hospital."

I wince. "Yeah."

"I'm so sorry that happened, Hayes. But . . . I just—"

"You don't feel like you can trust me."

"Bad things are bound to happen in life. Over and over again. Things that are out of our control, and I need to know that I'm with someone that can confide in me. Someone that I can confide in myself."

"You can confide in me, Em," I say. "I swear."

"I wanted to last night. I needed to see you so that we could talk about something serious, and you all but blew me off. You think I wanted to go to some party when we're both reeling?"

I move to sit on the edge of her mattress. "What happened, baby?"

She turns away, breaking eye contact. "Nothing."

"Em."

"You know what? I think I'd like some space."

My heart sinks. *Space.* That's the last thing I want, but I know I'm in no position to argue. I've hurt her, broken her trust, and now I have to give her what she needs—even if that's more time away from me.

"Okay," I say softly. "I understand. Take all the time you need. But I meant what I said—I'm going to do whatever it takes to make this right between us. I'm not giving up on you, on us." We sit in silence for a few moments before I move to stand. "I should get going. But thank you for hearing me out. And if you need anything —anything at all—I'm here. I promise I'm going to put in the work."

I make my way to her door, pausing to look back at her one

more time. She sits on the bed, staring down at her hands folded in her lap. Even now, after everything, she takes my breath away.

"Maybe," she whispers, "you should just focus on your own stuff for now."

"I can do both," I say, steeling myself. I'm resolved to make things right, not just with a grand gesture but with consistent effort, patience, and understanding. "And you should know that I'll wait for you, Em. However long it takes."

Chapter Twenty-Eight

IN A BURST OF RECKLESS OPTIMISM, I asked Matty about throwing a Sunday brunch at our apartment. I want to claw myself out of this rut of self-pity, to stop wallowing. So, I reached out to my former squad again—the girls who used to be my whole world.

Mimosas, pastries, and a side of life updates seemed like an easy bet. And, tucked away in my chest, there's this hope that maybe, with a little luck, I can bridge the gap that's grown between us.

The plan is to open up about my diagnosis, lay all my cards on the table. It's a big step, but it feels necessary. With everything lately, there's a part of me that's starving for the kind of support only old friends can give, even if we've all drifted into different orbits.

But as the clock ticks closer to the agreed-upon time, the only person who's confirmed so far is Shannon. That trusty, reliable fairy princess of a girl. The one who's stuck by me through thick and thin.

The silence from everyone else, however, is thundering, a chorus of nonresponses that has me second-guessing my decision. There's this deep-seated fear that it'll just be the two of us, wading in a sea of orange juice and champagne.

But I'm holding on to hope, clinging to the possibility that they'll surprise me. That we can somehow find our way back to each other, despite the time, distance, and all the unsaid things lying between us.

So, I set the table, lay out an array of bagels and toppings, and chill the champagne. The apartment smells like fresh coffee and flowers, a strange mix that has my stomach doing somersaults.

I've thrown open the windows, letting in the crisp morning air and the sounds of the city waking up. It's a beautiful day, the kind that feels full of possibilities, of hope. The kind that can distract me from the recent implosion of my relationship with Hayes.

As I adjust the tulips in the center of the table, my phone buzzes with a message from Shannon, letting me know she's almost here. I suck in a breath, steadying myself for whatever this day might bring. Whether it's just Shannon and me, talking and drinking, or if, by some miracle, the others decide to show up, I'm ready. Today, I'm facing the world head-on, with a bit of hope and a lot of carbs.

Shannon breezes inside a few minutes later, her energy a welcome burst of sunlight in the tense atmosphere. "If it's just us today, I'm fully prepared to drown in mimosas with you," she says, dropping her bag on the couch and heading straight for the kitchen.

Laughter squeaks out of me, the sound bubbling up from somewhere deep inside, easing the tightness in my chest. "You always know how to make me feel better."

She pops the cork on the champagne with practiced ease, pouring us each a generous amount. "That's what I'm here for. Now, tell me, how are you really doing?"

"I think I'm ok—" Before I can finish, the doorbell rings, cutting through the moment. My heart leaps into my throat, and I shoot up from my chair, nearly tripping over my own feet in my haste to get to the door.

I pull it open to find Cassidy and a few of the other girls—

Lena, Kyra, and Aubrey—standing there, hesitant but smiling. "Hope we're not too late," Cassidy says, raising one perfect brow.

"No, no, you're just in time," I say. "Come in!"

As they step inside, shedding coats and exchanging awkward hellos, Shannon appears at my side. "Looks like it's going to be a real party after all," she murmurs.

We all settle around the table, the initial awkwardness slowly giving way to a more comfortable chatter. Shannon, in an attempt to break the ice, launches into a recap of her date with the lip-biter, Alex, and I'm thankful for the distraction.

"So, Em," Cassidy says once the laughter dies down, "you mentioned you had some news?"

"Yeah, that's part of why I wanted to get us all together today." I flatten my palms against my thighs, scrubbing away the damp sweat. "Back when I quit the squad, it felt like the only option I had. I was . . . exhausted all the time. And honestly, it hasn't gotten much better. I'm not laid up in bed for days anymore, but I'm still not doing great. So, I went back to the doctor recently . . . and I was diagnosed with something called chronic fatigue syndrome."

The table goes quiet, all eyes on me. "It's been strange, figuring everything out. But I'm learning to manage, to adjust. And I just . . . I wanted you guys to know that I didn't just quit on you for no reason. I didn't leave because I don't care about you guys, about the team. And that, um, despite everything, you're still my friends, and I've missed you."

There's a beat of silence, and then Lena reaches across the table, squeezing my hand. "Thank you for telling us. We've missed you, too. And we're sorry for not reaching out sooner. We thought —well, we assumed a lot of things we shouldn't have."

The warmth from her gesture spreads through me, melting some of the ice that had formed around my heart over these past few months.

"We really had no idea, Em," Kyra says gently. "We should

have been there, should have asked more questions instead of just letting you drift away."

"You were always the one holding us together, grounding us," Cassidy adds, her words unusually sincere. She's always been more of the cutthroat type—cold and calculating on the outside—but there's a softness there that most people don't recognize. "We didn't realize how much until you weren't there anymore. I'm sorry about what you're going through. But we're here for you now, if you'll have us."

I blink back tears. "Yeah, I'd like that," I manage to say, my voice thick with emotion. "I really have missed you guys."

Shannon raises her glass. "To new beginnings, then. To understanding, to forgiveness, and most importantly, to friendship."

We all join her in a toast, the sound of clinking glass echoing around the room like a promise. And as I take a sip of my drink, a warmth spreads through me that has nothing to do with the alcohol. Despite everything that's happened, in this moment, surrounded by my friends, I feel lighter than I have in months.

As October edges closer to Halloween, Dayton's campus is alive with the crisp chill of autumn. It's another Thursday, unfolding with its familiar routines, and I'm feeling a little better already.

I'm weaving through the paths between buildings, lost in thought, when the unexpected sight of Hayes stops me in my tracks. He's not in the quad this time but cleaning up around the science buildings, a part of campus that's a little quieter, more tucked away.

I instinctively pivot, hoping to avoid an encounter, but it's too late. He's already seen me, and with that familiar, effortless jog, he closes the distance between us. His crooked smile, disarmingly handsome, hits me first.

"Hi, Em," he says. "How are you?"

"Just fine, thanks."

"That's good. I really miss you," he says, simple and straightforward, and my heart does an involuntary skip.

"Um, thank you." I look down, quickly searching for a way to change the subject, needing the safety of neutral ground. "How's Bash doing?"

"Thank you, er, for asking. For caring." His throat works over a heavy swallow. "Bash is good. Recovering well. He should be playing again by the end of next month."

"That's great news," I say, a genuine smile touching my lips. Bash's recovery is a relief, a happy little spark in a sea of complications.

"I had my seventh session with Dr. Vargas this week. We, uh, we talked about you."

"Is that so?" My voice is light, but my guard is up.

"Yeah, we talk about you a lot."

"Hayes." There's a warning in my tone, a gentle nudge to tread carefully.

"I wrote you something." He's suddenly earnest, fishing a scrap of paper from his pocket, unfolding it with a care that suggests its contents are precious. "You don't have to read it now, but just . . . sometime."

I pluck the paper from his hand, staring down at the scribbled words. "Is this a love letter?"

"Not exactly." His grin is sheepish, charming in its vulnerability. "It's, like, a poem of sorts."

My brows shoot up. "A poem? You wrote me a poem?"

He chuckles, the sound warm and a bit self-deprecating. "I tried. Vargas said poetry is romantic, thoughtful. She said it might help me work through some of what I'm feeling in a new way. I know it's really fucking dorky, but I thought maybe you'd read it anyway."

"Okay," I say, curiosity piqued despite myself. "I'll read it."

"Thanks." He looks relieved, almost hopeful. "Well, I better get back to work. Can I come by tomorrow, drop something off for you?"

I scrunch my nose, playing along. "Another poem?"

"No, something even better."

"Another blanket? A fruit basket?"

"Just you wait, Em. It's gonna blow your fucking mind."

I laugh, the sound surprising me with its lightness. "Okay, fine. But you can't stay."

"Why? 'Cause Matty would kick my ass if I did?"

"No, because *I* would."

Our laughter mingles for a brief moment, a soft, easy sound that feels like a bridge over troubled waters. It's a reminder of what was and, maybe, a hint of what could be again.

It's not that I want to be done with Hayes forever, but my mom was right before. I can't let a man walk all over me, and I have no evidence that he's ready for everything a real relationship entails. Not yet anyway.

As he heads back to his cleanup duty, I'm left standing there, clutching the folded piece of paper like it's a secret key. *A poem.* He actually wrote me a fucking poem.

My heart doesn't know whether to leap or to settle into a quiet rhythm of curiosity. The thought of him putting pen to paper, trying to weave his feelings into words, is unexpectedly touching.

It's a side of Hayes I've rarely seen, one that Dr. Vargas has somehow coaxed out of him. And despite my reservations, despite the careful distance I've tried to maintain, a flicker of warmth stirs inside of me.

Seeking solace before my next class, I wander to another forgotten corner of campus, a little courtyard hidden by the history building. It's a place where the world seems to quiet down, where I can hear my own thoughts without the constant buzz of student life.

Settling on a worn stone bench beneath the shade of an oak tree, I allow myself a moment of stillness. And then, I'm reading, my eyes tracing over Hayes' loopy handwriting.

Madison Emilia Fuller,

Roses are red,
Violets are kinda blue,
I'm not much for poems,
But I really miss you.

I know I've been a fool,
And sometimes a bit of a tool,
Although my jokes aren't the best,
My feelings for you are no jest.

Remember our attempts to craft paper stars,
I tried my best, but my skills were subpar.
And I know I have a lot to fix,
More than just my lack of folding tricks.

But if you give me a chance, you'll see,
I'm really trying, just for thee.
I hope this brings a smile, or even a laugh,
Because Emmy, you're my better half.

With Love,
Hayes Grecco

By the time I reach the end, I'm smiling, a genuine, unguarded smile. It's so endearingly Hayes—funny, a little childish, and utterly goofy. Yet, beneath the humor, there's an earnestness there, a vulnerability that he keeps hidden beneath layers of jokes and charm.

This poem, in all its quirky glory, is a testament to the guy I fell for—the one who can make me laugh even when I'm trying hard not to, the one who's not afraid to make a fool of himself if it means getting a smile out of me.

And even more so, it's the first step in the right direction. A simple, tangible thing that shows me he's putting his money where his mouth is.

Chapter Twenty-Nine

HAYES

It's almost time for me to head over to Emmy's. I told her I'd come by to drop off this ridiculous gift, but I'm still not finished with it yet. We've had craft supplies spread across our living room all week. Jars of paper stars, string, and everything we needed to make this twenty-foot garland happen.

I have paper cuts on every nook and cranny of my hands, and the Donovan brothers are less than happy with me. Of course, I forced them to help via a mixture of old-fashioned coercion and blackmail.

Now, we're about five minutes away from stringing on the last few stars. Liam squints at the garland for a long moment. It's stretched out like a constellation across our floor, and he's been fumbling with it for the last half hour. His section is embarrassing, to put it lightly, but at least he tried.

"I think this will help," he says, attaching a particularly crumpled star—one that looks more like a meteorite after a rough landing.

I snort a laugh. "Yeah, because when she sees that disaster, she'll definitely want me back."

He leans against the couch, eyeing his handiwork. "I, for one, think it looks great."

"Yeah," I say. "If you squint really hard, you can make anything look good."

He huffs. "Is that what you tell yourself when you look in the mirror?"

I grab the throw pillow behind my hand and toss it directly at his face. "I thought you said I was an 8.6."

"Yeah, well, your behavior lately brings you down a few notches."

"Good God," I mutter. "Why is everyone against me?"

"Uh, maybe because you should've treated Emmy better?" He leans over and smacks me hard on the back of the head. "She's good people. She likes cake."

I give him an odd look. "Who doesn't like cake?"

"Lots of people," he says matter-of-factly. "You'd be surprised."

"Whatever." I turn to his brother instead, gesturing to the garland with a flourish. "James, what do you think?"

"Someone alert the church elders," he says. "We've performed a miracle here."

I perk up, trying to ignore the ugly parts in favor of the rest. "You think?"

"It's a masterpiece," he says firmly. "Truly, the Sistine Chapel of paper garlands."

Liam nods, still defending his creation. "Exactly. When Emmy sees this, she'll be so overwhelmed by emotion, she'll have no choice but to crawl back into your waiting arms."

"I think the emotion might be confusion," I say, giving our work a skeptical look. "Or maybe fear."

"You're wrong." Liam gives me a sideways grin. "I think, when you present it to her, you should say something like, 'I've brought you the galaxy. Because my love for you is out of this world.'"

I cock my head, actually deliberating on it for a few good seconds. "Yeah, no, thanks. I'll stick to something normal this time around."

"God, you're boring."

I wave him off. "I'm sure she heard enough of my poetry the other day."

"No fucking way. You wrote a poem?" James asks, clapping his hands together with exaggerated enthusiasm. "You need to read it to us right this very second."

"Yeah, whip it out," Liam says.

They glance at each other, and then, "Read it, read it, read it!" comes a loud chorus of chants that echo around the room.

My face heats up, embarrassment bubbling up inside me. "No fuckin' way, you vultures. That's private."

"Aw, our little Hayes is flustered. Look at those rosy cheeks," Liam teases, a wide grin spreading across his face. "It's very cute."

"I am not," I protest, but the more I try to defend myself, the more amused they seem to get.

"Well, if you're not," James says, "then just go ahead and read it to us."

"No, I need to get going, anyway. Take this shit over to Emmy's." I gesture to the mess in front of us. "And you can both fuck right off. I don't have a spare copy hidden somewhere, so don't bother looking while I'm gone."

I scoop up the garland, which seems to sprawl endlessly across the floor. As I gather it into my arms, trying to avoid further damaging our shoddy handiwork, their taunts follow me to the door. "A poet and a shortstop, what a package!"

"You know, James, I never pegged him for the sensitive type."

"Yeah, he's always given me more of a *'baby girl, let me do you against the wall'* vibe."

I simply ignore them, choosing instead to slam the door behind me. They can be assholes sometimes, both of them. But at least they're helpful assholes. Caring assholes. The kind of assholes who helped me acknowledge my faults, pushed me to grow, and pressured me to make amends.

The kind of assholes I consider family.

· · ·

I'm at Emmy's door, heart hammering in my chest like it's trying to escape. I tap my foot on the floor, impatient. Stare up at the ceiling and count the tiny indents, all the little imperfections that come from years of wear and tear.

It's miserable out here. I feel like I'm waiting for a sentencing, preparing for the possibility of the death penalty. But when she finally opens the door to greet me, her hesitant smile is like the sunrise after a long, dark night.

"Oh, hi," she says softly, a gentle whisper in the air.

"Hey," I say, giving her a dorky little wave. "I come bearing gifts. Well, *gift*."

I pull out the garland, watching her face for any sign of reaction. For a long moment, she just stares at it, eyes wide, sparkling with . . . something. Amusement? Horror? I can't quite tell.

And then, she laughs. Not just a giggle but a long, hearty laugh that fills the space between us with warmth. "Oh my gosh, I love it. It's so . . . ugly."

My jaw practically hits the floor. "Ugly?"

"Like, perfectly ugly."

"Goddammit, I knew it. I swear to you, all the good parts are the pieces I worked on. James and Liam fucking suck at paper folding. They half-assed it," I defend, feeling oddly indignant, somehow protective of my creation.

"And you certainly full-assed it," she says, still laughing.

I grin at her. "You like it, though?"

"I love it, even if it's an ungodly color combination." She's looking at the garland now, as if seeing it in a new light. The colors are a chaotic mix of orange, blue, and bright green. I'll admit it wasn't the best of choices, but it's all we had to work with. "Honestly, I don't even know how you pulled this off. It must have taken *hours*."

"Twenty-eight hours," I murmur under my breath, almost embarrassed to admit it.

Her head whips up. "What?"

"I worked on it every night after classes. Stayed up last night until three in the morning because I was worried that it wouldn't be ready in time. Really put the guys to work, too. A lot of manpower went into this garland."

"Jesus, Hayes." There's a softness in her voice now, a tenderness that wasn't there before.

"It was worth it to see the look on your face," I say, and I mean it. Every second, every tiny paper cut, every moment of frustration—it's all worth it for this. For her.

She smiles, that beautiful, heart-stopping smile that's haunted my dreams all week.

"Do you . . . think I could come in for a minute?" I ask. "Help you hang it up?"

Her eyes narrow. "I thought we agreed you weren't coming in?"

"Eh, you agreed, and I followed," I say. "But we both know I'm more of a leader."

She laughs again, and for a moment, everything feels right in the world. "Okay, you can come in. But just for a few minutes. We can tack this up on my bedroom ceiling."

"Fine by me," I agree readily, stepping into her apartment with the garland in tow.

As I follow her down the hall, stars clutched carefully in my hands, I'm hoping this is another turning point for us. Maybe not a grand gesture that will fix everything, but a step. A small, imperfectly ugly step toward something better. And right now, that's all I can ask for.

In Emmy's room, the air feels different, heavier, charged with unspoken thoughts and lingering regrets. The last time I was here, almost two weeks ago, I left abruptly after we slept together. That night, I didn't think much of it, treating the moment as just another physical release, a way to escape the chaos of my thoughts. But standing here now, with her, the weight of that decision pushes against me.

I realize that my need for space, my habitual retreat after intimacy, probably left her feeling abandoned, maybe even used. It's a realization that stings, because with Emmy, it's never been just about the sex. It's always been so much more.

As we hang the garland, the soft glow of her bedside lamp lighting the room, a strand of hair falls gently across her face. It's a simple, mundane thing, but in the moment, it takes my breath away. She's so fucking gorgeous.

Before I can stop myself, the most chaotic sentence tumbles out of my mouth. "I hope you know that I really, really enjoy having sex with you."

She freezes, nearly dropping the string. "*Sorry?*"

"Shit, can we just . . . pretend I didn't say that?" I'm backpedaling now, wishing I could snatch the words right out of the air. "Reel this back to about thirty seconds ago?"

"Uh, no, we can't." There's a hint of amusement in her eyes now, but her cheeks are flushed with what I hope is more than just embarrassment.

I puff a breath, trying to salvage the situation. "What I meant to say was that when we're together, *like that*, it means something to me. It's more than just . . . sex. And I shouldn't have left so quickly after we were . . . together the last time. That was wrong."

"Oh." A bit of tension eases from her shoulders. "Well, thank you for saying that. If I'm being honest, it didn't feel too great."

"I'm sorry," I say. "I guess I'm just . . . used to dealing with things alone, especially stuff with Bash. And I've never really had sex with anyone that I . . . cared about the way I do you. I know it means more than just the physical, and so I need to treat it that way."

She gives me a tiny smile. "You can still want sex just for the sake of it, Hayes. You can need time and space to yourself, too. But you're right. I don't want to feel used when you're not willing to actually communicate in the end."

"And I completely get that," I say, feeling a shift between us, as if we're closing the gap I had unwittingly opened.

"I won't settle for being a simple distraction for you."

"You are so much fucking more than that." The words come out more forcefully than I intend, but they're true. "You—you own me, Fuller. All of me."

She quirks a brow, scarlet kissing her cheeks. "Really? Because handling even half of you is a bit much." I can't resist the opening, my smirk stretching wide with innuendo. She shoves me lightly on the chest, clarifying, "Not like that."

"Hey." I hold both hands up in mock defense. "You said it, not me."

"You're a . . . menace. You know that?"

Gently, I sweep the hair out of her eyes, cupping her cheek in my hand. "And yet here I am, asking you for one last chance."

"Hayes . . . I—I don't—"

Her words fade as she looks up at me, hazel eyes swimming with emotion. I know this is a lot for her, that I'm asking too much after the callous way I treated her. But I need her to understand how much she means to me.

My fingers trail down to tip her chin up, angling her face toward me. Her breath hitches, lips parting slightly. Our noses brush.

"Emmy," I whisper, reveling in the way her name feels on my tongue. "I know I don't deserve it. But I promise if you give me another chance, I won't waste it. I'll spend every day making sure you never regret taking this leap with me."

My thumb caresses her cheek, touch featherlight. Her eyes flutter closed, and she leans into me, her lips finding mine in a soft, tentative kiss. It's different than our other kisses, not fueled by simple desire or by reckless passion.

It's laced with hope and promise, a new beginning rising from the ashes of old mistakes. My hand slides into her hair as our lips move together—soft, unhurried. And God, she tastes like honey and feels like home. This sweet, comforting place that I never want to leave.

Chapter Thirty

"Oh God, what is that?" I grimace as Matty pulls out a tattered, neon pink fanny pack from an overflowing bin. This place is filled to the brim with what can only be described as the castoffs of several bygone eras.

"Dude, it's vintage," Matty says, slinging it over his shoulder. He's wearing a grin that's way too pleased for someone holding a literal piece of trash.

"Vintage is just a nice way of saying old, and probably used by someone's sweaty uncle," I say, sidestepping a rack crammed with Hawaiian shirts.

We're elbow-deep in the chaos of the fifth thrift shop of the morning, on a mission that's got us combing through every bin of crayons in a five-mile radius of campus. And not just any crayons—I'm talking about the elusive dandelion crayons, retired from production and now, apparently, a collector's item, according to the gospel of Emmy.

Matty agreed to help me out with this mission. Partially out of the goodness of his heart, and partially because I hinted that the Donovans might murder me in my sleep if I dragged them here. Another facet of Hayes Grecco's romantic gesture escapade.

After Emmy and I kissed last night, I left her apartment feeling better than I have in weeks. She didn't make me any promises, but I think it gave her a lot to think about nonetheless. And now, I need to keep the momentum going. To keep showing her that I mean business.

"So, remind me again why we're on this wild crayon chase?" Matty asks, tossing the fanny pack back into the bin with a look of regret.

"I'm still shocked she never told you about her obsession," I say, digging through a box labeled Art Supplies.

"Maybe she was just embarrassed, and rightly so."

I roll my eyes. "I think it's kinda cool, actually. And I thought it'd be even cooler to find her one."

He chuckles, shaking his head. "You are so extremely whipped it's uncanny."

"Am not." I unearth a crayon box that looks promising, only to find it's filled with every shade of green known to man. "It's just thoughtful."

"Thoughtful or whipped like cream, it's a fine line," he teases, moving on to the next shelf, cluttered with an assortment of items that defy categorization.

We spend the next hour sifting through decades of junk, our search turning up everything but the coveted dandelion crayon. At one point, Matty holds up a pair of roller skates, complete with fuzzy dice hanging from the laces.

"Find what you were looking for?" I ask.

"Just contemplating a new mode of transportation to practice," he says, setting them down with a clatter. "Imagine rolling into the locker room on these bad boys."

I give him the ghost of a smile, choking on a cough. "I'd pay to see Coach's face."

He turns to me, serious now. "You know you're gonna play this season, right? The terms of your plea bargain will be met before the end of next month. The dean has no reason to keep you from the team."

"Right, well, unless Sebastian . . . I don't know, decides to throw himself from an even taller building."

He nudges me. "Did you need me to go out there, knock some sense into him?"

"Nah, I think he got the hint last time," I say, forcing a laugh.

"Then all is well. You're gonna play, man."

"You sound like Emmy," I say. "Hopelessly optimistic."

"That is my girl, after all."

I shoot him a side-eye. "Watch out, Brooks. I'll fight you for her."

He chuckles, a sound that's too carefree for the cramped, dusty space we're standing in. "If I liked Emmy that way, you wouldn't stand a chance. But I . . . I've got somebody else, actually."

"Oh, yeah?"

He lifts his chin. "Yeah, my very own linebacker."

"No shit?"

"None given."

"Well, hey, congrats, buddy," I say. "I'm happy for you."

The urge to run through the entire football team's roster is strong, but I use all my willpower to resist. If he wanted me to know, I would.

It's not Matty's intention for me to feel like an outsider amongst my own friends, my teammates. In fact, it's likely the opposite. But life is moving forward for everyone around me. And sometimes I feel like I'm stuck on the outside, just waiting here in limbo.

As much as I'm focused on securing my future with Emmy, I can't ignore this intense longing I have to rejoin my team this spring. To stand with them again, not just as a player but side by side with Matty as a captain. As a leader who's learned his lessons —the hard way—and is prepared to fight for what he wants.

· · ·

By the time I drop Matty off, there's a sense of accomplishment swelling inside me. I'm in a better place now, more so than I've been since before Bash's accident. But I didn't ask to go upstairs because I was already toeing the line last night.

The last thing I want to do is to push Emmy too far. So, I head out of their neighborhood, pulling onto the main road, and make a call to Bash on speakerphone.

"Hey, Bashy," I say when he answers. "How's things?"

"All is well," he says, upbeat but notably cautious. "Uh, it's good you called, actually."

"Because you desperately missed the sound of my voice?"

"Well, that, too," he says. "But, uh, I've been meaning to talk to you about Mom and Dad. Apparently, they wanna come out here once I'm all healed up. See the training facility and stuff."

The excitement in his voice should make me happy, and on some level, it does. But all I can think about is how our parents have a knack for building up hopes just to let them down.

Like the fucking Sizzle Fest, or like Bash's graduation weekend —when a convention of hungry bikers rolled into town—something else is bound to come up. They'll bail, and I'll be there, trying to glue Bash back together.

Lost in thought and half listening to Bash's plans for their visit, I roll straight on past a stop sign. There's a brief, heart-stopping moment of realization, and then the sound of a siren snaps me back to reality.

Isn't that just my fucking luck?

"Sorry, Bash, I gotta go," I say, rushing to end the call. "Talk later."

The cop car slowly pulls up behind me, a singular light flashing before it dims. I veer to the side of the road, roll down my window, and kick myself for being so careless. The wait for the officer to approach is endless, every second amplifying my anxiety. Finally, he reaches my window, expression unreadable behind the glare of his sunglasses.

"Do you know why I pulled you over?" he asks, already scribbling on his notepad.

"That stop sign back there," I say, turning on my most charming smile. "Sorry about that."

"And speeding, you were going 34 in a 30," he states matter-of-factly. "License and registration, please."

I offer up my documents with another sincere apology. Going four miles over the speed limit doesn't seem like much of an offense, but I turn on the charm anyway.

Despite my efforts, the man is wholly unmoved; perhaps he has a quota to meet, or maybe he just doesn't like the way my face looks. Either way, I'm fucked.

"Sorry, pal, can't let you off with a warning this time," he says sternly, handing me a ticket.

I curse under my breath as he walks back to his car. And that's when the panic officially sets in, spreading through my veins like wildfire. My plea bargain terms are clear—no further offenses. Even something as minor as a traffic infraction could jeopardize everything.

For a fleeting moment, I consider just hiding it from my attorney, burying the ticket in a drawer and hoping for the best. It's a tempting thought, one born out of fear rather than logic. Deep down, I know it's likely a bad decision, a gamble I can't afford. But the thought of losing what I've worked so hard to maintain is crushing me.

Right now, there's only one place I want to be—one person I want to see.

Without fully thinking it through, driven more by a need for comfort and understanding than any concrete plan, I turn the car around and head back to Emmy's place. It's an instinctual move, one that speaks volumes about where my heart lies.

When I arrive, Matty answers the door, a brow suspiciously cocked. "Did I . . . forget something?" he asks, and when I shake my head, he finally notices the panic written on my face.

So, he turns and calls down the hall for Emmy. Without further hesitation, he grabs his jacket and steps past me out the front door. It's a not-so-subtle attempt to give us privacy, and it's one I appreciate more than he knows.

Emmy appears less than a minute later. "Hayes, um, hi? What's going on?"

I'm breathing hard, the weight of the day, of the past few months, too much to bear alone. "I know we left things open-ended last night," I say. "We kissed, and that was it. But I just . . . I needed someone reasonable to talk me down. You can tell me to go if you want."

"Of course I won't." Her response is immediate, her voice soft but firm. "This is exactly what I wanted from you all along. For you to come to me when things got hard. To open up so we can be there for each other."

I swallow past the lump in my throat. "Then can I come in?"

"Please," she says.

The journey to her room is a blur of motion, my footsteps heavy, solemn. The door closes behind us with a soft click, and now, it's just Emmy and me, surrounded by the familiarity of her space.

I sink onto the edge of her bed, tension rolling off of me in waves. She joins me there, the heat of her thigh pressing against mine, and there's a momentary comfort in the closeness, a sense of solace I find in her mere presence.

"Talk to me," she says, her voice a gentle invitation.

"It's . . . my parents. They told Bash they want to visit."

Her brows draw tight. "And that's . . . a bad thing?"

"It's just not gonna happen," I mutter, palms pressed flat

against my thighs. "They're gonna find a way to weasel their way out of it at the last minute. It's what they've always done."

"Then why bother getting his hopes up?"

"So they can feel like good parents, involved parents, at least for a brief moment in time. It's fake pleasantries, and somehow, Bash still doesn't see right through their bullshit."

"But you do?"

"Yeah, I have for a long time. There was this turning point for me, years ago, and I haven't been able to trust them since."

"What happened then?"

"Bash was only twelve at the time, a sixth grader who was a little on the shy side. He got beat up pretty bad by a group of bullies on the playground. The school's office called, and I guess Bash was full-on bawling over the phone."

She frowns. "Oh, that's so sad."

"Yeah, it was even more sad when my parents asked me if I could pick him up. I had just gotten my license, and they didn't want to leave work. Because it's not like they own the fuckin' company or anything." I give a bitter laugh. "When I got to his school, Bash was basically inconsolable, asking for our mom. She didn't come home until he was already passed out in bed that night."

Her shoulders slump as she leans closer to me. "They put so much on both of you at a young age."

"Yeah, they never gave a shit. When Bash told me they called earlier . . . I just *blanked*. I spaced out and fucked up," I say, the words tumbling out in a rush, my gaze fixed on the pattern of the quilt beneath us. "Got a ticket for running a stop sign and . . . and slightly speeding. It seems like a small thing, I know. But with my plea bargain . . ."

"Did you already talk to your attorney?"

"Not yet. I just—I don't know, I was thinking that maybe—"

"Don't try to hide it, Hayes," she says firmly, pressing a finger to her lips. "Nothing good can come from that. You should call him first thing in the morning tomorrow. It might not be as bad as you think."

Her practical advice slices through the fog of my panic, grounding me. "You think so?" I ask, desperate for that sliver of hope.

"I do."

"Okay, yeah, then that's what I'll do." I rub the back of my neck, give her a sheepish smile. "Thank you . . . for talking through it with me. For listening."

Her hand finds mine, fingers intertwining in silent support. The touch is charged, calming—like a direct line to something steady inside of her. It's in this moment of quiet connection that I'm reminded of how her presence, her belief in me, can make the chaos recede.

But it's not just about my own problems, either. Emmy's been a constant, a steadfast presence despite everything I've put her through these past weeks. I've been so wrapped up in my own head I've nearly missed seeing how much she's held up for me.

And here she is, still offering her support, her understanding, without a second thought. I know I need to focus on her, too, to give back some of the immense support she's given me. It's as if my heart knows before my head that it's time to flip the spotlight.

"You know, you mentioned . . . before the party, there was something you wanted to tell me," I say, my thumb rubbing a small circle on the back of her hand. "If you're ready, I want to hear it. All of it."

It's not just a gesture of reciprocation; it's a need, a yearning to understand her more, to be there for her as she has been for me. Her willingness to open up, to share her vulnerabilities with me, is a gift—one I'm now ready to fully appreciate.

She worries over her bottom lip. "Are you sure you have room to think about my problems right now?"

"Of course I do." I slide my hand up the side of her arm, fingertips trailing a searing path to her chin. "This is a two-way street."

"It's . . . about why I quit the squad," she says, scrunching her nose. "Um, I mentioned before that I couldn't keep up with the physical demands anymore. Well, it's a little more than just that. The day of the party, I finally got some real answers. A diagnosis from a doctor who actually listened to me."

My expression slides into a frown. "Is it . . . something serious?"

"Kind of," she murmurs. "It's called chronic fatigue syndrome. It affects my energy and mood, but there's not much known about exact causes. It's been . . . a lot, coming to terms with it. But I feel better, in some ways, because at least I know I wasn't just . . . exaggerating my symptoms, I guess."

"Of course you weren't. You're strong, Em. And you always seem so happy, so light," I say, tipping her chin up. "Ready and willing to look on the bright side of things."

"That's just my way of coping. You shut down, and I . . . bloom, I guess."

"I like that—watching you bloom. But you can share the bad stuff with me, too, you know?"

Her eyes light up. "Can I?"

"Yeah, Emmy, I want that. I *really* want that," I say. "For both of us."

Chapter Thirty-One
HAYES

A GARLAND of ugly paper stars hangs above us, the soft light from Emmy's bedside lamp illuminating the room. She's nestled against me, her head resting on my chest, drifting in and out of sleep. My fingers roam through her hair, tracing the soft ends and occasionally gliding over her cheekbones.

"Hayes?" she murmurs, eyes half-lidded as she looks up at me. There's a hint of playfulness in her tone, a softness that tugs at something deep within my chest.

"Yeah, baby?" I whisper back, my voice low.

"You're officially off probation."

I chuckle softly, the sound vibrating through us both. "Was I still only on probation? I thought maybe I'd been expelled by now."

"Nah, can't seem to get rid of you," she teases, her smile growing wider. I continue to stroke her hair, savoring the warmth of her body against mine.

"That's so true. I'm like . . ."

"A fungus," she cuts in.

I scoff. "Yeah, the best-looking fungus you've ever seen."

"You know, actually, that *is* a problem. There are a lot of fungi that look edible in nature, wild mushrooms and stuff, but they're actually toxic."

I squeeze her hip with my free hand. "So now I'm toxic?"

"Mm, no," she whispers, gaze roaming across my face. "I'm

saying I need to be careful, really take my time checking you over first."

"Before you eat me, you mean?"

Her breath is warm against my lips, eyes locked onto mine, our noses nearly touching. "Exactly."

"What about me, then? Do I need to take my time before I . . . eat you?" My fingertips press against the soft spot just above her hip bone, teasing. "Or are you wanting me now?"

"I . . ."

The rest of her words are lost in a breathy sigh as I lean in, closing the remaining space between our mouths. Her lips are soft and sweet, and no matter what I do, I can't seem to get enough of her.

My hand moves higher up her shirt, sliding along the bare expanse of her stomach, leaving goose bumps in its wake. "I want you, Hayes," she whispers between kisses. And I can taste the truth in her words, hear it in the tremble of her voice.

"I want you, too. So badly, baby." I cup her face, holding her gaze. "But . . . you know this isn't about sex for me, right? I just need you to know that—"

"Hayes, stop. *You* should know that I really, really enjoy having sex with you." She laughs, throwing my own words back at me. "And . . . I trust you."

Trust. A five-letter word that makes my chest expand, makes me want to prove myself even more. "I trust you, too, Em. And I want to . . . take care of you."

I flip us over, laying her flat on her back, slowly making my way down her body. Her skin is soft and warm like a summer's day. She lifts her hips, and I slide her little sleep shorts down her legs. Then, I nudge the damp heat of her panties with my nose.

"Want to taste this sweet pussy," I murmur. "Do you . . . do you have any toys you like, Em?"

Her breath hitches. "Toys?"

"Uh-huh. How do you get yourself off when I'm not around?"

"Well, I . . . I don't . . . that often."

I look up at her from between her thighs, arching a brow. "Yeah, okay."

"I don't!" she protests, her cheeks flushing a deep shade of pink. "I mean . . . not as much as I probably should."

I grin, my cock impossibly hard as I picture her touching herself, using a toy, moaning my name silently into her pillow. I nip the soft skin of her inner thigh. "You've never taken a toy out . . . maybe fantasized about me fucking this pussy with my fingers? Or . . . maybe you sank down onto it, thought about riding me?"

"I . . . um, maybe once. Or twice."

"Good girl. And?"

"Er, and there's a . . . a little pink one that vibrates, um, fast. I keep it in the top drawer of my dresser."

I smile to myself as I slide her panties aside. "Tell me you want me to use it on you."

"Hayes . . ."

"Tell me, Em."

"Will you?" she asks, voice breathless as I tease her clit with my tongue, slowly circling but never quite touching the slick center of her desire.

"Yeah, baby, I will. When you beg for it."

"Please, Hayes," she whimpers, her hashed breaths fanning across my cheek. "I . . . I want you to. Please . . . use it on me."

"That's more like it," I say, sitting up on my heels. "Stay right there. Don't move."

I stand and head to her dresser, only to return moments later, her little pink vibrator in my grasp, a devilish grin on my face. Her eyes widen at the sight, a deeper shade of red painting her cheeks.

"You're blushing," I tease, crawling back onto the bed.

"Hardly."

"Extremely," I counter, running the smooth tip of the vibrator against her damp folds before flicking it on to its lowest setting. "And I can think of lots of ways to make you blush even more."

She moans, her head falling back against the pillow as I tease her clit with the toy, upping the vibration. I lift her shirt to suck on a swollen nipple at the same time, alternating between pulling at it and licking it softly.

"Hayes, Hayes . . ." Her breath hitches as I slip a finger inside her, curling it upward.

"Mmm?" I ask, pulling my mouth away from her breast.

"Please . . ."

"Please what?"

"More," she whimpers. "More. Faster."

I comply, tracing the vibrator over her clit in figure eights while thrusting a finger inside her. She's so tight, gripping me like a vise, and it takes everything in me not to plunge my cock into her right then and there.

"That feel good, baby?" I ask in her ear as she moans uncontrollably into my shoulder. "You like it when I make you beg?"

"Yes . . . yes," she pants out, arching her hips toward me as her orgasm crests. And then she shatters apart in my arms. Her nails dig into my biceps as wave after wave of pleasure washes over her.

"That's it, Em," I say, slowing down the vibrator as I continue to massage her gently. "So. Fucking. Sexy."

She collapses back onto the bed, spent, her chest heaving. As I plant a series of kisses along her jawline, my cock is still throbbing for her, pulsing against her warm thigh. I pull my own T-shirt over my head, using it to wipe her up before tossing it onto the floor.

"Hayes?" Her voice is thick with satisfaction as she rolls onto her side, eyes half-lidded.

"What is it?" I ask, stroking her damp hair from her forehead.

"Just thinking that . . ." Her cheeks redden again. "I should return the favor."

I grin, shaking my head and tucking her in close to me. "Em, it's okay. Getting you off gets *me* off."

"So, you don't want me to suck your dick, then?"

"I, uh, I didn't say that," I sputter.

She laughs. "Good, because I'd really like to."

I clear my throat, trying to sound casual, but my dick is about to jump out of my fucking pants. "Well, um, if you insist. I don't want to put you out, though."

"Oh, I insist."

She makes quick work of unbuttoning my pants, and then we push down my boxers together. Her hand slowly wraps around my cock, and I groan, low and deep.

"Fuck, Emmy." She looks up at me through hooded eyes, her hair a mess, her lips swollen from my kisses, and I think I might explode right then and there.

"You okay?" she asks.

"Never been better," I manage, guiding her down between my legs.

Slowly, she takes me into her mouth, lapping at the head of my cock as if it were her favorite flavor of ice cream. She sucks, her tongue swirling around the sensitive underside of my shaft before she takes me even deeper. And then, I bottom out at the back of her throat.

"Jesus, fuck," I moan, gripping the sheets to steel myself. I don't want to come just yet; I want to savor this.

I grunt, hips shifting, trying not to thrust too hard for fear of spooking her. Her pace is slow and deliberate, teasing every inch of me before she works her way back to the very tip.

"Emmy," I grit out as she massages my balls with her free hand. "Shit, baby . . ." She moans around my cock, the vibrations sending me over the edge. I can't take it anymore. "I'm—" I croak, trying to warn her, but it's no use.

My orgasm rockets through me like a freight train, and I come hard in her mouth, my hips bucking as she swallows every drop. I collapse onto the mattress, utterly wasted, as she wipes her mouth daintily with the edge of her shirt.

"Well, that was fun." She grins up at me before nestling into my chest. My dick twitches against my abdomen, and I laugh despite myself.

"Very fun," I say.

The quiet of the room wraps around us, broken only by the gentle rustle of fabric as we adjust ourselves on the bed, drawing closer to one another. And that's when I remember the gift I brought for her, still in the pocket of my jeans discarded on the floor. Without a word, I lean over the edge of the bed to fish out the little package.

"I had plans to wrap this up nicely," I say, turning back to face her. "But then, you know, got a bit sidetracked when that cop pulled me over."

I hand her the gift, grinning as she eagerly unwraps it. The lone dandelion crayon emerges from its protective bubble wrap, and her reaction is immediate—a gasp of delight, eyes sparkling with unfettered joy.

"Oh, my God," she says. "You actually found one."

"Yeah, and I figured it deserved a home with you. Matty and I went on the hunt this morning."

"So that's what you two goofballs were up to." She throws her arms around me. "I love it, Hayes. Thank you so much."

With a slight hesitation, she moves to dig around in her night-stand for a small journal. She hands it to me, her cheeks tinged a bashful pink.

"I actually have a present for you, too," she says, her voice soft, almost timid. "I started on this after you told me about your love language. Words of affirmation, *supposedly*. And I know you're finishing up with Dr. Vargas soon. I thought . . . maybe this could help you keep expressing yourself."

The journal is simple, yet the thought and care she's put into it show in every detail. I flip through the pages, each topped with a handwritten note of encouragement or prompt.

"Every pitch is a home run in the making."

"Writing it down is like setting it free!"

"Life throws curveballs, but every swing brings you closer to a grand slam."

"Keep flexing those mental muscles!"

"Life's a marathon, not a sprint."

Each page, each line, reads like Emmy's speaking directly to me, her optimism and belief in me captured in ink. At the back, there's even pages of blank diamonds where I can "write down my wins for the day." It's the most thoughtful, most wholesome, thing that anyone has ever done for me.

"It's a bit cheesy, I know," she adds, watching me closely, searching my face for a reaction. "Hopelessly optimistic, as you'd say."

I close the journal, looking up at her with a smile that feels like it might split my fucking face in two. "Cheesy? Maybe. But it's fucking golden, Em. And your optimism? It's one of the many things about you that I . . . that I love."

"Yeah?" Her lips part in a beaming smile. "That's good, then, because there are a lot of things that I love about you."

"Yeah?" I parrot. "Like what?"

She laughs, the sound filling the room. "I'll make you a list. But for now, let's just say . . . your determination is a big one. Definitely a top contender."

I pull her into a tighter embrace, the journal nestled between us, her dandelion crayon perched carefully on the nightstand. "You know I'm gonna hold you to that list," I say, "I'm dying to hear the rest."

"Oh, of course you are," she says. "I'd expect nothing less."

Chapter Thirty-Two

EMMY

I'VE MADE a little shrine for my dandelion crayon on top of my dresser. It sits there, surrounded by some of my favorite books and a small succulent, a tiny spark of joy smack-dab in the center.

I've collected a few others over the years, but I've kept them all at home, tucked safely away at my mom's place. This one, though? It's a daily reminder of the lengths Hayes would go to just to make me smile.

All week, he's been sending me selfies of him writing in the journal I made, adding his "wins" to the baseball diamonds in the back. "Made Emmy laugh today," "Finished a project for class," "Got to see Emmy's tits."

It's goofy, sure, but it's also the most endearing thing. Every little message from him lifts my spirits, the brightest spots in my longest days. The ones that are filled to the brim with classes, with studying, with trying not to fall asleep before seven o'clock at night.

As the week finally draws to a close, I'm eager for us to spend more time together. To forget about the recent strain on our newfound relationship and just enjoy the night. We have a Halloween party lined up, and due to Hayes' latest mishap, I'm on driving duty.

I'm still pulling my costume together—a Little Bo Peep outfit complete with stockings and a pair of Mary Janes—when another message comes through.

HAYES

send pics

EMMY

I'm gonna see you in, like, 10 minutes!

HAYES

don't care

I roll my eyes, moving to the mirror to snap a quick picture for him. The costume is short, a frilly dress that accentuates my greatest assets. My boobs, according to Hayes. Or maybe it's my smile, my eyes, or my hair, depending on which day you ask him.

After about ten half-hearted attempts, I finally find the perfect angle and hit Send.

HAYES

damn. you are the prettiest girl I've ever seen

you ready to herd us, bo peep?

EMMY

only if you promise to be good. no wandering off.

With a final check in the mirror, I grab my bag and head out to the living room. Matty, already in his sheep costume, emerges wearing a ridiculous headpiece. It's huge, spattered with cotton fluff, and it makes him look more like a cloud than an actual sheep.

"You look . . . very fluffy," I say.

He gives me a quick once-over, grinning from ear to ear. "And you, my dear, look baa-eautiful."

I wince. "Really, Matty?"

"What? Not a fan of sheep puns?"

I snort a laugh. "I just think you can do better."

"Oh, I can, and I will. I've got a killer one stored up here"—he taps his temple with a sly quirk of his lips—"but I'm saving it for your boyfriend."

"Still not technically my boyfriend."

He rears back. "Are you serious, Em?"

"What? He didn't ask!"

He levels me with an incredulous stare. "Emmy, you had this man digging through decades of garbage for you on a Saturday morning. Making you *crafts*. Writing you goddamn *poetry*. If he's not your boyfriend by now, then you've both got some serious issues."

"I need to be asked, Matty," I say dismissively. "It's a simple thing, but I think it's important. For all my luck with dating over the years, I've . . . never actually been asked before."

He pops a piece of candy into his mouth, chewing thoughtfully. "Well, maybe he'll ask you tonight . . . while dressed like a sheep. Isn't that romantic?"

"What every little girl's dreams are made of."

He chuckles and tosses an arm over my shoulder. "Let's get going, Bo Peep. The boys are waiting."

"Oh, don't want to disappoint '*the boys*.'"

"Well, *your boy* in particular is the one with the ants in his pants. He won't quit messaging me."

I take the phone from his waiting hand, quickly reading over their text exchange.

HAYES

what the fuck is taking so long???

MATTY

hold your horses. it's not easy to look this good

HAYES

I guarantee you I look better

MATTY

bet's on

A wide smile quirks my lips. I hand the phone back, and then we head out to my car. The short drive to Hayes' house is filled with the sounds of Matty chomping on Halloween candy.

He's usually an overtly healthy eater—with his meal preps, his zoodles, and his penchant for green salads—but he's been waiting for this night all month. Halloween has always been his favorite holiday, and he's never once skimped on the treats.

When we pull up to the house, the boys are already waiting outside on the curb for us. Hayes looks unfairly handsome, even in his makeshift sheep costume—a white T-shirt with cotton balls glued on, complete with a double-horned headband.

Next to him, the Donovans are dressed much the same, except Liam's opted to wear black. I'm not sure if it's a commentary on being the family outcast or if he just wanted to be different from the rest of the group. Either way, he stands out like he always does.

When I step out of the car to greet them, Hayes' entire face lights up. His eyes sweep over me from head to toe, that charming, crooked smile spreading across his face. "There's my girl," he says appreciatively. "We've been waiting ages for you."

I tilt my head. "I told you we'd be here at nine o'clock."

"Yeah, exactly." He checks his watch with an exaggerated flare. "And it's 9:03."

"Well, pardon me."

"You're pardoned." He slides a hand around my waist, tugging me into a little spin. "But only because you look so fucking cute in your costume."

"Yeah, Emmy," Liam says as he approaches, taking a good long look at me. "Very sexy. The baby blue really makes your eyes pop."

Hayes' jaw hinges wide open, and he shoves Liam away from me with a flat palm. "Her *eyes?*" he all but shouts. "Jesus Christ. Get your own girl, Donovan."

"I would if I could," he says with a shrug. "Oh, and Em, can we stop by A&W on the way to the party?"

"No," Hayes cuts in before I can answer.

I roll my eyes. "Sure, Liam. What did you want to get?"

Liam smiles, unfazed by his friend's possessiveness. "Just a root beer float."

"No problem," I say. "We can make a quick pit stop."

Hayes frowns, clearly displeased with this plan. But before he can protest further, James jumps in. "Alright, alright, enough chitchat. Let's get this show on the road." He claps his hands together. "I could really use some hunch punch right now."

Matty makes a face. "Gross."

"You just shoved a Reese's and a sour strip into your mouth at the same time," James says pointedly. "Don't talk to me about gross."

Matty chuckles. "Fair point."

We pile into my car—Hayes in shotgun, of course—and the rest of the guys in the back. As I turn onto the main road, Hayes flips around in his seat, directing his attention to the youngest boy stuffed in the middle.

"Why do you need a root beer float at nine o'clock at night, by the way?"

"Is there any other time for it?" Liam asks.

I take a quick glance in the rearview mirror, laughing at the sight of all three of them. A group of collegiate athletes are crammed together in my back seat, practically sitting on each other's laps, and they don't seem bothered by it in the slightest.

"Is this part of your birthday thing?" I ask Liam. "Or just a random craving?"

"Birthday thing, of course," he says.

"Oh," Matty's deep voice cuts in. "Happy birthday, man."

"Thank you."

"It's not your birthday, dipshit," James says, and there's an audible smack to the back of his little brother's head.

Matty snorts. "Do I even want to know?"

"No," James and Hayes say in unison.

"Speaking of dipshits," Matty says, placing a firm hand on the seat in front of him. "I have a joke for the runt of the flock."

Hayes scoffs beside me, loud and overly dramatic. "You better not be referring to me, Brooks."

"Oh, but I am, you little convict," Matty says. "I'm sure you of all people can tell me why the sheep got arrested."

"What if I *told you* that I don't give a shit?" Hayes mutters, jerking away from Matty's playful touch.

He tsks. "Well, I'd say that's too damn baaa-d."

"It's because he tried to pull the wool over the officer's eyes," Liam chimes in, stealing the punchline for himself.

I laugh, but the rest of the car remains oddly silent. That is, until Matty breaks it with a drawn-out sigh. "You ruined my joke, bud."

"No," Liam says, "I just finished what you started."

Hayes wraps a hand around my thigh, thumb tracing over the edge of my stockings. "Did Emmy tell you I got pulled over last weekend?" He looks right at me, but the question is clearly directed at the menace behind him—the only person in this car who doesn't know the full truth of his arrest. "Right after I dropped you off?"

"Ah, so that's what was wrong with your face."

"Exactly." Hayes chuckles, tapping his fingers against me. "But Em made me call my attorney the next morning. We figured our shit out. Apparently, I can ask the judge for a PJC since it's my first traffic violation. It shouldn't affect the plea bargain at all."

"So, you freaked out for no reason, then?" Matty asks.

Hayes' grip tightens around my thigh. "Shut up."

Liam snorts. "Classic Grecco move."

"*Anyway*, all is well," Hayes continues. "So you can stop with the jail jokes now."

Matty reaches over the seat to flick the horns on Hayes' head. "Not a chance, my little sheep."

"You know, all of the men in this car are currently dressed as sheep," Hayes mutters. "That's not the insult you think it is."

Matty snickers. "It's not an *insult*. It's a term of endearment."

The boys continue to bicker for the next twenty minutes, hitting a peak when we pull up to the drive-through at A&W. Hayes insists that Liam buy fries for the car, and Liam—the non-birthday boy—adamantly refuses. Instead, he offers to share a singular sip of his drink with each of us.

We all decline except for Matty, who's really taking this Halloween treat thing to the next level. According to him, it would be a cardinal sin to deny an offering of something sweet. And he's not interested in testing the spirits tonight.

By the time we make it to the party, there's a flicker of excitement dancing through me, tinged with a trace of nervous energy. It's not just the baseball team here tonight; it's practically half of campus—athletes and coeds from all pockets of life.

I find a place to park the car around back, and the five of us clamber out. Hayes, ever attuned to my shifting moods, draws me closer. His voice is a soothing rumble against my ear as he says, "Don't sweat it, Em. I'm right here with you."

"Thanks," I whisper, leaning into his side.

We all enter the house together, but it doesn't take long for the rest of my flock to scatter. Hayes and I, still glued, head to the kitchen in search of a drink. He grabs some fruity spiked lemonade. Since I'm DD, I opt for a bottle of water.

As the night deepens, Hayes' spirits rise, buoyed by the sweet drink in his cup. He's a little past tipsy by now, the liquid courage making him even flirtier than usual, if that's possible. Every so often, he dips down to whisper something new in my ear.

"As much as I like the way you look in this outfit," he says this time, palming my ass as we wait in line for the bathroom, "I can't wait to take it off you later."

"Yeah." I giggle, swatting his hand. "If you can even make it that far."

Time blurs—eyeball beer pong, trick or drink, and apple bobbing blending into one big party haze. Until suddenly, I notice Hayes has disappeared. A flicker of worry sparks as I search, only to find him lounging on a couch downstairs, absorbed in his phone.

At first, I'm worried that something else has happened to his brother—another near-fatal mishap—but then I spot the amused crinkle in his brow. I know that expression, and it usually means he's up to no good.

Intrigued, I settle in beside him, bumping his shoulder with mine. "So, what are you up to?"

Without missing a beat, he shoots me a boyish grin, his fingers a blur across the screen. "Just sending us to the moon," he declares, as if it's the most natural thing in the world.

I arch a brow, a laugh catching in my throat. "Come again?"

"Sending our names to the moon, Em, keep up." He finally glances at me, his eyes twinkling with mischief as he flashes his screen. "The VIPER rover is headed up there later this year. There's a trip from the Kennedy Space Center, and I'm putting our names on a boarding pass. It's pretty simple."

"Wow, that is . . ." I search for the right word, toggling between disbelief and amusement. "Goofy but really cool. I'm gonna be in *space*."

"*We're* gonna be in space, baby." His smile widens, and he tucks his phone away, turning his full attention to me.

"Speaking of, your jar of stars is barely hanging on," I say. "It's really starting to pale in comparison to mine."

"Okay, add the hundreds of stars from your garland and we'll see who comes out on top."

"James and Liam helped with those." I shake my head. "Doesn't count."

"Didn't know there were so many rules to this."

I gesture to my outfit, then tweak him on the nose. "Well, I'm in charge. I can make as many rules as I'd like."

"Is that right?" He nuzzles closer, nose pressed just below my ear. "Because you're my little . . . *shepherdess.*"

I laugh, and when he pulls me in for another kiss, it's all I can do not to jump his bones right then and there. It's these small, simple moments between us that give me hope. A glimpse into the future where my partner isn't just my nightly homecoming but also my best friend.

"Em," he murmurs. "You want to be my girlfriend, don't you? I mean . . . Fuck, I know this isn't how I'm supposed to do things. But I feel like I've been sitting on this question for ages, and I'm impatient now. A little bit tipsy, but that's beside the point."

I press my palms to both cheeks, warm from the heat. "It's not about doing everything right. I love these easy, carefree moments with you, and I don't ever expect you to follow some imaginary guidebook. There are no secret steps to being the perfect boyfriend."

"So, does that mean you will?" A deep frown creases his brow. "Be my girlfriend, I mean? Let me be your boyfriend?"

"Yeah, Hayes," I say, soft laughter spilling out of me. "I will."

Chapter Thirty-Three

THE FIRST WEEKEND of November rolls around, and our football team is squaring off against the Blue Devils. Hayes and I decided to join Jade for the game; she's here cheering on West, the star running back in his last season before the draft. And I figured it would be nice to support my former squad.

We file into the stands, and Hayes slides his arm around my shoulders, pulling me close. "You doin' okay?" he asks.

I smile up at him. "Yeah. I'm actually excited to be here, to cheer everyone on. It feels good to be back supporting the squad, even if I'm not out there on the sidelines."

He gives me a little squeeze. "That's my girl. I know the team meant a lot to you over the past three years. But I'm happy you're taking care of yourself now."

My cheeks flush at his sweet words. But before I can properly respond, the crowd erupts into ear-splitting cheers. Players burst through the giant inflated helmet at the end of the field, officially kicking off the start of the game. The three of us join in, eagerly shouting for our team.

The game starts off well for our Eagles. West plows through the defense time and time again, the team scoring two touchdowns in the first quarter alone. By halftime, we're up 21-7.

As the marching band takes the field for their show, Hayes stands and stretches. "I'm going to grab some drinks. Want anything?"

"Just a bottle of water would be great," I tell him.

"You got it, babe. Jade?"

She gives him a polite smile. "No, thanks. I'm all good."

He makes his way up the steps until he disappears into the sea of people. Turning my attention back to the field, I take in the familiar sights and sounds that used to be such a monumental part of my life. The squad performing their halftime routine, the band marching in perfect formation, the crowd hyped up from a competitive first half.

A pang of nostalgia sweeps over me. I really did love being a part of the team, pushing myself to be the best athlete that I could possibly be. But my health has to come first, and in the end, I don't regret my decision in the slightest.

Beyond my diagnosis, there were things about the team that I struggled with. The culture could be toxic at times—the intense competition between us, the pressure to be on mat for nationals, the occasional weigh-ins, and the fact that our self-esteem hinged on maintaining a certain look.

As much as I loved cheering, the negatives had started to outweigh the positives. My pain and fatigue may have been the ultimate deciding factor, but it certainly wasn't the only one.

"Hey, you little daydreamer." Jade nudges me with her elbow, knocking me out of my thoughts. "It looks like things are getting pretty serious between you and Hayes."

"Yeah, they are." My heart swells. "We finally made things official last weekend."

"That's so great, Em," she says. "I can tell he really cares about you. And you seem so happy lately."

"I am," I say with a sincere smile. "We worked through some issues, and things have been going well. I know he has a bit of a reputation, but he's been very sweet and supportive with me."

She grins. "Good. He better keep treating you right."

"How about you two?" I nod toward the field. "I'm assuming West is still on my good side."

She rolls her eyes, chuckling. "Oh yeah, Theo is . . . absolutely smitten. He's always finding little ways to surprise me and show me how much he cares. I swear he's trying to win an award or something."

I snort. "Yeah, mine's the same. Maybe we should get them some gold stars. Start an actual reward system, little stickers for a job well done."

She presses her fingers to her lips, hiding a chuckle. "You know, I think you're onto something there."

Hayes returns a few minutes later, large ICEE in hand, and passes off a bottle of water. "Thank you," I say, twisting the cap and taking a long sip.

The third quarter starts with significantly less fanfare than the first half. The energy has shifted; our opponents have found their footing. We're neck and neck through most of the quarter, neither team able to pull ahead.

It's not until much later on that the action picks up. The Blue Devils march down the field methodically. Their quarterback fakes a handoff and launches a bomb into the end zone. A receiver leaps up and snags the ball over the outstretched hands of another cornerback.

The crowd collectively groans as the Blue Devils close the gap to 21-14. Our lead has been cut in half with only one quarter remaining.

"Come on, defense!" Hayes shouts, cupping his hands around his mouth.

I clap loudly along with the cheers from our student section. We need a big stop here to swing the momentum back in our favor. We hunker down and force a three-and-out on the next series. Now it's up to our offense to chew up some clock and extend the lead once again.

West takes a handoff and finds a seam, bursting through for a thirty-yard gain. The crowd jumps to their feet as he races down the sideline, finally pushed out of bounds at the fifteen-yard line.

"Go, Theo!" Jade screams, pride shining through her voice.

Two plays later, Noah Elliot, my once failed date, plunges into the end zone on a quarterback sneak. We're now up 28-14 as the clock winds down in the final quarter. And, luckily, the defense holds strong, sealing the win for our Eagles.

Hayes sweeps me up into a spinning hug once the clock hits zero. "Hell yeah!" he exclaims. "That's how it's done, boys."

Beside us, Jade is on her feet, shouting her own praises. I grin, my heart swelling with pride for our school. I may not be on the squad anymore, but I'm still an Eagle. And school spirit is easy enough to muster when you're surrounded by such an energetic crowd.

As the crowd continues to cheer, Jade yells over to us, "I'm going down there," her dark eyes sparkling under the stadium lights. Without waiting for a response, she darts off, merging with the wave of students rushing the field. They're all there to celebrate together, but Jade's got her own star in mind.

Hayes and I watch her go, sharing a look of amusement before he sets me back on my feet. With the crowd's focus shifted, we make a quiet exit, slipping out the back of the stadium.

"Well," I say, "that was an exciting game."

"Yeah," Hayes murmurs, wistful. "Makes me miss playing baseball, you know?"

"Have you heard anything else?"

A shadow passes over his features. "Nope, nothing new. I have two more sessions with Vargas, and my last few hours of community service will be finished before Thanksgiving break. Then, I guess, I have to keep playing this waiting game."

My heart aches for him, caught in limbo, tethered to hope and the uncertainty that goes along with it. "The waiting must be so hard," I say gently. "But you've done everything you can at this point. Do you . . . are you planning to spend the break with Bash?"

"Yeah, I'll probably go up there. We'll do something together at his place, just us."

"Your parents don't host?"

"No, they work Thanksgiving. Big day for the business and all. Not many local places are open."

I give him a sympathetic smile. "Should have suspected."

"Yeah, it's whatever."

"Would you and Bash want to come to my mom's place instead?"

"Really? You want us to crash your Thanksgiving?"

I give him an earnest nod. "Of course! We always make way too much food anyway. It'll be nice to have more people to share it with."

He rubs the back of his neck, looking unsure. "I don't want to impose . . ."

"You wouldn't be imposing at all," I insist. "Please come. It's usually just the two of us. I know she'd love the company." He's visibly wavering, so I press on. "We watch the parade together in the morning while the turkey cooks. And we tell bad jokes over dinner until our stomachs hurt from laughing. You should experience a real Thanksgiving meal."

Finally, he relents. "Alright, if you're sure we won't be in the way, we'll come. It does sound a lot better than takeout and video games at Bash's place."

"Yes!" I give his bicep a firm squeeze. "We'll cook, and you two can just come hungry."

He chuckles, the sound warm and rich. "We can do that. I'll let Bash know. Seriously, thanks for the invite, Em. This means a lot."

We walk in comfortable silence for a few moments, the cheers from the stadium fading behind. Most of the students are still out celebrating our win, but the parking lot is slowly emptying, and I can spot Hayes' car a few rows away from us.

"Your mom seems really cool, by the way," he says, eyes warm in the dim light. "I can see where you get your big heart from."

I bump my shoulder against his. "She's going to love you guys. You know, I've actually . . . never brought home a boy I've dated before."

He smiles, cheeks dimpled. "Really? I would've thought you'd have had to beat them off with a stick in high school."

"Nope, I was pretty focused on cheer, on classes. Never really made time for dating. I told you my Dayton track record hasn't been too great, either. There have been lots of dates, but nothing long-term."

"Well, I'm honored to be the first, then," he says, giving me a playful nudge. "I'll have to be on my very best behavior. Don't want to fuck up and have your mom ban me from the house."

I laugh. "I'm pretty sure you could charm your way out of anything."

"Yet to be determined."

When we reach his car, he joins me at the passenger side, pulling open the door for me. I step back to give him space. As he guides me inside, his hand brushes against the small of my back.

"Always the gentleman," I say.

"Just giving you the respect you deserve."

He closes my door with a soft click and then jogs around to hop into the driver's seat. When he leans over me to click my seat belt in place, our eyes lock, and something shifts. Without thinking, I reach over the center console, threading my fingers through his hair, pulling him over to me.

Our lips meet in a kiss, soft at first and then more urgent.

I slip my tongue into his mouth, and he groans, a sound that vibrates right through me. His hand finds the back of my head, fingers tangling in my hair, pulling me closer, deepening the kiss.

The world outside melts away, leaving nothing but the heat of his mouth on mine and the tight, thrilling coil of desire building inside of me.

His other hand tracks down my arm, leaving a trail of goose bumps in its wake, before gently gripping my waist, pulling me closer still.

Eventually, the need for air forces us apart, but only slightly. Our foreheads rest against one another, our breaths coming fast and heavy. His eyes search mine, dark with want but also filled with something softer, something that makes my heart skip.

"Em," he whispers, his voice rough with emotion. "You have no idea what you do to me."

I smile, my thumb tracing the line of his jaw. "I think I'm starting to get the idea."

He lets out a soft laugh, the tension easing. "We should probably get going before we give someone a real show."

I settle back into my own seat, the echo of his lips lingering on mine. As the car comes alive, he adjusts the rearview mirrors, and the lights from the streetlamps catch on his chiseled features. I marvel at him—this charming, larger-than-life man who's opened his heart, bared the best and worst parts of his soul to me.

In the past few months, he's become my best friend, my rock. He's shown me his vulnerabilities and accepted mine in return. And that's all I've ever wanted in a man, in a partner. Someone who doesn't shy away from emotions, someone who's willing to share himself with me wholeheartedly.

Someone exactly like the person Hayes Grecco has become.

Chapter Thirty-Four
HAYES

I LEAN BACK on the chair in Dr. Vargas' office, kicking my feet up on the small table between us. She cocks a brow, unimpressed. So I quickly drop them back to the floor with a sheepish grin.

"Sorry, force of habit," I say.

She leans forward, folding her hands on her lap. "It's quite alright, Hayes. It's our last session; I suppose a bit of informality is to be expected." Her voice is gentle, but there's a hint of something bittersweet in her tone.

"Yeah, last session," I repeat. "Kinda hard to believe we're here already."

She smiles softly. "Indeed, it is. But it's a testament to how far you've come. You've worked hard, confronted your challenges head-on. How are you feeling about it all?"

I pause, reflecting on the journey that led me here—months of unpacking emotions, wrestling with my past, and learning to navigate my future with a clearer head. In the beginning, I was irritated that these sessions were wrapped into my plea bargain. That taking the fall for Bash meant I had to sacrifice more than I wanted.

But now, all I feel is relief.

"Good, I think. Better than good, actually," I say. "Proud, but also . . . I don't know, a little scared?"

"Scared?" Dr. Vargas prompts gently.

"Yeah," I admit, running a hand through my hair. "Scared of falling back into old habits, of turning in on myself when things get hard, I guess. That I'll somehow forget everything we've worked on here."

"That's a normal fear," she reassures me. "But you have the tools now, Hayes. And remember, growth isn't linear. There will be ups and downs, but what matters is how you handle them. And know that my door is always open if you need to return."

I let out a deep breath, comforted by her words. "Thank you. Honestly, I couldn't have gotten to this point without your help."

"We did the work *together*," she says. "I merely guided you. You were the one brave enough to face everything head-on."

As our session comes to an end, I stand, a tangible weight lifted off my shoulders—a weight I've carried for far too long. "I guess this is goodbye, then," I say, extending my hand.

She takes it, her grip firm and reassuring. "Don't be a stranger."

"Don't worry, I hear I'm pretty hard to get rid of."

With a final nod, I turn to leave, stepping into the washed-out gray of a late-November morning. I'm not the same person who walked into this office all those months ago, and for that, I'm beyond thankful.

THE OPEN ROAD stretches out before us, an endless ribbon winding through the rain-soaked afternoon. Emmy's beside me, curled up in my passenger seat, her favorite playlist humming softly through the speakers.

She insisted this was the perfect road trip soundtrack, and when Tracy Chapman's "Fast Car" starts playing, I know she's onto something.

"So, tell me more about your mom," I say, glancing over at my girlfriend. The topic of her childhood came up miles back, and I'm still turning over the sacrifices she mentioned.

A small smile plays on her lips. "She's always been my biggest supporter. Paid for my camps, uniforms, travel—you name it. She worked overtime, took on extra shifts. Just so I could cheer across the state and, eventually, the country."

I whistle softly. "That's . . . a lot."

It's hard to imagine, honestly. My parents paid for baseball, sure, but they've always had money in spades. The closest they got to sacrifice was opening one of their locations for me after hours. My club team had just crushed regionals, and they let us all come over and grab some food that night.

Looking back, I know it was just another strategic marketing decision.

"It was," she agrees, her gaze drifting out the window. "But she never made it feel like a burden, you know? She always said, 'You just chase your dreams, honey. I've got the practical stuff covered.'"

"Sounds like an incredible woman," I say, and I mean it. The warmth and love Emmy always speaks of when it comes to her mom . . . it's something special, something I can't quite relate to but admire deeply.

She turns to me, her eyes soft. "She is. And she's really excited to meet you. Bash, too."

My brother's headed over to her mom's place now. He left earlier this morning, driving in from his house near the complex. "Can't wait to see the look on his face when he tries your mom's cooking," I say. "Bet it'll beat the takeout we usually end up with."

She laughs, the sound light and easy. "Oh, definitely. I'm prepared for him to be a permanent fixture from here on out."

The conversation shifts naturally, the way it always does with us, and somehow, we land on the topic of the future—of family and aspirations. It's a thread I've been pulling at lately, trying to unravel my own desires from all my unmet expectations.

"A lot of people grow up wanting that," I start, keeping my eyes on the road as I navigate a curve. "A close-knit family. They picture their future and see a partner, kids . . ."

She's quiet, attention centered on me, one hand holding up her chin.

"My parents?" I continue, a rueful chuckle escaping me. "I swear they've envisioned a barbecue pit, some stacks of fucking cash, from the moment they could walk. Six locations and counting."

There's a pause, and then she reaches over, her hand finding mine. "And you? What do you picture?"

The question throws me for a loop, a direct hit to the chaos of thoughts in my head. I squeeze her hand. "I used to think I didn't care one way or another. But lately?" I glance at her, then back at the road. "Lately, I'm not so sure. Being with you, talking about the way you grew up . . . It's got me thinking about the kind of future I actually want."

"And?" she prompts, her voice gentle.

"And I think . . . I want more than just my individual success, more than the legacy of *Grecco's Barbecue* to my name." The words are a confession, a truth I've only recently allowed myself to acknowledge. "I want a family. Not like my parents, obsessed with work. But something real, something warm. Like what you have with your mom. Like . . . what we could maybe have one day."

The admission hangs between us. She shifts in her seat to face me, her expression earnest. "That's all I've ever wanted, too. To build something real, a family, with the person I love."

I gulp low in my throat. "And you . . ."

"Love you?" she asks softly. "Yeah, I really do."

"I love you, too, Em. More than I even knew possible."

I glance at her then, her face illuminated by the occasional passing light, and see the future I hadn't dared to envision. One where love is the cornerstone and dreams are built together, not apart. A future that suddenly feels well within my reach.

And I find myself wanting it, needing it. The future that just weeks ago felt so uncertain, so murky, is now unmistakable—shining in front of me like the northern lights.

If this baseball season doesn't work out, if somehow Bash continues to spiral, at least I'll still have Emmy by my side. She's my brightest spot—my starlit girl—and she's more than enough for me.

WE ARRIVE at Emmy's late, Bash trailing closely behind, and find her mom already tucked into bed. The house is quiet, save for the soft ticking of the kitchen clock and our whispered conversations as we help my brother settle in.

There's a makeshift guest space in her mom's office, and I practically have to slam the door on Bash's face to keep him inside. He can save his attempts to grill Emmy—to embarrass me into oblivion —until we're all well rested in the morning.

Emmy and I shuffle into her old room together, and it's like stepping back in time. Each corner is filled with remnants of her childhood, from the faded posters on the walls to the trophies lining the shelves. But what catches my attention most are the photographs—snapshots of a girl with boundless energy and an infectious smile.

My gaze roams the room, lingering on each picture, tracing her journey from a beaming child in oversized pom-poms to a confident teen commanding the room.

"Wow, look at you go." I chuckle, pointing to a picture of her in action. She's standing strong, bright blue bow in her hair, focus intense as she supports a flyer above her head. "You're really fucking strong, aren't you?"

She laughs. "Yeah, kind of. Or I used to be, anyway. I always liked being the one others could count on."

It's an aspect of her I've come to know and love—the steadfast support, the unwavering strength she offers freely, not just in cheer but in everything she does. We move from picture to picture, Emmy narrating the stories behind each, her words filled with passion.

It's nice to see this side of her—light, happy, nostalgic. There's a comfort in this space, surrounded by memories of her past, and I'm grateful she's allowed me to take part.

Once she's finished with her tour, we settle onto her bed together. I lean against the headboard, and she slots her body between my open thighs. Carefully, I encircle her waist, lifting her shirt ever so slightly to trace patterns along her stomach—little constellations I've made up inside my head.

Just as we're settling into the cozy quiet, my phone cuts right through it, its harsh vibrations startling us both. The screen lights up with a name that makes my stomach drop—Coach Hartwell. It's nearly midnight, the day before Thanksgiving, and anxiety is clawing at my throat.

Emmy's hand finds mine, a silent offering of strength as I hesitate to pick up. But her touch gives me the courage to answer, steeling myself for whatever comes next.

"Hey, Grecco," Coach's voice comes through, not stern or disappointed but unexpectedly light. "Wanted to get this to you before the holiday. Figured you could use some good news."

My grip on the phone tightens, confusion giving way to cautious optimism. "Okay."

"I hear you've completed the terms of your plea bargain?"

"That's right," I say.

"Well, your attorney got the paperwork through to the courts. The dean's seen it, and he's on board. Looks like you're off academic probation, and . . . your athletic suspension has been lifted, too. You'll be back on the team for spring term, assuming the judge clears you in a few weeks."

The words hit me like a wave, relief and disbelief mingling in equal measure. This is the break I've been waiting for, the hope I've held on to for the last three months.

"Thank you, Coach," I manage to say. "I won't let you down."

"That was a close call. But we'll see you in the spring, buddy. Enjoy your Thanksgiving," he adds before hanging up.

The phone slips from my hand, landing softly on the bed as I turn to Emmy, her eyes wide with anticipation. "I'm officially back on the team," I say, the reality of the statement sinking in. "For the whole regular season."

Her response is immediate, her arms wrapping around me in a tight embrace. "I knew you would be," she whispers, voice thick with emotion.

The room around us, filled with the echoes of her past, is now charged with the promise of new beginnings. It's a silent reminder of where we've been and where we're headed, the struggles we've faced individually and together, converging into a moment of pure, unbridled hope.

"I've been so fucking stressed," I say, my voice muffled against her hair. "Worried I wouldn't come back from this. That maybe part of me would grow to resent Bash. I know it was my choice in the end, but I—"

"I always had faith," she says, pulling back just enough to look me in the eyes. "Sometimes good things *do* happen to good people, Hayes. And it helps that you didn't give up, even when it would've been easier to."

Her belief in me, unwavering and absolute, fills me with a sense of determination I've never felt before. "With you by my side," I say, "how could I lose?"

Chapter Thirty-Five

The holiday season came and went, winter break stretching out with more visits to my mom's place, a quiet Christmas with just the two of us, and the Grecco boys attempting to reconcile with their parents.

Hayes spent Christmas Day with all of them, just a quick trip, not quite enough time to allow for disappointment. And then he joined me for a New Year's celebration. It was the perfect winter break, but now that spring term's underway, my boys have been gearing up for the season.

Co-captains in their senior year, Matty and Hayes carry a certain gravity between them now. A sense of determination, a synergy, that's seemingly unbeatable.

Today is their first showcase of the year, a non-conference game to highlight all their preseason training. Aside from his dedication to me, Hayes has been putting nearly all of his effort into the team. Extra practices, intra-squad scrimmages, and conditioning to make up for lost time.

Now, I sit here in the bleachers, clutching a steaming cup of hot chocolate against the chill of February air. Jade and Shannon sit beside me, the stands filled to the brim with friends, family, and fellow student fans.

Below us on the field, the team's gearing up for the game, my boys standing tall. They're natural leaders—Matty with his calm composure and Hayes with his fiery passion. And they're better together than they ever were apart.

Hayes smiles up at me, hazel eyes twinkling with excitement. I wave back, my heart swelling with pride. Everything he's gone through, all the uncertainties and fears, have led him here, back to the field where he belongs.

He'd been skeptical before, waiting on bated breath until the judge officially cleared him, hardly daring to believe it was real. But now, standing on the diamond, that #5 jersey gleaming under the field lights, there's no mistaking that Hayes Grecco is back.

The game begins in a flurry of action. Shouts from the crowd mingle with the sharp calls of the players on the field. Matty pitches a wicked curveball, striking out their opponent's opening batter, while Hayes backs him up at shortstop, ready to spring into action at a moment's notice.

Despite my excitement for Hayes, my support for the game, there's a small, silent part of me that still worries. All the effort he's put in over the last few months has been incredible to witness. But I also know how easy it is to burn out when you're pushing yourself so hard.

By the time the third inning hits, my heart's racing as Hayes steps up to bat. He takes a moment to adjust his grip before the pitcher winds up and sends a blistering fastball toward him.

With a powerful swing, Hayes connects, and the ball rockets off his bat. There's a resounding crack, and then it sails high into the sky before dropping perfectly into left field. It may not be a home run, but it's enough to send him sprinting toward second base.

The stadium erupts into cheers, and I join in, jumping up and down with my friends beside me. We hug each other tightly. I look to the field where Hayes is grinning over at me. And when he taps the brim of his helmet, tipping his head in our direction, a wave of emotion surges through me.

I know, beyond any doubt, that this man—so full of life, of love—will always be the one for me.

The game carries on, a blend of cheers and groans from the crowd, cleats carving lines in the field dirt, and that crackling sound of bat meeting ball. Hayes is at the core of it all, in his element.

He doesn't just play the game; he lives it. It's as if everything he does on the field is an extension of who he is—confident, dynamic, unyielding. It's not just about winning or losing for him anymore. It's about being there in the moment, living his passion.

When the final inning rolls around, the score is tied. The fans are on edge, hardly daring to breathe. Across the field, Hayes stands on third base, ready to dash home at the slightest opportunity.

Matty steps up to the plate. There's a hush in the crowd as he adjusts his grip on the bat, staring down the pitcher. Then it happens—the pitch is thrown, a screaming slider whizzing through the air toward Matty. Time seems to slow as he swings, connecting with a satisfying thwack that sends the ball hurtling toward right field.

Hayes bolts from third base as soon as he sees the ball in motion. His legs pump furiously beneath him, and dust billows from his cleats as he charges to home plate. The right fielder is sprinting for the ball, but it's too late—he can't reach it before Hayes crosses over. And when he finally slides home, the crowd goes wild.

I jump up from my seat, my cheers ringing out across the field. We've won the game! Hayes turns, and our eyes lock once more.

My heart's so full it could burst. That's the man I love right there, this strong, resilient person who's been through so much yet managed to rise above it all. And that victorious smile on his face is more than just a win for his team—it's a personal victory.

Afterward, amid countless congratulations and excited chatter,

Hayes finds me in the crowd. He takes me into his arms, spins me around, and says, "We're back, baby."

I smile up at him. "You did so good."

"Fuck yeah, we did," he says. "You ready to celebrate?"

"What's the plan?"

He sets me down, kisses me on the forehead. "The boys have something planned back at our place. A party for the team, and for me, I guess. Liam's already rushed home to set up."

I laugh. "Who left Liam in charge?"

"Someone with a penchant for chaos, I'm sure."

After Hayes grabs a quick shower, all of us head out for a meal together. We order our usual pizzas: extra black olives for Hayes and me, jalapeños for Jade, and something a little plainer for Shannon.

By the time we arrive at his place, the party's already in full swing. The front door's thrown wide open, music spilling into the yard, where clusters of my old friends stand—girls from my former squad, faces both new and old.

Inside, the boys from Hayes' team are dotted around, some lounging on the sofas while others huddle around a makeshift bar. Liam's standing there behind it, grinning wide. He's wearing an orange jumpsuit and shaking a cocktail mixer.

Hayes squeezes my hand, peppers a soft kiss to my temple, and we navigate through the sea of people. He's instantly swarmed by his teammates who take every opportunity to congratulate him.

Eventually, the crowd clears, and that's when I spot a banner hanging from the ceiling. It reads, "Free at Last." The gears didn't quite click into place before, but now it's all making sense. Liam's choice of attire isn't, in fact, a random fashion statement; he's dressing to the theme.

"Hey, babe?"

"What's up?" Hayes asks, and I point to the banner in front of us.

"Free at . . . oh, fuck no." A grin of disbelief spreads across his face, mouth agape. "Liam Alexander Donovan, you goddamn weasel."

He takes my hand, weaving us back over to the bar where Liam stands. This time, there's no mistaking his intent. Handcuffs litter the counter. Stacks of mock "Get Out of Jail Free" cards are spread out next to an array of colorful drinks.

Liam looks up from his cocktail crafting, the smirk on his face widening as he catches sight of us.

"Don't you think this is a little much?" Hayes asks. "Even for you?"

"It's not enough, actually. The rest of the guys are putting on their stripes as we speak."

He gestures to the crowd, where several of their teammates are, indeed, changing into matching black and white. As Hayes' gaze sweeps over the room, a loud laugh escapes him. He looks back at Liam, shaking his head.

"Only you could turn an arrest into a party theme."

"What can I say?" Liam shrugs before winking at me. "I'm just glad our boy is finally free."

Hayes huffs a chuckle, patting Liam's shoulder before pulling me in closer to his side. "You're a piece of shit, I hope you know that."

"Thanks, buddy," Liam says. "I love you, too."

After another couple of drinks, Hayes spends the next hour being the life and soul of the party, occasionally breaking away to steal a few moments with me. He tucks me under his arm, whispering in my ear about how much he loves me, how pretty I look, how he can't wait to take me upstairs later.

As the party winds down, James drags a tipsy Hayes to the center of the room for a toast. With beer in hand, his own striped outfit notably stained, he raises his glass high. "To Captain Grecco," he begins, "for showing us all what it means to be *free*. We're so fucking glad you made it out alive, buddy."

The room fills with applause, whistles echoing off the walls as everyone raises a drink. Hayes stands tall amidst it all, his gaze meeting mine across the room.

Once the applause dies down, he settles back into the space beside me. His arm loops around my shoulder and tugs me close. We're cozy and content for a moment, a crooked smile on his face, but then a shove from behind sends his cup flying.

Beer soaks through my shirt, and my mouth pops open in a gasp.

"Shit, baby, I'm so sorry," he blurts out, his face a mix of horror and apology. It's a scene oddly reminiscent of that first night we spent here together, and it sends me into a fit of giggles.

"Is this gonna become a tradition now?" I ask, clutching my soaked shirt away from my chest. "You drenching me at parties?"

His eyes light up with recognition, lips twitching into a smirk. "It could be arranged."

I look down at my wet T-shirt—practically transparent now—and then back up. We lock eyes, and there's a heat there that rackets down my spine.

"You know how you're looking at me, don't you?" he asks.

"How's that?"

"Like you want me to take what I want." His gaze flicks down, eyes darkening. "Right. This. Very. Second."

"And what you *want* is to take me upstairs, right?"

His fingers trace over my collarbone, then press flat against my wet chest. "And leave my own party?"

"Like you said, it's *your* party," I say, lifting a brow. "You can do *whatever* you want."

Eyes flashing, he grabs my hand, pulling me up the stairs. We tumble into his room; the door shuts with a resounding thud as he leans against it, his playful demeanor shifting into one of intensity.

He looks at me like I'm his entire world, and a fluttery sensation invades my chest. Striding toward me, he cradles my face in his hands, our lips meeting in a slow, perfect kiss. When he pulls back, the dim light catches the glimmer in his hazel eyes.

"Em," he murmurs, fingers brushing through my hair. "God, you know how pretty you are?"

I bite my lip, flushing, and take a measured step back. He watches me intently as I pull the beer-soaked fabric over my head, tossing it aside.

When he moves closer, and I let him. His head dips, lips trailing kisses down my neck while confident fingers trace the edges of my bra. A finger hooks beneath the straps and pulls them down slowly, igniting sparks along my rib cage.

"You know . . ." A low chuckle rumbles in his chest. "I kind of like this tradition."

"Oh, I'm sure you do. You probably couldn't last a single day without a glimpse of my boobs."

"If it's any consolation," he says, "you have really great ones."

We both laugh. "Yeah? That sounds . . . oddly familiar."

"What can I say?" A thumb circles my nipple. "You make it very hard to be a gentleman."

I instinctively reach out to steady myself against his chest, and his heart thrums rapidly beneath my fingertips.

"Em," he groans softly, pressing his forehead against mine.

"Yes?" I say, breathless.

"Need you." He finally unclasps my bra, lip pulling between his teeth as it drops to the floor. One hand gently cups my breast. "Really want to fuck these."

I tilt my head. "Yeah?"

"Been dying to for ages, baby."

"All you had to do was ask."

"Is that so?"

His grin is sly as he pushes me back toward his mattress. I climb on, propping myself up as he grabs a bottle of lube from his top drawer. When he returns to my side, he shoves his boxers down just enough to free himself, dripping the liquid onto both of us.

"Lean back," he instructs, and I oblige. Our eyes connect as he climbs over me, takes the base of his shaft, and guides it directly to my cleavage. As if in slow motion, he thrusts forward, nesting himself between my breasts.

A gentle finger curls around my necklace, thumb tracing a pattern over my initials. It's strangely intimate considering the circumstances, and the concentration on his face crinkles my brow.

"You okay?" he asks, eyes soft. They're the same shade as a mossy meadow after it rains, flecked with gold.

"Mhmm."

"Good," he says, letting my necklace fall.

His hips move in earnest, sliding in and out with an unexpected sense of leisure. He's taking his time, savoring the feeling. I smile up at him through half-lidded eyes and push my tits together to urge him on.

He braces his hands on the headboard, and a ragged groan spills from his throat. His hips pull back before they meet my chest —again and again—until he's a trembling mess on top of me.

His brow is furrowed, beads of sweat dripping from his forehead. His thick arms are shaking. It's obvious he's struggling to maintain his control, and I think it might be the hottest thing I've ever witnessed.

"Em, is it . . . alright if I . . ."

"Come, Hayes, please," I beg, arching into him. And like the good boy that he is, he does exactly as he's told.

Chapter Thirty-Six

"Good morning, gorgeous."

"Good morning, sweet boy," Emmy says, head on my chest, my hand in her hair. "What do you want to do today?"

I let out a contented sigh. "How about we just stay right here in bed?"

"All day?"

I grin down at her. "It'd be a sacrifice, but I'm willing to fight the good fight."

She props herself up on one elbow, trailing a finger down my chest. "You're very funny, you know that?"

"Yeah, I told you about that already," I say, flashing her a grin. "And don't forget cute, handsome, and also deep. The full package, really."

"Aren't I a lucky girl?"

"The luckiest."

"It only makes sense that we'd work so well together," she says, her eyes lighting up. "Our star signs are very compatible."

I let out a dry chuckle. "That's like saying we were destined to be together since the day we were born."

Her nose wrinkles. "I do say that."

"Which I love," I say, backtracking. "That's one of my favorite things about you."

She gives a tiny giggle. "I'm kidding. Although, if I'm being completely honest, I did have . . . a secret crush on you for a while."

"Before Showergate, you mean?"

"Mhm."

"Aw, Emmy, baby," I say with a crooked smile. "I kind of figured that out already."

She gasps, swatting me on the chest. "God, you're so full of yourself."

"It's not that." I tilt my head, correcting myself. "Well, it's partially that. But when you told me about bumping into me before practice all that time ago . . ."

She winces, curling into me. "You knew, even then?"

"You're not that subtle."

Her laughter fills the room, light and carefree. "Okay, smart-ass. Since we're sharing, when did you first know you were falling for me?"

I pretend to ponder, a theatrical hand to my chin. "Hmm, shortly after that time you drenched yourself in beer, trying to impress me. The *first* time."

"Hey!" she protests, but her eyes are dancing with amusement. "That was completely your fault."

"Maybe, or maybe the guy who bumped into me that night was a paid actor," I say, tucking a loose strand of hair behind her ear. "Either way, it gave me the perfect excuse to take care of you. And somewhere between leaving you naked in my shower and sharing a picnic with you in the park, I realized I didn't want to be without you."

Her expression softens, a cheeky smile playing on her lips. "So, would you say . . . the stars aligned that day?"

"Yeah, baby, I'll give you that one."

And there it is, the simple truth. Maybe the universe initially brought us together, set us down our predestined paths. But now, it's about the moments we choose each other, again and again. Emmy, with her clever comebacks and endless kindness, has become my constant, my north star. In her, I've found not just a partner but a part of myself I didn't know was missing.

As she snuggles closer, her breath warm against my skin, I know this is where I'm meant to be. Where I belong. Because when I look into her eyes, I see my whole future spread out before me, fuller and brighter than it's ever been before.

THE END

Epilogue

EMMY

A warm August breeze brushes against my skin. I settle deeper into the plush rooftop patio furniture and look up. It's a clear night, the sky a tapestry of darkness speckled with stars, Mercury hanging low on the horizon.

Hayes' voice, muffled by the phone, carries softly to where I'm lounging. He's finishing up a call with Bash, who's ending his first minor league year in High A. We attended a few of his games earlier in the season, and he's been killing it ever since.

Somehow, he's managed not to get himself into any more trouble. It didn't take much for Hayes to convince him to try therapy on his own. Sharing how much it helped him, how it changed his view on love and relationships, made his little brother curious. Now, he's seeing the benefits, too, making real progress.

It's been a source of pride and relief for Hayes—heavy on the latter—and their relationship has only grown stronger because of it. It seems Bash has finally learned to fend for himself, and it's been heartening to watch him come into his own.

Hayes often jokes that it took a broken leg and a bit of space for him to find his footing, but there's no denying the truth in it. The distance has been a necessary evil for both of them. And though they wish they could be closer now, their biweekly calls have become a regular part of our lives, a means to bridge the gap.

Moving into our new Dayton apartment together was a leap of faith. Hayes made the choice to stay close by after graduation, taking on the role of assistant coach for his old team in the upcoming school year. On my end, I secured a digital marketing job at a local startup.

It marks a fresh start for both of us—close to what we know yet on the verge of exciting change. And though I'm still chronically tired and hopelessly romantic, I'm more at peace than I've ever been before.

When Hayes finally joins me, the call ends with a click, and the quiet wraps around us like a comfortable blanket. "Bash says hi, by the way," he says as he settles in beside me.

I lean into him, my head finding its favorite spot on his shoulder. "That's sweet."

"Yeah, it was, until he asked me how your mom was doing. I think you can guess where that led."

"My *mom?*" I sit up, eyes wide. "Seriously?"

"What can I say, my dear brother has a thing for MILFs."

"Hayes!" I grimace, unable to stifle my laughter. "That's horrifying."

"Respectfully." He holds both his hands up. "Your mom looks like you but . . . older. She's a beautiful woman."

I rear back. "If Bash hits on my mom this Thanksgiving, I might have to pass away."

"Don't worry," he says, chuckling. "I'll rein him in."

We settle into a peaceful quiet, with only the soft whisper of the wind whirling around us. He pulls me closer, and my gaze drifts to the bracelet on his wrist, a simple banded piece that I haven't seen before. Curiosity nudges me, and I reach out, turning it over in my hands.

There, inscribed on the inside, are my initials: M.E.F.

A tender warmth blooms in my chest. "When did you get this?" I ask, tracing the letters with my fingertip.

"Last week."

Emotion clogs my throat. "Wh—why didn't you tell me?"

He shrugs, a casual lift of his broad shoulders. "I wanted it to be a surprise. Do you like it?"

"Love it." I curl a finger under the pendant on my necklace, gently tugging it. "Now we match."

His warm chuckle rumbles through the quiet night. Holding me tight, he hums into my hair, "What can I say? I'm a sucker for symbolism."

Silence descends once again, but it's the comfortable kind, the sort that lulls us into contemplation. Now, I'm counting the stars, tracing constellations with my mind. Hayes's chest rises and falls beneath my cheek—his deep, steady breaths a calming rhythm.

"You know, Theo's off at training already, Jade's starting her master's soon, and Shannon's still over at summer camp. But I've been thinking, when they have some free time, we should do another triple date."

An amused expression quirks up the side of his mouth. "You want me to call up Alex?"

"No, thank you." I stifle a wince. "She's actually back with the guy she was seeing last summer. *Camp flings.* They're just one of those things that are hard to shake, I guess."

"Well, good for her."

"Yeah," I say, brushing my palms together. "Wouldn't it be fun for us all to go bowling or something?"

"*Bowling?* Oh, hell no."

My shoulders slump, and I give him a faux pout. "Why not?"

"I'm fucking terrible at bowling."

My eyes narrow. "Didn't you once tell me that you were good at *everything you set your mind to?*"

"Yeah, but Em . . . bowling?" A flicker of a smile passes his lips. "Come on, you can either be good at bowling, or you can be good in bed. Those are the only options."

I burst into laughter, leaning back to stare up at him. "What kind of logic is that?"

"Grecco logic," he says. "It's foolproof."

"Okay, well, in that case . . . I guess I'll take the latter."

"Wise choice, baby."

He kisses the top of my head, a soft, lingering gesture that forces me to melt into him. The warmth of his body beside me, the softness of his voice, the gentle strength of his embrace—these are my anchors, grounding me in a world that often feels too big, too loud.

In his arms, I find not just love but a promise of forever.

As the evening wanes, Mercury fades from view, and the stars seem to shine even brighter. It's a showcase just for us. I turn my hand in his, playing with the bracelet, the imprint of my initials pressing against my skin.

"Such a pretty night," I say, staring up at the sky.

"That's true." His gaze slowly traces my path and then shifts back to my face, flitting across my features. "But the view's got nothing on you."

"Cheesy," I murmur.

He breathes off an easy laugh. "I know, but at least I tried."

"Well," I say, "I love you, anyway."

"Yeah, and I love you more."

Acknowledgments

Thank you, as always, to my husband and our baby girl. It's been a struggle to get through these last eight months without my second half, but we are so looking forward to you coming home in June.

To my best gals—Becka, Erin, and Hannah—for being my constants. You're always there when I need you.

To my editor, Sandra, for finishing our sixth project together. You are always a delight to work with.

To my assistant, Taylor, for enabling me to keep my focus on writing and for taking care of all the nitty gritty details.

To my beta readers—Megan, Sierra, Madeleine, Arley, and Taylor—for all of your encouraging comments.

To my agent, Emily, for letting me do my thing, and for lending me a hand when I need it.

And to all the lovely readers, book bloggers, indie bookshops, etc. who make my world go round and round. Love you all with a million hearts.

I'm so beyond grateful that this is my life now. Can't wait for all the stories still to come.

About the Author

Ki Stephens is a romance enthusiast who finds comfort in the happily-ever-after . . . with just a little bit of angst along the way. She has a special interest in works that include neurodivergent characters like herself. When she's not daydreaming about books, Ki enjoys working with kids, creating art in her backyard studio, and spending loads of time with her baby girl, her husband, and their three pets.

She released her debut novel, Spring Tide—Book 1 in the Coastal University Series, in December of 2022.

www.kistephens.com

www.ingramcontent.com/pod-product-compliance
Lightning Source LLC
Chambersburg PA
CBHW022027310726
48972CB00006B/1834